FATAL SHOT

FATAL SHOT

DC Mel Cotton Thrillers
Book 6

BRIAN PRICE

This edition produced in Great Britain in 2025

by Hobeck Books Limited, 24 Brookside Business Park, Stone, Staffordshire ST15 0RZ

www.hobeck.net

ISBN 978-1-913-817-93-8 (pbk)

ISBN 978-1-913-793-92-1 (ebook)

Cover design by Jayne Mapp Design

Printed and bound in Great Britain

Are you a thriller seeker?

Hobeck Books is an independent publisher of crime, thrillers and suspense fiction and we have one aim – to bring you the books you want to read.

For more details about our books, our authors and our plans, plus the chance to download free novellas, sign up for our newsletter at **www.hobeck.net**.

You can also find us on Twitter **@hobeckbooks** or on Facebook **www.facebook.com/hobeckbooks10**.

To all those working for truth, peace and justice in an increasingly hate-filled and misinformed world

Note from the Author

The main part of this novel starts immediately after the events described in *Fatal Image*. Jenny Pike's body has been discovered, various offenders featuring in the book have been committed for trial and DC Sally Erskine is about to return to work.

As always, I have tried to keep police procedures reasonably accurate, without burdening the reader with excessive, tedious procedural details. I have shortened the timescale for the investigation somewhat, notably relating to tracing mobile phone activity and vehicle movements, and the exploration of electronic devices. I hope I will be forgiven for this. I would be happy to hear of any serious mistakes. If any of the abbreviations or police terms are unfamiliar, you will find them in the Glossary at the end.

The 3D-printed firearm described in *Fatal Shot* is based on reality, as is the conversion of blank-firing starting pistols to handle lethal ammunition. The *Real CSI* and *Woman's Hour* references are true.

As usual, there are some Easter Eggs hidden in the text. Look out for references to, among other things, Pink Floyd and Traffic, as well as a number of important scientists. You may also spot references to a comic song by Bernard Cribbins. The answers will appear on the Hobeck website in due course.

I hope you enjoy the latest instalment in the DC Mel Cotton saga. If you do, please leave a review. If you don't, please let me know.

I hope you will subscribe to my newsletter – please go to my website at www.brianpriceauthor.co.uk.

Prologue

THE GIRL LAY motionless in the alley, blue and white lights strobing across her bloodless face.

'Too late for naloxone,' said the paramedic, 'and the woman who found her tried CPR. Fucking hell, another victim of some bastard pusher. And she can't have been more than fifteen. Sometimes I could murder people, you know?'

'Come on, Steve,' his partner Callie said, taking his arm. 'Wait in the rig for the police. I don't envy the poor bastard who's got to tell the parents. It's the third overdose this week. There must be some really nasty gear going around. Contaminated, I expect. That's usually what finishes them off.' She shook her head. 'What a waste. An utter bloody waste.'

Mr Francis Garrett's eyes scanned the Directors' Lounge at Mexton Golf Club. The great and the good were gathered there, following the annual Founders Dinner – an excuse to eat and drink extravagantly on the club's anniversary. Not a drinker himself, Mr Garrett took advantage of the less-than-sober conditions of his fellow celebrants, whose looseness of tongue was in direct proportion to the amount of alcohol consumed. Information was valuable to Mr Garrett, even if it did not bear directly on his business – a business that the club membership would, almost universally, regard with horror. Titbits from careless councillors, grumbles from other businessmen and unguarded remarks by senior police officers were all squirreled away, especially the last of these. One never knew when they might prove useful.

Mr Garrett was expanding his business into Mexton, so he needed to develop a respectable presence in the town, a convenient veneer for his more nefarious activities. Not one for public demonstrations of charity, he avoided such organisations as the Rotary Club and the Lions. The golf club, however, was the perfect place to start – not for the game, although he was a passable player, but for the contacts and the gossip.

Tonight had proved profitable. He had listened to the Assistant Chief Constable bemoaning the shortage of officers on the county's streets and had arranged to play golf with him the following Sunday. He had heard the Chief Planning Officer describe how the Eastside Estate was a drug-infested rat run that, because of its labyrinth of walkways and alleys, was a virtual no-go area, and had chatted to the owner of a chain of estate agents about vacant premises in town that proved impossible to sell or let. As the event concluded, and the members departed in an atmosphere of boozy bonhomie, Mr Garrett smiled to himself and strolled to his sleek Mercedes in which his chauffeur-cum-bodyguard waited. *A very useful night,* he thought. *No doubt the first of many.*

Chapter One

Day 1

Three months later

'D'you want to earn ten grand?'

The wiry youth, a scruffy mongrel on a piece of string by his side, called out to Michael Crompton as he sat on a park bench eating a burger.

'Yeah. And I'd like to shag Taylor Swift and see Mexton Rovers win the premier league. None of which is going to happen. Fuck off, you idiot.'

'No. I'm serious. I know who you are and why you're pissed off. But this is solid.'

The youth briefly flashed a roll of notes.

'So what's it all about?'

'You know Frankie Garrett?'

'Heard of 'im. He's a hard bastard. Taking over the gear and blow scene, they say.'

'That's 'im. So this is the job. He's got a laptop with everything on it. Dealers, customers, suppliers. The whole fucking lot.

A bloke I know wants that, and he'll pay for it. Get it and the ten grand's yours.'

'Nick it from Frankie? You're fuckin' crazy. I might get away with it for a while, but he has contacts. One of these days he'd find me and cut me into little pieces. He's got a really nasty rep. Why are you asking me? D'you think I've got a fuckin' death wish?'

The youth shrugged and lit a roll-up.

'I heard about your daughter overdosing. Sorry and all that. Thought you might want to have a go at a big dealer.'

'That's bollocks. I'm not some fuckin' crusader. I'm dealing with the two arseholes who killed Kerry with dirty gear. I don't need to start a war. 'Cos whoever wants that laptop aint gonna play computer games on it. Why are you doing this, anyway?'

The youth took a deep breath before answering and coughed up a gobbet of tobacco-stained phlegm.

'I work for Frankie. I didn't have a choice. Me and my sister had a patch selling the odd bit of gear and Frankie wanted to take over. I agreed, but Shania refused. Two of his goons raped her and half killed her. She's now been sectioned. When I heard some bloke from Bristol wanted to expand in Mexton, I got in touch. He's a player here already and he wants Frankie's trade. He promised to deal with the bastards who did my sister if I helped him. So, are you interested?'

Crompton tossed the remains of his burger to the delighted dog and stretched, looking around to see if anyone was watching.

'Possibly. How would this work?'

'Frankie keeps the laptop with 'im most of the time, but his accountant, Bernie Simpson, also has to use it. He's the weak point. You'll have to watch for a time when he has it and Frankie's somewhere else. I might be able to tip you off, but I'm just a street dealer. I don't have his bleedin' diary. Have you got a shooter?'

'Yeah. I'm getting one. This Bernie aint gonna be on his own, is he?'

'No. He'll have a minder. You'll have to deal with 'im or get 'im away from Bernie somehow.'

'Christ, it's getting complicated. I'll think about it. Give me your number and I'll call you. What's yer name?'

'Billy.'

'OK, Billy. If I do this, I'll want a wedge up front. And no way is my name mentioned to anyone, OK?'

'Yeah. You got it. Call me later.'

Billy shambled off, the dog trotting happily beside him, leaving a conflicted Michael Crompton sitting on the bench and considering his options. Three hours later, he made a phone call.

'I'll do it.'

'So what's it like? Policing an area like this?'

Assistant Chief Constable Roger Collins frowned, regarding his companion through the filter of a bottle and a half of fine burgundy and several large brandies.

'Why d'you wanna know?' he slurred.

'Oh, I was a magistrate where I lived before. I thought I might apply here.'

'Good man. Good man. We need good chaps on the bench. Not these woke types. Easy on the villains 'cos someone pinched their teddies when they were four.'

He paused.

'S'pose it's like any county in the south. Loads of countryside. A few biggish towns. Lot of shut down industry. Couple of good golf courses. Decent folks who've made it. Usual lot of work dodgers and petty criminals. Pretty quiet in most places.'

He took another swig of brandy.

'Mind you, Mexton's had a lot of excitement recently. Gangs, bombs, a poisoner. And the MP's up at the Bailey for multiple murders. Biggest problem is the Eastside. Damn great estate. Full of scrotes. Impossible to police. Bloody no-go area.'

'Sounds terrible. And I suppose you don't have enough officers to cope.'

'No, we don't. Bloody cuts. Not enough coppers on the streets. Some good chaps in major crimes, though. Usually get a result. There's a DC, a girl. Connor or something. Rising star. Prob'ly get my job when she's older.'

He thought for a moment and looked concerned.

'Not sure I should be telling you all this.'

'Don't worry, Roger. You know what they say. What happens at golf club stays at golf club. Can I get you another drink?'

The ACC chuckled and tapped the side of his nose with his forefinger.

'Yes, please. Very decent of you.'

Francis Garrett smiled to himself as he stood at the bar waiting to be served. Mexton was becoming very profitable indeed.

Chapter Two

DC Sally Erskine poked morosely at her limp tuna salad in the police canteen. She hadn't had time to prepare her lunch before leaving the house and had to fall back on the efforts of the catering contractors. She wished she'd picked up a sandwich from a petrol station instead. Her attention was caught by the conversation of two uniformed PCs on the table behind her.

'You should have seen her, Steve. A plastic bag on her head, no knickers and porn running on her laptop.'

PC Halligan chuckled at the recollection.

'Go on!' replied his companion. He paused. 'What sort of porn?'

'Nothing weird, just a bloke and a woman going at it like knives. Reckon she was doing that asphyxiation thing while playing with herself. And guess who it was.'

'No idea.'

'Jenny Pike. That journalist who's given us so much shit. She won't be having a go at us anymore, that's for sure.'

Sally's mind jolted into focus. *Something's not right there.* Turning round, and masking her dislike of the officers' attitudes, she asked who was dealing with the incident.

'Your boss, DI Thorpe,' replied Halligan. 'She took a look and reckoned it was probably misadventure, but there'll be a PM anyway. Why do you ask?'

'Something's niggling. I'll have a word with the DI. Thanks.'

Sally rose, dumped her salad in the food waste bin and headed for Emma Thorpe's office, leaving the PCs to their sniggering.

'Have you got a minute, guv,' Sally asked, knocking on Emma's open door.

'Sure, lass. What's up? I didn't think you were back at work yet.'

'I've a meeting with HR shortly to discuss that. Now that the Ventham business has been settled, I believe I'm ready. I should be back full-time tomorrow. With a bit of luck, I'll start back this afternoon.'

'That's great news. Are you OK? You had a couple of pretty nasty experiences.'

'Yeah, yeah, I'm fine, apart from some sore ribs. Mel's been brilliant. Anyway, I just heard a couple of PCs talking about Jenny Pike and something's worrying me.'

'Go on.'

'Well, they said she was watching hetero porn – a bloke and a woman – and she died accidentally from autoerotic asphyxiation.'

'Aye, that was my initial thought, though Dr Durbridge will be taking a look.'

'Well, that doesn't seem likely. Jenny was gay.'

'What? How do you know?'

'I'm on an LGBTQ+ chat forum – not under my own name, I should say – and so was she. She was really outspoken about the exploitation of women in porn. No way would she look at that.'

'Oh shit. So what are you saying?'

'I'm saying it's suspicious, that's all.'

Emma though for a moment.

'You reckon it could have been staged?'

'Maybe. Anyway, I thought I'd better let you know.'

'Yes. Thanks Sally. Good spot. I'll get forensics round there to take a look and discuss it with the DCI. But who would want to murder a journalist like Jenny Pike?'

'Me for one', Emma mused, as Sally left her office, then checked herself and picked up the phone to call forensics.

Three hours later Mark Talbot, the crime scene manager, phoned Emma.

'We've had a look round,' he reported, 'and there was nothing unusual. There were a few scratches around the lock on the front door, which may have been the result of someone picking it, but they could equally have come from someone fumbling with the key. The body had already been moved, so we couldn't document it, but we took some shots of the bed. We dusted a range of surfaces, and most of the prints came from one person, presumably the occupant. There was one unidentified set, however, in several rooms. We found only one set on the laptop. In short, nothing much to help you, I'm afraid. I'll get a full report to you tomorrow. Oh, I retrieved the laptop – do you want me to send it to digital forensics?'

'Yes, please, Mark. And thanks. I took some photos on my phone when I attended the scene, so at least we've got some images. I'll let you get off home.'

'I should be so lucky. I've got that shooting on the Eastside to look at. DS Vaughan's there.'

'OK. Thanks again.'

She wondered whether she should attend the shooting scene. She knew Jack was perfectly competent to take charge, but, nevertheless, she was the DI. Still, he would call her, or DCI Farlowe, if necessary, and she had to get home. Slightly irritated, she turned her thoughts back to Jenny Pike. She appreciated Sally's suggestion, but there didn't seem to be enough to open a full-scale investigation. She would wait until she saw the pathologist's report. She switched off her computer, gathered her things and left the office, heading eagerly to home, husband and baby Genevieve.

Chapter Three

Day 2

'I DON'T THINK the boss is taking it seriously,' said Sally to DC Mel Cotton, as they queued for coffee. 'No way would Jenny Pike be looking at that sort of porn. I think it was a set-up, by someone clever enough to leave no forensics.'

'You could be right,' replied Mel, 'but you know that we haven't got the resources to launch a full investigation on the basis of the wrong type of smut.' She thought for a moment. 'Tell you what, give me the address and I'll knock on a couple of doors on my way home. See if any of the neighbours saw anything.'

'Thanks, Mel. I suppose the PM might show something up, but if the killer's that clever, there probably won't be anything. Hang on, sounds like we're being summoned.'

DCI Farlowe's voice sounded above the chatter of detectives and the whirrs of equipment.

'Briefing room, everybody, now, please.'

'Ladies and gentlemen,' began Farlowe. 'Welcome to the first briefing of Operation Athlete. Late yesterday afternoon, we received an anonymous tipoff that shots had been fired on the Eastside Estate. Officers attended and discovered the bodies of two young men, apparently with gunshot wounds, in an empty flat. DS Vaughan was called to the scene and supervised its preservation and the arrival of CSIs. What can you tell us, Jack?'

'Thanks, guv. The deceased were Shane Hopton and Tyson Harper, both Eastside residents and both with previous for theft, vandalism, assault and possession of Class A. We suspect they were dealing, but they've never been convicted. Harper was twenty-one and Hopton was two years older. Forensics are still processing the scene and will be another couple of hours, Mark Talbot reckons. When they've finished, the PoLSA team will go in to look for drugs, weapons and so on.

'What about the firearm?' asked Mel. 'Pistol, shotgun, or what?'

'The paramedic who pronounced death, an ex-army guy, said it looked like a small-calibre pistol had been used. They had been shot in the back of the neck, and the victims were found face-down.'

'Execution-style?' queried Emma.

Jack shrugged.

'Could be. It didn't look like a firefight. Dr Durbridge is doing the PMs today – he's postponed Jenny Pike as these are more urgent. We'll get the bullets off to NABIS, to see if they match with samples from any other offences.'

'Any witnesses?' asked Sally.

'It's the Eastside,' interjected Mel. 'You could throw a couple of grenades around and people would say they never heard anything.'

'Mel's right,' said Jack. 'We knocked on a couple of doors near the flat and no one had anything to tell us. Uniform will try a few more doors, in pairs, later today, but most of the locals don't get up until lunchtime. And before you ask about CCTV, the average lifetime of a camera in that area is three hours. Despite the prevalence of intoxicants, some of the residents are remarkably accurate with airguns.'

'Thanks, Jack,' said Farlowe. 'Let's get moving on this one. Gun crime makes me shudder. We need to check ANPR footage on roads leading from the estate for out-of-place vehicles, assuming that some cameras still work. See if IT can get anything useful from the phone call. Talk to the drug squad about the victims and see if they have any relatives or friends who would be prepared to talk to us. Contact any informants we have, too. DI Thorpe will be the SIO, with me assisting, so please report to her in the first instance. Can you divvy up the jobs, please, Jack? Thanks, everyone. Crack on!'

Chapter Four

Michael Crompton's phone rang just as his 3D printer stopped whirring.

'It's Billy,' the whispered voice said. 'You're on. Frankie and Bernie are going to a health spa down south for a meeting and Frankie usually stays for the afternoon. I'll text you the address. He'll probably send Bernie back into town, with a minder. That's your chance.'

'So how the fuck do I deal with the minder?'

'I dunno. That's your problem. Drug him or something. There's a waiter in the spa restaurant. Buys a bit of Frankie's blow off me. I knew him from way back. Bung him a few quid and he could put some stuff in the minder's drink. Just a thought.'

'All right. What's he look like?'

'Thin. Black hair. Small scar above his nose. Name's Istvan.'

'OK. I'll think of something. What do I do with the laptop?'

'I'm not touching it. I'll give you an address in Bristol. Take it there and you'll get the rest of your money.'

'OK. There's something I've got to do tonight. I'll take it down there tomorrow.'

Billy provided the address and rang off, leaving Crompton to find a suitable drug. Sending the minder off to sleep while driving seemed a bad idea. The car could crash and destroy the laptop. He remembered a box of old medicines left behind when his mother died. He'd never got round to clearing it out. Perhaps there was something there.

He found the box at the back of a cupboard. There were seven different types of tablets so he spent ten minutes Googling their names. *That should do*, he thought, when the properties of furosemide came up on the screen. He ground up three of the tablets between two spoons and put the powder in a small baggie. Then he set off for the spa in search of the obliging Istvan.

***

'I think I'll stay here for a bit,' said Francis Garrett, looking around the well-appointed health spa. 'I've got someone else I'd like to meet. I'll give them a call. See if they're around. Marcus, you take Bernie back to the club in your car. He's got some work to do on my spreadsheets.'

The middle-aged accountant in the shabby pinstripe suit failed to hide his delight at the prospect of encountering the naked women in Garrett's gentleman's establishment.

'Max, you stay here and keep your eyes open for anything dodgy. You'll drive me back in my car. And, Marcus, don't let that laptop out of your sight.'

'Sure thing, boss.' Marcus drained his coffee. 'Come on Bernie. Let's not keep the ladies waiting. I know you're dying to see them.'

Bernie blushed and followed Marcus to the car park.

***

The accountant clutched Garrett's laptop tightly to his chest as Marcus escorted him to the car. This did not go unnoticed by Michael Crompton, watching from a car parked three spaces further on. He contemplated making a rush for the machine, but Marcus's bulk, and the bulge under his coat, deterred him. He decided to follow the car instead and stick to his initial plan. It was a good hour's drive back to Mexton and the powerful diuretic, which he'd paid Istvan to slip into Marcus's drink, would begin to act soon.

As expected, Marcus pulled the car into the first services they encountered. Parking it across two disabled bays, he leapt out and dashed towards the toilets, leaving Bernie in the vehicle. Crompton put on a face mask, pulled his hoodie down and tapped on the passenger-side window. Bernie shrank away at the sight, gripping the laptop like a lifebelt. Crompton signalled to Bernie to open the window, indicating the firearm concealed beneath his coat. Bernie shook his head in refusal but when the weapon was shoved emphatically up against the window, he complied.

'Laptop, now, or I'll kill you.'

'I can't. My boss'll beat me to death. And Marcus will kill you when he finds you.'

'I'll fucking shoot you now. Give it.'

Tears streaming down his face, Bernie passed the machine through the window, and his assailant vanished. Marcus returned to the car to find a sobbing accountant, a stench of urine and no laptop. He turned away and vomited for a full three minutes.

'You fucking what?' screamed Garrett, who rarely swore, when Marcus phoned him. 'My fucking laptop? Have you any idea what this means? Everything I've done and everything I'm planning is on that machine.'

'B-b-b-but Bernie said it's all backed up offline, so you haven't lost anything.'

'That's not the point, you total fucking moron. If the police or those turnip-heads from Bristol get hold of it, they'll know everything. And I'll be royally screwed.'

Garrett thought for a while as Marcus trembled, the silence frightening him more than his boss's tirade.

'Right. This is what you'll do. First, get rid of Bernie. He's let me down and knows too much. I can always get another bent accountant.'

'But boss, he had a shooter aimed at him. What was he supposed—'

'Don't argue. I don't care how you do it as long as it doesn't get back to me. Then, you'll find my laptop, before anyone else manages to open it. If you don't, whatever you do to Bernie will seem like a minor inconvenience compared with what I'll do to you. Understand?'

'Yes, boss.'

'Now get a fucking move on.'

Marcus turned to a quaking Bernie.

'Did you recognise this bloke?'

'N-n-no, Marcus. He had a mask and a hood.'

'How about his voice? Any accent?'

'He only said a few words. I suppose he sounded just like you and me.'

'OK. That's good. Now, Frankie's pleased the stuff on his laptop's all backed up, but he still wants the machine back. So, we'll head back to Mexton. I want to take the back roads, so I can see if anyone's following us. I'll probably need to stop for another piss, anyway. Hop in.'

Bernie complied and Marcus drove out of the services, his thoughts a mixture of terror and fury.

Two days later, a dog walker discovered the decomposing body of a middle-aged man in a Hampshire forest. The man's throat had been cut, and any documents likely to identify him had been removed. It was a week before he was identified as Bernie Simpson.

Chapter Five

MEL DROVE SLOWLY down the well-kept street of 1930s semis. There was nothing to indicate anything untoward had happened in Jenny's house – the CSIs had long since departed, and there was no crime scene tape, simply because it wasn't considered a crime scene. Parking her car, she scanned the area for CCTV cameras. Seeing none, she sighed and rang Jenny's immediate neighbour's bell. A few moments later, a middle-aged man in cavalry twill trousers and a checked shirt opened the door, a golden retriever beside him.

'Yes?' he said, before Mel could introduce herself.

'I'm Detective Constable Cotton,' she replied, showing her warrant card. 'I'm sure you know that your neighbour, Ms Pike, passed away three days ago. I wonder if you saw anything suspicious that evening?'

The man shrugged. 'I saw her getting out of a taxi and stumbling to her door when I was walking the dog. Nothing suspicious about that. She often came back half-cut.'

'I see. What time was this?'

'Quite late. Maggie, here, likes a walk when things are quiet. About eleven-thirty, I suppose.'

'And did you see anyone else around?'

'No. The odd car passed but didn't stop. She sometimes came back with a woman, but she was alone that time. Never seen her with a chap. I did wonder about her.'

'Did you have a problem with her?'

'No. Not at all. She was perfectly civil whenever we spoke, but we had nothing in common. Why are you asking?'

'Just routine, sir. Tying up loose ends, as it were. Thank you for your help, Mr...?'

'Bentley. Giles Bentley. If that's all, I'll return to my supper.'

'Yes. That's fine. Thanks again. Good evening.'

Jenny's neighbour on the other side had nothing to add to Bentley comments, but, crossing the road, Mel's spirits lifted when she spotted a doorbell camera. She rang the bell and crossed her fingers that some footage from the night of Jenny's death remained. The door opened a hand's width and a woman's voice called out.

'Who is it? I'm not buying anything, and I don't believe in gods. Any of 'em.'

'It's the police, madam. Detective Constable Cotton. May I have a quick word?'

She held her warrant card up to the gap and waited while it was perused. Eventually, the door chain was released and the door opened to reveal a woman, in her mid-forties, Mel guessed, wearing loose jogging trousers and a T-shirt bearing an image of Charles Darwin.

'What's this about?' she asked, crisply.

'I noticed you have a doorbell camera, and I wondered if you have any footage from the night of the second. You probably know that the woman who lived at number twenty-seven passed away that night, and I'm trying to find out whether she had any visitors before she died. It's an outside chance, but maybe your camera picked up something?'

'Jenny Pike, you mean? I knew her vaguely. How did she die?'

'We're still looking into that.'

'You'd better come in. The recording's on my laptop.'

The woman ushered her into a well-organised study full of books on evolutionary biology and geology, occupying two sides of the room. A laptop sat on a modern desk that faced a bay window, and an arrangement of fossils decorated a mantlepiece, above which was fixed a poster advocating humanism. A Burmese cat perched haughtily on the arm of a sofa, regarding Mel with disdain.

'So, you're a scientist Ms...?' began Mel.

'Doctor. Doctor Regina Mowlem. I was a lecturer in geology at the university until ill-health forced me to retire from full-time work. I still do a bit of research and teach for the Open University. Anyway, you wanted the footage.'

Dr Mowlem opened up the laptop, signed in and clicked on a folder labelled 'Door cam'. She found the recording and swivelled the machine so that Mel could view it.

'Do sit down,' she said, indicating the chair. 'The camera's motion activated so it shouldn't take you long. Would you like tea or coffee?'

'No, thank you. I'm fine.'

There were very few recordings from the date in question. Dr Mowlem had been in and out twice, the postie had called, and a courier had left a card for an undeliverable parcel. But there was one, time-stamped twelve forty-seven, which caught Mel's eye. She opened it eagerly, only to be disappointed at the sight of a fox walking up Dr Mowlem's drive. On the verge of giving up, she froze.

'Find anything?' asked the scientist.

'Maybe. The camera picked up a fox in the drive, but I think I can make out a pale figure on the other side of the road, by Jenny's front door. Could you email the file to me, please? I'll get our technical guys to take a look at it.'

Dr Mowlem looked at Mel shrewdly.

'You think something's wrong, don't you? Give me the email address and I'll send it over.'

Mel smiled, put her business card on the desk but refrained from answering the question.

Ten minutes later, having thanked Dr Mowlem, she was heading for home, tingling with anticipation. Was Jenny Pike murdered? She had certainly made enemies, not least among the police, but would any of them hate her enough to kill? Surely the DI would open an investigation, with Sally's insight and, now, the camera footage. She tried not to get ahead of herself. Perhaps the image was just of a large cat? But she couldn't wait to see what IT Support came up with. She pulled up outside her home, eager to tell Tom about the development and to spend some quality time with the parrots.

Chapter Six

Marcus Forrest sat in the Fife and Drum, the third double whisky burning its way down his throat and into his sore stomach. *How the fuck am I gonna find who nicked Frankie's laptop?* He wracked his brains. *Bernie didn't recognise the toerag and he'd gone when I got back to the car. It was planned. Must've been. Some arsehole must've put some shit in my coffee to make me piss and followed us. No one brings a shooter to nick a laptop in a car park on the off chance. That shooter, though. Bernie said it looked plastic. Still scared the shit out of him. And what do fucking accountants know about guns. Still, it could be a lead. And the best place in Mexton to find out about shooters is this bleedin' pub.*

'Anybody know anything about plastic guns?' he called out to his fellow drinkers.

Most of the men in the pub ignored him. Three gave him a hard stare. A youngish man, in a black hoodie and camo trousers, quickly finished his drink, spilling half, and left the pub in a hurry. Marcus caught up with him in the car park as he tried to unlock a black Corsa.

'Oi! You know something. Fucking tell me.'

'Nah, mate. I just came out for me fags.'

'Bollocks.'

Marcus hit him in the stomach; he doubled over in pain.

'I won't fucking ask you again. What d'you know?'

'Honestly, nothing.'

The next blow broke his nose.

'I can keep this up all night. And Frankie Garrett can keep going even longer. Your choice.'

At the mention of Garrett's name, the bits of the lad's face that weren't covered in blood shone deathly pale.

'All right. All right.' He wiped the blood from his face and spoke with a gargling snuffle. 'I got talking to this bloke. In the pub. We was sayin' that getting hold of a piece aint easy. I said that you could make one with a 3D printer and the instructions are on the dark web. He kept wantin' details. He was really hot for them. I told him all I knew, then he bought me a drink and fucked off.'

'What was his name?'

'I...I can't...'

Marcus raised his fist again.

'Crompton. Michael Crompton.'

'Where does he live?'

'Dunno.'

Another raised fist.

'A flat in town, I think. With a girl called Josie. She's a hairdresser. I heard him speak to her on the phone. I've never seen 'im before. I don't reckon he was from the Eastside. That's all I know. Honest.'

Marcus said nothing, wiped his bloodied fist on the lad's hoodie and walked away.

Marcus called Garrett to report that he had a possible name for the thief and was assured that Frankie's crew would be looking for him. It was made clear to him that his own life expectancy was extremely short if he didn't find the laptop quickly, and what there was left of it would be extraordinarily painful. When the call ended, Marcus took a gulp of whisky from a hip flask and set about finding Crompton's flat and girlfriend.

Chapter Seven

THE THUMPING MUSIC from an early-evening pole dancing session percolated into the upstairs room of the club where Frankie Garrett held court.

'This afternoon somebody stole my laptop,' he announced to his senior employees. 'Marcus left it in the car with Bernie while he used the toilet and some cheeky bastard took it. Bernie is with us no more and Marcus is looking for the machine. What happens to him will depend on his success in retrieving it. I need to know two things. Who took it? And why? Marcus has a possible name, Michael Crompton, and is investigating. I want him found.'

'Could it have been a random mugging, boss?' asked Max the Plank.

'No. It was targeted. The thief knew it was there and asked for it. And Marcus swears somebody must have put something in his drink at the spa to make him need the toilet. Someone knew Bernie and I would be at the spa and took the chance that I would stay while Bernie headed back here with the machine. So I need to know who put whatever it was in Marcus's drink and who tipped off the thief. The waiter who served us was foreign looking, maybe Eastern European. And when you find them, bring them to the warehouse and I will make my displeasure felt.'

'Why d'you think he nicked it, boss?' asked Speedy. 'He wouldn't get more than twenty quid for it in the pub.'

Garrett spoke patiently.

'No one would go to this trouble just to steal a machine to sell in a pub. He knew what was on it. There are two possible reasons. Either he thought he could sell it back to me, or he thought he could blackmail me with it.'

'He must have a fucking death wish,' interjected Max.

Garrett gave him a sharp look.

'Or,' he continued, 'he took it on behalf of someone else. Someone who wants to use its contents.'

'You mean those Bristol twats?' said Speedy.

'Exactly. I'm hearing of incidents where they're straying from the deal and trying to take over selling my products. There's that business with the Jones kid that needs sorting. If they've got the laptop and can crack the password, they'll be able to take over everything. So, I want you to set up a meet with Jasper Burnham as soon as possible. Guarantee him safe conduct, but come armed, anyway. Any questions?'

No one answered.

'Well, get on with it.'

Chapter Eight

Michael Crompton leaned on the top of his car and cradled the weapon against his cheek, the rudimentary sights lining up with his target's chest a few metres away. His heart thumped, his palms sweated, and he fought against the tremor in his arms. He'd waited months for this: the moment when Nathan Jones would pay for what he'd done to Kerry. This wouldn't bring back his daughter, but that wasn't the point. This was payback. Retribution. An eye for an eye, like it said in the Bible his nan used to read to him.

He'd followed Nathan for days and knew his habits: which pub he visited, who he called on, presumably to sell drugs, and who his mates were. Nathan Jones would die, in this respectable-looking neighbourhood where, Crompton presumed, he had dropped off some blow to a customer reluctant to venture into the Eastside for his marching powder. Now the wait was over. And Nathan, walking blithely along the street, would never know what hit him, which was a pity.

Michael took a deep breath and then exhaled, stilling himself as he imagined a trained sniper would do. Then he slowly squeezed the trigger. A flash. A bang. And a scream from

Michael, as shards of viciously sharp plastic ripped through his face.

By the time the smoke cleared, his target had disappeared, although the blood dripping into Michael's eyes would have stopped him seeing Nathan, even if he had been standing in front of his would-be killer. Howling with pain, Michael threw the remains of the gun over a nearby wall and ran for his car, his ears ringing from the explosion. Still half blind, he fumbled for his keys, lurched into the driver's seat and revved the engine. He roared down the street. Confused about where he was, he ended up in a cul-de-sac. Throwing the car into reverse, he hit thirty before he struck the lamppost he'd not seen. He knew nothing more until he woke up in hospital to the chorus of bleeps from the equipment at his bedside.

'What,' he moaned, 'the fuck happened?'

Clutching the packet of tablets the nurse had given him, Michael sidled out of the hospital, trying to avoid CCTV cameras. He cursed himself for giving his real name, but he'd been so confused when he'd woken up that he didn't think to use a false one. Anyway, they could have looked at his wallet and discovered his identity from his cards. The car could be traced to him, too. He'd have some explaining to do when Josie realised that he'd crashed it. But that was the least of his problems. Firstly, would anyone realise he'd been injured by an exploding firearm, rather than broken glass, and tell the police? Would they be allowed to? Secondly, and more importantly, would Nathan realise what had happened and come after him with a gang of mates? Surely he wouldn't know who'd fired the shot, but he was scared, none-theless.

Chapter Nine

Day 3

'WE HAD a funny one came in yesterday evening, Sam,' said Victoria Adeyemo to her husband, as he picked her up at the end of her night shift at Mexton General Hospital. 'This guy came in with concussion and some facial lacerations the registrar had never seen before. The patient claimed he'd fallen against a window that broke and cut him, but it didn't look right.'

'Is that all?' asked PC Samuel 'Addy' Adeyemo, as he pushed the car park ticket into the barrier machine.

'Well, we couldn't find any glass in the wounds, just bits of plastic. And, weirdest of all, his hair smelt just like yours does when you've been practising on the firing range.'

'What? Gun smoke?'

'I suppose so. There were also some dark marks on his cheek that we washed off before we could stitch and dress his wounds.'

'Is your patient still there?'

'He wanted to discharge himself, much against the doctor's advice, as he needed monitoring. We tried to persuade him to stay in overnight in case the head injury was serious. He'd been unconscious. He left halfway through my shift, with some painkillers and antibiotics and an appointment for a follow-up in clinic, when he'll have the stitches removed and they'll decide if he needs more surgery. Why are you interested, anyway?'

'Something's ringing a bell. I know you can't tell me his name, but what sort of bloke was he?'

'Late thirties. Physically fit. Rather a lot of tattoos. He didn't say much. Beneath the pain I sensed a lot of anger. He couldn't wait to leave and muttered something about finishing the job.'

'How did he get to the hospital?'

'He reversed his car into a lamppost, passed out, and somebody called an ambulance. I think your guys were meant to attend but he was taken away before they arrived. Someone turned up at the hospital to test his breath, but he wasn't fit enough for that. He couldn't have blown into the tube. Anyway, he didn't smell of alcohol. The PC was called away before he could see the patient and said he'd come back in the morning.'

'OK. I think I'd better mention this to someone in CID. They'll probably have a word with Traffic about the RTC. Thanks, Vic. Fancy some breakfast?'

As Emma sat in her office wrestling with the overtime budget, DC Kamal Chabra knocked on her door.

'Can I have a word, guv?'

'Of course.' Emma smiled.

'PC Adeyemo – Addy – told me about something odd this morning. His wife's a nurse at Mexton General and they had a patient last night with odd facial injuries and smelling of gunshot residues. Apparently, the guy said he'd cut himself on broken glass, but the doctor didn't believe him. Addy wondered if some kind of firearm or explosive was involved.'

'Oh shit. Not more guns. OK, thanks, Kamal. That's perceptive of Addy, and Victoria. I'll have a word with him, and we can try to contact the patient. Hopefully it'll be nothing, but you never know. Thanks for passing it on.'

Several detectives, who had worked with Addy before he joined the Firearms Unit, waved at him as Emma led him to her office. He smiled in response.

'So what's on your mind, Addy?' asked Emma. 'Kamal said you suspect a firearms incident.'

'Yes, guv. One of Victoria's patients had bits of plastic in some facial wounds and smelt of gun smoke. He claimed it was glass that cut him but there was no glass. I've been thinking about a briefing we had a while ago. Apparently, you can download files from the internet that will let you print the components of a firearm using a 3D printer. The bits are plastic, and you need to get some metal for springs and barrels and so on, but the weapons do work. The thing is, they can blow up when fired, especially if they're not made correctly. I reckon that could have happened here.'

'Bloody hell. So the patient tried to shoot someone, and it backfired. Literally. I never knew plastic guns really worked. Still, one was used in that film with Clint Eastwood and John Malkovich. Is Hollywood coming to Mexton?'

Addy smiled grimly.

'Did you get the patient's name?'

'There's the problem. Victoria spoke to the registrar and he wouldn't let her pass it on. The British Medical Association guidelines say that doctors can disclose patient details when a firearm is involved if there is a possible danger to life. The doctor felt that this wasn't the case since the weapon, if that's what it was, would have been destroyed.'

'Well, what about the gunman? Isn't he likely to be in danger from the target? Presumably he missed, as the only gunshot victims we've got at the moment are the two apparently executed on the Eastside.'

Addy shrugged.

'There is one thing, though. The patient was brought in following an RTC. Traffic was notified and someone turned up at the hospital to do a breath test. However, it wasn't possible. He couldn't have blown into the machine properly because of his injuries. They should have got a name from the staff, but they didn't. We should be able to trace him through the car. Unless it was nicked.'

'That's great, Addy. Thanks for letting us know. You should join us for a drink, sometime. I'm sure your old colleagues would like to catch up with you.'

'I'd like to, but I don't drink much these days in case I'm called out. Firearms and alcohol don't mix. But if I'm on leave, great.'

As Addy left her office, she picked up her phone and dialled.

'Colin,' she said, when the call was answered. 'We have another problem.'

Chapter Ten

'Where's that bloody laptop to?' demanded Jasper Burnham. 'Crompton should 'ave delivered it by now. He's had half the bloody money.'

'Dunno, boss,' replied Wayne Fletcher. 'Last I heard he'd got hold of it as planned and was bringing it down last night, after he'd taken care of something. Aint heard from him since. His phone's dead 'n' all.'

'Right. Well get you off to Mexton and find out what the fuck's going on. Oi don't like being pissed about. He shouldn't be taking care of anything else if he's working for me.'

'On my way. I know where he lives. I'll give him a bit of a shake.'

'You do that.'

'We've traced the car we believe the shooter used, boss,' said Kamal to Emma as they queued for coffee. 'It's registered to a Josie Lambert. She's not known to us and her driving record's clean.'

'OK. Can you go talk to her and find out who was using it that night? Also, what happened to the vehicle? There could be forensic traces in it. Take someone with you and let Jack know where you're going. Thanks, Kamal.'

'Will do,' he replied, and looked around the office for someone to accompany him.

Josie Lambert cautiously opened the door of her first-floor flat, a swirl of weed smoke coiling through the gap.

'Ms Lambert?' queried DC Trevor Blake, looking meaningfully at the young woman, whose piercings would have set off airport security monitors from metres away.

'Police. DC Blake and DC Chabra. Can we have a word?'

Josie blinked at the officers' warrant cards and replied sullenly.

'What about?'

'Your car. We believe it was involved in a collision last night. Can we come in?'

'Er... it's not convenient. We can talk here. What about it?'

'We're anxious to trace the driver. We're concerned about how he received some injuries to his face. So did you lend your car to anyone?'

Josie shuffled her feet and looked away.

'This bloke – I didn't know him – offered me fifty quid for a loan of the car for a couple of hours. I'm skint so it seemed a good deal. I didn't know he was gonna smash it up.'

'You expect us to believe you lent a complete stranger your car?' said Kamal, incredulously.

'Like I said, I'm skint. And now I've gotta pay for the sodding repairs.'

'Where is the car now? We'd like to take a look at it,' said Trevor.

'At a mate's garage.'

'OK. So what did this bloke look like? Where did you meet him.'

'The Fife and Drum. If someone there asks for a favour, it aint a good idea to refuse. He was just a bloke. White, tall, shaven head. Just a bloke.'

Trevor nodded to Kamal who spoke next.

'We'd like you to come to the station to make a formal statement and look at some photos, please.'

Alarm flared in Josie's eyes.

'No way. I'm not a grass. And I aint going down the nick unless you arrest—'

Josie was shoved violently aside and a bulky figure in a wife-beater vest and joggers cannoned into Kamal, knocking him into Trevor who fell over and took Kamal with him. Leaping over the officers' entangled limbs, the figure hurtled down the stairs and out the front door. By the time Kamal and Trevor reached the street, he was nowhere to be seen.

'Fuck!' said a breathless Trevor. 'He was there all along. Did you see his face?'

'Briefly,' replied Kamal. 'It was bandaged so I couldn't make out any features. Short dark hair, a tattoo on his neck – someone's name. More tats on his arms.'

'Yeah. That's about all I got. OK. We'll arrest Josie for obstruction and take a look around the flat for any obvious clues to the guy's identity. A proper search can wait. And we need the address of the garage before any forensics are lost.'

Josie provided the name of the garage, reluctantly. Trevor called the details in as Kamal drove back to the station, a mute and angry Josie in the back seat of the car.

Chapter Eleven

It took Wayne five seconds to slip back the tongue of the cheap rim lock on the door to Michael Crompton's empty flat and ten minutes to rip it apart. It was clear, even to Wayne, that the flat hadn't been used for some time, so he searched for some indication of where its former occupant was living. It wasn't the type of premises where notes were pinned to a cork board or magnetically clamped to a fridge. There was no address book, also no surprise, but Wayne did find a pile of official correspondence on a table, underneath an empty pizza box. Most of it was addressed to Crompton, but there was a final demand for council tax, addressed to Miss Josie Lambert, at a different address. Someone had scrawled 'What's this shit?' across it and torn it almost in half.

Crompton's bird? thought Wayne. *Better go and have a chat.*

'So you really think there's enough to open an investigation, Emma?'

DCI Farlowe sipped his tea and regarded his colleague appraisingly.

'Yes, I do. I accept Sally's argument that Jenny Pike would be unlikely to watch that particular type of porn on her laptop, and Mel found footage of what looks like someone outside her house, some time after a witness saw her return home. Apparently, a fox triggered a neighbour's doorbell camera, and it picked up a distant image of a person. It's blurred, but we've asked IT support to clean it up.'

Farlowe grunted.

'Well, they can't enhance what isn't there. Worth a try, I suppose. OK. I'm inclined to agree. Get the team together and set up a briefing. When do we get the results of the PM?'

'This afternoon, I believe. I'll give Dr Durbridge a ring.'

'I'll leave this in your hands, then. Keep me informed. By the way, how's Genevieve?'

'Gorgeous if a little fractious. I think she's teething. She seems quite happy with Mike looking after her while I'm at work.'

'That's good. I expect the new part-time DI to start shortly, which should make things easier for you.'

'I hope so,' she smiled, a little half-heartedly.

Emma left Farlowe's office half apprehensive about sharing her job with a stranger. She had always been a team player but had never actually shared a role before.

Chapter Twelve

'You shouldn't eat so many biscuits, Trevor,' teased Mel, when the two detectives described the suspect's escape. 'You'd be able to run faster.'

'Sod off. I passed the bleep test. I'm fit for duty. Anyway, you can talk. You're always pinching them.'

Mel grinned and reached for a custard cream on Trevor's desk.

'Sally and I are interviewing Josie Lambert later on, when the duty solicitor gets here. We'll threaten her with an obstruction charge if she doesn't tell us who the bloke in her flat was, but I doubt that the CPS will go with it. Still, it's a card in our hand.'

'Good luck. I'm going back to the flat shortly for a more thorough look around. See if there's anything related to weapons. You'd better call me if Josie's no longer under arrest. I'll have to leave the premises if she's released.'

'Be careful.' Mel frowned. 'The suspect might come back.'

'Shouldn't think so. He's not that stupid, surely. Anyway, you know where I'll be.'

Mel nodded and went to find Sally to prepare for the interview.

Wayne pulled up across the road from Josie Lambert's flat to see a chunky-looking man get out of a car and enter the building. *Shit! One of Frankie's boys?* He grabbed a baseball bat from the boot, crossed the road and crept up the stairs to the flat. He pushed the half-open door and followed the sounds of someone moving in one of the rooms.

Trevor looked around Josie Lambert's flat and grimaced. The smell of weed had dissipated, giving way to a combination of unsavoury odours. Damp walls, unwashed bedding and stale food blended into a dismal cocktail. On balance, Trevor preferred the smell of weed.

The flat was small, consisting of one bedroom, heaped with dirty clothing, which Trevor searched first. There was a kitchen-diner, a bathroom and toilet and a lounge featuring a collapsing sofa and a large TV connected to a PlayStation. Lager cans, saucers full of cigarette and spliff ends, and piles of computer games decorated the floor, covering a worn and grubby carpet. A laptop sat on a rickety coffee table, next to an older-model mobile phone and a tablet. Resisting the urge to open the phone, Trevor put it in a plastic evidence bag and slipped it into his pocket. He had just reached for the laptop when he heard a noise behind him. He turned, too late. A glimpse of a balaclava, a swish of a baseball bat and a flash of agony. Trevor fell to the floor, unconscious and bleeding. He didn't see his attacker or the baseball bat. He didn't see anything at all, for quite some time.

Wayne snatched the laptop from the table, did a quick search of the flat to check there wasn't another one, and fled, the bloodied baseball bat under his arm. Two hours later, he knocked on the door of an anonymous house in south Bristol, beaming with pride.

'I've got it, Jasper, I've got it!' he said when his boss opened the door.

Chapter Thirteen

MEL PACED THE FLOOR, wondering why Trevor hadn't made an appearance yet. It shouldn't be taking him and hour and a half to look round a poky flat. With a growing feeling of unease, she picked up her jacket and car keys, told Jack where she was going and headed for Josie's flat. Ten minutes later, she was outside the building. The front door was open and the hairs on the back of her neck prickled. *That can only be bad*, she thought. She debated whether to wait for backup. *If Trevor's hurt, there's no time.* She texted Jack, withdrew her baton from the glovebox and cautiously approached the flat.

The first thing she noticed on entering the flat was the smell of vomit, with an overtone of blood. Seconds later she heard a faint groan coming from the doorway to the lounge. She rushed forward and her heart nearly stopped at the sight of Trevor, lying on the floor, just inside the room. Blood covered the side of his head and had spread over the rancid carpet. A bloody trail showed where he had tried to crawl to the door, dragging himself through a pool of sick. Nearly slipping on the vomit, she leapt over him and crouched down.

'Fuck, Trevor. What's happened?' she almost sobbed.

Trevor was barely breathing and had relapsed into unconsciousness. Mel checked his airway was clear, pulled out her phone and dialled.

'Ambulance. Send a fucking ambulance. Police officer injured, bleeding and unconscious. Head wound. Hurry.'

She had barely given the address to the call handler and ended the call when her phone rang again. It was Jack.

'Mel. What's happened?'

'Trevor's been injured. Badly. Very fucking badly. I've called an ambulance. They reckon five minutes.'

'Is the assailant still there?'

'Don't know. Haven't been able to check.'

'Then get out and wait for backup.'

'Not fucking likely. I'm staying with Trevor.'

'Mel, think of your own safety. Get out.'

She hung up.

***

Fifteen minutes later, after grim-faced paramedics had stretchered Trevor into the ambulance, he was blue-lighted to the hospital. Police tape, guarded by a uniformed officer, fluttered in the breeze at the bottom of the external staircase and a forensic team was on its way. Mel sat in her car, overcome with dread. She really liked Trevor – he came second only to her husband in her affections – and the thought of him dying was too awful to contemplate. She debated whether to go to the hospital to check on him or return to the station to apologise to Jack. Realising that it was too soon for a prognosis, she opted for the latter. But first, she had to call in at home to change her malodorous shoes and trousers. And, all the way, she told herself *whoever did this is going to fucking pay.*

Chapter Fourteen

'I JUST WANT a quick word with her.' Mel pleaded with Tim Hodgkin, the custody sergeant.

'You know I can't let you interview her in her cell. And without her solicitor.'

'It's not an interview. I just need to ask her something. Trevor Blake is in hospital, possibly dying. And I think she knows who attacked him.'

Tim thought for a moment, looking doubtful.

'You promise not to intimidate her?'

'Course I won't. You can stand outside the door if you want.'

Reluctantly, the sergeant agreed and led Mel to the cell.

'How much bleedin' longer are you keeping me here?' Josie snarled.

'Until we decide what we can charge you with,' said Mel, perching on the stainless-steel toilet, just out of range of the cell's camera.

'What do you mean?'

'One of my colleagues is fighting for his life. He was attacked in your flat. If he dies, we will be looking to charge someone with murder. And you could be charged as an accessory.'

Josie looked terrified, not realising that Mel was bluffing.

'I don't know nothing about murder. Believe me. Please.'

'Then you'd better help us.'

'What do you want?'

'Firstly, you tell me the name of the person you lent your car to. I assume it's the same person we saw at your flat. Then you agree to make a statement, in a formal interview, giving his name and all the circumstances. Understand?'

Josie nodded, gave the information, whimpering slightly, and Mel slammed the cell door behind her.

'Thanks, Tim,' she said. 'I owe you one.'

'Were you here?'

'Only if someone asks.'

Mel sped back to the incident room, aware that the DCI had called the team in for a briefing. At least she would be able to provide the name of a suspect. She would take the flak for the irregular conversation later.

***

'Ladies and gentlemen,' began DCI Farlowe. 'As many of you know, Trevor Blake is in a critical condition in Mexton General. He was assaulted while searching the flat belonging to Josie Lambert, the owner of the car in which an individual suspected of using a printed firearm travelled last night. Lambert refused to name the suspect, and we still don't know where...'

'Michael Crompton,' called Mel, crashing into the room. 'He was driving the car and was at the flat when Kamal and Trevor called.'

'How do you know?' asked Farlowe, astonished.

'She just told me.'

'What? You interviewed her without telling anyone or offering her a brief?'

'No, boss. It wasn't an interview. I just had a quick chat, to save time. She's prepared to make a full statement.'

'Well, the name is useful. But we'll talk about procedure later. OK, everyone, find out everything you can about Michael Crompton. I gather his face is still bandaged, so that might help us trace him through CCTV. Haunts, relatives, known associates, any previous – you know the drill. I'll ask some uniforms to look around the site of the RTC for any sign of the weapon. We need to recover it as a matter of urgency. I know you're busy with the Eastside shootings, but this is a priority. I will not have members of my team killed,' the word slipped out, 'and we will get this bastard.'

The DCI's mistake, and his uncharacteristic swearing, shocked the team and they dispersed to their desks, determined to catch Trevor's assailant.

Mel looked at the half-eaten packet of biscuits on Trevor's desk and wondered, sick at heart, whether he would ever be able to finish them.

Chapter Fifteen

THE PREVIOUS NIGHT's trawl of social media, in an attempt to track down Michael Crompton, had proved fruitless, and Marcus awoke from a fraught couple of hours sleep with a feeling of dread. Never the most patient of men, Frankie would be expecting results and Marcus had nothing to give him. He had asked around pubs until they all closed, and planned to continue when they re-opened, but either no one had heard of Michael and Josie, or they weren't going to tell this stranger, with a malevolent gleam in his eye, anything about them.

Eventually, he decided on a different tack and traipsed around Mexton's hairdressers enquiring after Josie. He drew blank after blank, the only Josie he encountered being a middle-aged woman, wearing wedding and engagement rings, who denied any knowledge of Michael Crompton. She was unlikely to be Crompton's bit on the side.

On the verge of giving up, he called at Mexton Magic Curls just as they were closing. The manager told him that Josie Lambert did, indeed, work there, but she hadn't been in to work that day. She confirmed that Josie's boyfriend was called Michael. Putting on his best efforts at charm, Marcus persuaded the manager to give him Josie's address, explaining that he was Michael's brother and that he was supposed to be going there for dinner that night. The address was on his phone, which had been stolen, and he couldn't remember it. Michael would be so disappointed if he didn't turn up, and they had no means of contacting each other.

Fifteen minutes later, Marcus looked with horror at the vestiges of the police tape still flapping around the steps up to Josie's flat. No police vehicles or officers were visible, so he decided to take a chance. He walked briskly up the steps and knocked on the door. No response. He tried again, speculating that Crompton could have been arrested or even taken by Frankie's boys. But Frankie hadn't told him he'd got the laptop back. Then the implications of the police getting hold of the laptop hit him like a concrete block in the balls.

He could almost feel Frankie's knives as he walked slowly down the stairs. On impulse, he rang the doorbell of the downstairs flat, to be greeted by an elderly man in cords, a cardigan and slippers.

'Sorry to bother you,' he said, 'but can you tell me what's happened upstairs? I'm Josie's brother and I haven't been able to contact her. Is she all right?'

'As far as I know,' replied the pensioner. 'She was taken away in a police car earlier today. Later on, there was quite a commotion. Police all over the place, an ambulance with its sirens going, just like on the telly. They said a copper had been hurt. He was in the ambulance, I suppose. I didn't see anything, but they asked me lots of questions. They seemed very angry.'

'I see,' said Marcus, fighting back the nausea. 'I'll come back later and see if Josie's come home. Thank you for your help.'

'That's OK, son. I hope your sister's all right.'

Once the door was closed, Marcus slipped round the side of the staircase and hid in the space beside the bins to wait for Josie to return. An outside chance, but the only one he had.

Chapter Sixteen

JASPER BURNHAM GAZED with unconcealed glee at Frankie Garrett's laptop. This was the key to his expansion. Bristol was getting more difficult, and his little empire was being eroded. Albanians, Scousers, Nigerians and Cypriots were all jostling for a piece of the market and Jasper had fought off several rival gangs, resulting in considerable business for the A&E department at Bristol Royal Infirmary and at least one body floating in the River Avon.

The drug trade in Mexton had been disorganised, following the elimination of the Albanian gang that had run it ruthlessly. Small-time dealers had proliferated, until Frankie Garrett expanded from his base in Portsmouth, by which time Jasper was supplying much of the weed, ecstasy and ketamine demanded by local users. There was a verbal agreement between the two gang leaders that Jasper would stick to his products and Frankie would supply the heroin and cocaine. But Jasper was sick of this. One of his suppliers had offered him a good deal on Turkish heroin and Colombian cocaine, and he begrudged Frankie's monopoly.

His first attempts at poaching street-level dealers from Frankie proved fatal for the youths in question. And accepting that blow off Nathan Jones was a mistake. He knew he would have to return it, and the money from its partial sale, and the loss of face rankled. But now he had the laptop, and he could systematically dismantle Frankie's network. And he would honour his promise. Two rapists would be killed. For all his ruthlessness, that was one crime he couldn't stomach. Retribution would be a pleasure.

In a small workshop on the edge of town Michael Crompton contemplated the 3D printer that had led to his injury and cursed it. His attempt at revenge was a dismal failure, and he wished he'd never listened to that idiot in the pub who said it was easy to make an untraceable gun. His wound was hurting and he'd run out of painkillers. It was starting to smell, and he feared it was infected. The antibiotics from the hospital didn't seem to be working. He needed more medicine, but he couldn't go back there.

Walking back to his flat, using back streets to avoid CCTV, his eyes alighted on a van, from a local pharmacy, delivering medicine to a patient. The driver had entered a ground floor flat and, to Michael's delight, had left the engine running. Michael ran to the van, wrenched open the door, leapt in and accelerated frantically, leaving streaks of rubber on the tarmac as he hurtled down the road, the yells from the returning driver inaudible above the noise. So far, he'd managed to evade the police, and what could they prove, anyway? He hadn't actually shot anyone. He'd lie low for a while and wait for his face to heal. Then he would deal with Nathan Jones, permanently. He was beginning to feel more confident, but, had he known that the entire Mexton police force was prioritising his arrest for the attempted murder, and possible actual murder, of their colleague, his confidence would have been shattered like a window hit by a flying brick.

Chapter Seventeen

Josie Lambert climbed the steps to her flat, irritated and tired after a tedious bus ride.

'The least the bastards could've done is given me a lift home,' she muttered to herself, 'and when do I get my bloody car back?'

As she opened the door, she was knocked off balance by Marcus crashing into her. She started to scream but a hand across her mouth stifled the noise before she could make a sound.

'Any noise and you're dead,' Marcus hissed. 'Understand?'

Josie nodded and Marcus released his hand from her mouth, transferring it to her throat.

'I've got two questions for you,' he said. 'Where is Michael and where is the laptop he stole?'

He started to squeeze.

'Michael's done a runner,' she gasped. 'He tried to shoot someone, and the bloody gun blew up. The cops are after him. They think he nearly killed a copper in this flat. I haven't a fucking clue where he is.'

He squeezed a little harder.

'And the laptop?'

'No idea. He brought one back here before the gun went off, but it's gone now. I expect the coppers took it.'

'Does Michael have anywhere else to go?'

'He had a flat. I'll give you the address.'

'Anywhere else?'

'He's... he's got a workshop somewhere. Please, I can't breathe.'

Marcus released his grip slightly.

'Where's this fucking workshop?'

'I don't know, I swear. Rented it a couple of weeks ago. He wouldn't tell me where it is, or why he wanted it.'

Josie started crying, her sobs inhibited by Marcus's hand around her throat. He relaxed his grip and threw her to the floor where she lay motionless, floods of tears dripping onto the mangy carpet.

Marcus picked up a takeaway menu from the floor and scribbled on it.

'Here's what's going to happen,' he said, his voice redolent with menace. 'If you hear from Michael, find out where he is and call me. If you remember where his workshop is, call me. And if you're lying to me, or go to the filth, you're dead. I work for Frankie Garrett and if he finds out you know anything and didn't tell me, you'll wish you were dead. Get it?'

Josie nodded and curled up on the floor, shivering in fear at the sound of Garrett's name.

Marcus left her there, attempting to suppress his own terror.

Chapter Eighteen

Day 4

'Any news on Trevor?' Mel asked, accosting Jack at the coffee machine.

'Sorry, Mel. No. They're keeping him in a medically induced coma to allow the swelling on his brain to go down. They don't know how long he'll be like that and what he'll be able to do when he comes round. Susie's by his bedside most of the time – I dropped in last night and she looked like a ghost.'

'Poor woman. I'll go and see her myself after work. She's always dreaded something like this would happen.'

'It could happen to any of us,' replied Jack, sourly. 'Come on, Mr Farlowe's waiting for us in the briefing room.'

The two detectives took their seats among their grim-faced colleagues, and the DCI started to speak. His update on Trevor's condition was much the same as Jack's account and he assured the team that Susie Blake would be supported as much as was humanly possible. He promised further updates as soon as he heard anything from the hospital.

'Now,' he began, 'where are we with Michael Crompton?'

'Forensics have finished at the flat,' reported Jack. 'They found a partial shoeprint in Trevor's blood but, apparently, it's a common brand and there was nothing distinctive about it – no cuts or odd wear patterns. The blood spatter guy said it looked as though Trevor was only hit once, which the hospital confirmed. The consultant looking after Trevor suggested that the weapon probably had a hard, smooth, rounded surface, so we could be looking for a length of pipe, a baseball bat or something similar. The only useable prints found were from Josie, Crompton and Trevor. They've taken a few tape lifts but the flat's in such a mess that they may not give us anything useful. One thing, there was a laptop charger on a table but no computer, so it looks like Crompton took it with him.'

'So Crompton's prints are on file?' said Sally.

'He's certainly known to us. A string of minor convictions for drugs, theft, affray, twocking and so on. Nothing to do with firearms, though, and we still haven't found the weapon. He's currently banned from driving because of repeated motoring offences. He got six months for assault when he set upon a couple of local dealers a few months back. He claimed they had sold his daughter the drugs that killed her. The court took pity on him and suspended the sentence.'

'Nice bloke,' commented Kamal.

'Find out who the dealers were, please,' said Farlowe. 'Any sightings?'

'I've been looking through CCTV, guv,' said Kamal. 'There's nothing from the council cameras and I've still got private CCTV and doorbell camera footage to retrieve. But a van driver working for Bantings Pharmacy said a man stole his van while he was making a delivery yesterday evening. He'd left the engine running, apparently, as he reckoned that he'd only be a minute. He thought the thief had a bandaged face.'

'Perhaps Crompton needed something for his injuries and didn't dare go to the hospital,' suggested Mel.

'Could be,' replied Jack. 'Is anyone looking for the van on CCTV and ANPR?'

'Me,' said Sally. 'I picked it up a kilometre from the site of the hijack, heading east, but I've seen nothing since. It's tagged and I'll keep looking.'

'Good. Thanks. Keep at it,' said Farlowe. 'How about the car?'

'It's being picked up from Vinnies Vehicles, a cut-and-shut shop that specialises in arranged mileages and filed-off VINs,' said Jack. 'They're reputed to do MOTs while you wait, even if the car's somewhere else.'

A couple of detectives grinned wryly.

'Oh, one more thing,' said Farlowe. 'Josie Lambert's made a full statement, naming Crompton as the man who was in her flat and who borrowed her car. They've been in a relationship for a couple of weeks, and she seemed a bit scared of him. She denies any knowledge of a firearm. Unlike Mel's conversation with her,' he scowled in Mel's direction, 'it's admissible in court. She's been bailed while the CPS decides what to charge her with, either obstruction or assisting an offender.'

The expressions on the team's faces suggested they would like to see her charged with the most serious offence possible.

'Are we saying anything to the press?' asked Mel, before the briefing broke up.

'Media Relations are preparing a statement,' replied Farlowe, 'and I'll hold a press conference later today, preferably when we have more news about Trevor. Speaking of the press, I need a word with you and Sally about Jenny Pike. Get some coffee and join us in my office, please.'

'What kind of idiot leaves a van full of drugs unattended and with the engine running?' said Sally, as they queued for the coffee machine. 'It could have had loads of dangerous, and saleable, things on board.'

'Someone who's probably looking for a new job,' replied Mel. 'Anyway, it looks as though the boss is taking your suspicions about Jenny seriously. He wants to see us.'

Sally smiled and, with full mugs, the two detectives set off for Farlowe's office.

'Firstly,' the DCI began, 'We've Jenny's PM results back from Dr Durbridge. They were delayed because of the Eastside shootings. Death was caused by asphyxiation, consistent with an auto-erotic practice going wrong. A credible scenario is that Ms Pike let things go too far and couldn't remove the plastic bag in time. There were finger marks on the bag, and fibres under her finger-nails from a ribbon tied around the bag, consistent with this hypothesis. There was no sign of a struggle involving anyone else. Given your suspicions, I pressed Dr Durbridge on this point. He said it wasn't impossible that someone had asphyxiated her by some other means and then rigged the scene to look like an acci-dent, but he wouldn't go so far as to put that in his report. Ms Pike had quite a lot of alcohol in her bloodstream, although no drugs, so it might have been reasonably easy to overpower her. She had no bruises, though. He did say that this practice was unusual in women.'

Mel and Sally looked disappointed.

'However,' he continued, 'the video you obtained, Mel, has been examined and it does seem as though she had a visitor within the time-of-death window. So, I'm happy for you two to spend some time looking into this. An inquest is scheduled for two days' time, so see what you can dig up by then. Talk to her work colleagues and friends. She has an occasional partner who's abroad I believe – have a word with her when she gets back. I'm sure you know what to do. But,' Farlowe emphasised, 'the priority is to find Crompton.'

'Thanks, boss,' said Mel, echoed by Sally.

The two detectives left the DCI's office pleased that their concerns hadn't been dismissed, yet well aware that they had little time in which to make progress. And they were determined to find Trevor's attacker.

Chapter Nineteen

Michael Crompton gazed at the boxes of stolen drugs with deep disappointment. He'd never heard of most of them and had no idea what they were used for. Co-codamol he recognised, and he gulped down a couple of tablets to ease the developing pain in his cheek, but he couldn't find anything suitable for his infection. The only thing he knew about antibiotics was that he was allergic to penicillin, and every drug for infections he looked at seemed to contain the stuff. Apart from some diazepam, which he could sell, there was nothing else of use and he began to regret taking the risk of stealing the van.

Getting rid of the vehicle presented a further problem. He would have liked to have torched it but, as it ran on diesel, he couldn't use its fuel to set it alight. He had no handy can of petrol, either. He decided to hide it in plain sight, and park it outside a DIY store in an out-of-town retail park, from where he could get a bus back into town. The bandage on his face made him feel conspicuous but he covered up most of it with a scarf and his hood. He could only hope that he hadn't left any traces in the van that could identify him. He realised that he could be arrested at any time, but he had a mission to complete. Once he had dealt with Nathan, nothing else would matter.

———

'Look, love, is this really a good idea?' Mel looked at her husband with concern as they walked across the retail park towards DIY-Easy.

'Of course,' replied Tom. 'It's just painting. I can at least manage that with a prosthetic hand. It's not bloody plumbing or bricklaying. Just choose the paint and I'll rub down the woodwork and paint it. No problem at all.'

'OK, if you're sure. But...hang on a moment. That van over there. Banting's Pharmacy. It looks like the one Crompton nicked. Put the paint on hold. I'm calling it in.'

Mel fumbled with her phone, stepping belatedly out of the way of a bus pulling out of a bay, and earning a toot on the horn from the irritated driver.

'Any sign of Crompton?' asked Jack, once Mel had read over the registration and he'd confirmed it was, indeed, the stolen van.

'No, Jack. But the engine's warm so he's been here recently. Shit! I bet he was on that bus. Two metres away and we bloody well missed him!'

Mel and Tom rushed back to their car as Mel asked Jack to contact the bus company for details of the service's route. They climbed in and Mel gunned the engine, nearly knocking over a shopping trolley full of plasterboard as she reversed out of the parking space. With no blue light and siren, she couldn't force other vehicles to get out of the way, and she seethed with frustration every time she met a bottleneck or a set of traffic lights. She caught up with the bus after a kilometre and swerved in front of it, just as it was about to pull away from a stop. She leapt out and banged on the bus door, brandishing her warrant card. The door wheezed open, and the driver let fly before she could introduce herself.

'You're that stupid cow that nearly got herself killed in the car park. What the bloody hell do you think you're doing?'

'I'm a police officer and I'm looking for someone who I think may be a passenger on your bus. I'm sure I can rely on your co-operation.'

She smiled sweetly.

'Knock yourself out,' replied the driver, sullenly.

Mel walked rapidly through the single-decker vehicle, scanning the passengers, failing to find Crompton. Just as she turned to leave, something greyish white on the floor caught her eye: a dirty bandage. She pulled on vinyl gloves, slipped the object into an evidence bag and labelled it. She turned back to the driver who was glowering and muttering about idiots holding up his passengers.

'Do you have any CCTV on this bus?' she asked.

'Yep.'

'Well, how can I view it?'

'You can go to the depot when I've finished my shift. They'll have it on their system.'

'And when does your shift end?'

'Not for another three hours. If you'll let me get on with it.'

'Alright. Did you see a man with a bandaged face get on in the retail park.'

The driver looked as though he was going to be obstructive but then thought better of it.

'Yeah. Dark hoodie pulled down over his face. He paid cash, though we normally expect people to use contactless.'

'Did you see where he got off.'

'A couple of stops back, I think. Can't be sure. I was busy. Can I go now?'

'OK. I've got your name from your badge, Mr Griffin, in case we need to talk to you again. I'll be sure to tell the depot manager how helpful you've been.'

Griffin scowled and shut the doors in Mel's face.

'Not putting him forward for a customer service award then,' grinned Tom, who had been waiting on the pavement.

The driver ground the gears angrily as the bus squeezed past Mel's car, while she reported her findings to Jack.

'Let's retrace the bus route,' said Tom. 'Perhaps we can get some idea of where he might have gone.'

'Good idea. I'm afraid your painting will have to wait. Don't look too disappointed,' she grinned.

Tom laughed as they plugged in their seatbelts. Mel executed a smart U-turn and headed back the way they came, eyes peeled for any sign of Crompton.

Chapter Twenty

'Could I speak to someone who's looking into Jenny Pike's death?' asked the smartly dressed, suntanned woman standing in front of the police station reception desk.

'Can I ask who you are?' asked the receptionist, cautiously.

'I'm Megan Lloyd, her partner. I've been away in the Canaries, and I've just returned. I need to know what happened.' Her voice caught in her throat.

'I'll phone through to CID, Ms Lloyd. Please take a seat.'

Two minutes later, Sally appeared, introduced herself, and guided Megan to the comfortable interview room.

'I'm sorry for your loss,' she began. 'Thank you for coming in: we were going to contact you. What do you know about Jenny's death?'

'Only that she was found on her bed, half-undressed, with a plastic bag over her head and pornography on her laptop. You're treating it as an accidental death, I believe.'

Sally looked aghast.

'How did you get that much detail? We've never disclosed that to the press.'

'Social media. It's on several platforms. It's disgusting what people are saying about Jenny.' She tried to hold back tears. 'I don't believe the horrible allegations and I want to find out the truth from you.'

Sally replied, uncomfortably, 'That's broadly what we think happened, I'm afraid. Please treat this in strict confidence, but a couple of things about the death concern us. Firstly, the porn on her laptop was hetero, an unlikely choice for a gay woman.'

Megan nodded her agreement.

'Secondly, we think someone visited her home around the time she probably died, although there was no trace of an intruder. But the fact remains that Jenny was found with a plastic bag over her head as if she was indulging in some kind of autoerotic...'

'Bollocks.'

'What?'

'That's bollocks. Jenny would never indulge in that sort of nonsense. She heard an item about strangulation on the radio – on *Woman's Hour*, in 2024, I believe. She wrote a piece for the *Messenger* emphasising the dangers and has also put stuff on social media. Someone must have killed her and arranged things to look as though it was an accident.'

Sally thought for a moment, unsure about how much she should disclose about the police's thinking. Then she spoke.

'Assuming that's possible, and we don't know that it is at this stage, can you think of anyone who would want to kill Jenny?'

'I suppose any journalist who works the crime beat, which she did for years, is bound to meet some unsavoury characters. Whether she upset any of them enough for them to take revenge, I can't say. You could ask her colleagues at the paper if any story stood out. She also pissed off a good few police officers, not,' she held up her hands, 'that I'm suggesting that any of them would commit murder.'

'How about her personal life. Any problems there?'

'I don't think so,' replied Megan, slowly. 'She had a few

friends, but I think her journalistic drive and commitment to her job put some people off. I guess it can be the same for police officers. I was her first serious partner in a long time, but I don't think there are any aggrieved exes in the background. I'll have a think and get back to you.'

Megan paused and asked, hesitantly, 'Will I be able to see her?'

'She hasn't been formally identified yet, and we haven't been able to trace her family. Would you be able to help us?'

Megan nodded.

'Yes. I can identify her. I really need to say goodbye. We loved each other so much and were planning to marry later this year. I'll send you her brother's contact details.'

'I'll arrange it with the hospital, then,' said Sally, placing a comforting arm around Megan's shoulders before showing her out. 'Feel free to contact me if I can help.'

'Thank you, DC Erskine,' said Megan, almost whispering, as she signed out in reception. 'I'll be in touch.'

She didn't bother to hide her tears as she left the police station and faced the brisk wind outside.

The *Mexton Messenger* will miss Jenny,' thought Sally, 'but nothing like as much as Megan. On the way back to the office an unwanted thought crept into her mind. *If Jenny's death was murder, then it was committed by someone extremely forensically aware. Could it actually have been a police officer? At least three of us have said they would like to see her dead. But surely not...*

'Look at my blaster, Dad,' cried five-year-old Davy Waters, brandishing an odd-shaped lump of plastic with a protruding steel tube. 'I'm Luke Skywalker, on a mission to defeat Darth Vader.'

'But I thought Luke had a lightsaber,' his father replied, indulgently.

'I haven't got a lightsaber so a blaster will have to do. Anyway, Han had a blaster.'

'Here, let me look at that. It seems to have some nasty sharp edges. Where did you get it?'

Davy handed over his toy reluctantly.

'It was in the garden, by the back fence. I just found it.'

His dad examined it, frowning, and recalled an episode of *The Real CSI* he'd watched on the iPlayer. It featured a home-made firearm that looked uncannily like his son's find.

'I think, Davy,' he said slowly, 'this could be rather dangerous. I'd better hang on to it. But,' he continued, in an effort to mitigate the boy's disappointment, 'I'll get you a lightsaber on eBay and you can go after the Dark Lord of the Sith with the proper gear. What do you reckon?'

Davy scowled for a moment and then cheered up, running off to play with his Star Wars action figures while his father phoned the police.

Chapter Twenty-One

'I THINK we've found the weapon,' called Kamal. 'This kid picked up something weird in his garden. His dad thinks it's a printed gun. He watches forensic programmes, and he said it looked familiar. He wants to know if he should bring it in.'

'He'd better not,' replied Jack. 'Tell him not to handle it any more. I'll ask for an AFO to collect it. Get the details and I'll make the request.'

An hour later, Crompton's printed firearm, tagged to show it was safe and in an evidence box, was on its way to the ballistics lab for examination. A report was promised by the following day, and photographs of the object had been sent to NABIS for their opinion.

'Come, on, love. This is a waste of time,' Tom complained. 'Crompton's hardly likely to hang around on a street corner waiting to get nicked.'

'OK, OK. Just another few minutes,' Mel replied, oozing frustration.

The couple had driven up and down the bus route three times in the hope of catching sight of Crompton, and patrol cars had also been alerted. Mel was just about to call it a day when something caught her eye.

'Why would someone be wearing a scarf over their face in this weather?' she asked.

'To hide something,' her husband replied.

'Like a wound. That's him!'

She swung the car across the road, infuriating a white van driver and frightening a cyclist, while Tom called in their position and asked for backup. Alerted by the noise, Crompton started running. Mel and Tom leapt out of the car and gave chase, pushing past pedestrians too slow, or too absorbed in their phones, to get out of the way.

Crompton's height and longer stride gave him an advantage, but the detectives were fitter and began gaining on him. In desperation their quarry tried to knock obstructions in their way – traffic cones from around a hole in the pavement, a sandwich board outside a fitness studio and a green recycling box left outside a shop – but they leapt them with ease. Then he turned down an alley lined with rubbish bins and a skip full of builder's debris. A dead end.

Crompton pulled a metre-long piece of timber, studded with rusty nails, from the skip and turned to face his pursuers, snarling.

'Piss off, or I'll fucking do you. And tell Frankie he'll get his laptop back. I just need to sort a few things out.'

'Put that down, Crompton. We're police officers,' called Mel.

"You can still piss off.' He swung the wood menacingly. 'I've got things to do and you're not gonna fucking stop me.'

Mel nodded to Tom, and they moved slowly towards him, spreading out with Tom on his left and Mel on his right. Confused, Crompton lunged with his weapon, first at Tom then at Mel. She leaned backwards and, as the timber swished past her chest, she pivoted and kicked Crompton in the knee. He staggered but regained his balance just in time for Tom to deliver a Tae Kwan Do kick to his solar plexus. He collapsed, wheezing, and Mel kicked the wood away before both detectives flung themselves on top of him. Crompton bucked and struggled until the blue lights of a patrol car appeared at the end of the alley. Then he gave up and sobbed.

With their captive handcuffed by two hefty, uniformed PCs, Mel turned to him, barely concealing her loathing.

'Michael Crompton, I am arresting you on suspicion of the attempted murder of Detective Constable Trevor Blake. You do not have to say anything...'

'What the fuck?' Crompton interrupted, incredulously. 'I just pushed him over. He got up and ran after me. Him and his brown mate. I never tried to kill him. You're fitting me up.'

Ignoring him, Mel completed the caution.

'You can give your side when we interview you with your solicitor present. Right now, our friend is in a coma because of what you did to him, and they don't know if he'll recover. Now get in the fucking car.'

Mel and Tom returned to their own vehicle to find a traffic warden in the process of issuing a ticket.

'Is this your car?' he asked. 'You've parked it on double yellow lines and it's been there for nearly half an hour. So you're getting a ticket.'

'Sorry, mate,' said Tom, using a conciliatory tone. 'We're police officers. We had to leave it there while we chased a suspect.'

'It's not a marked car. You're not in uniform. The law applies to everyone,' he grinned maliciously.

The two detectives showed their warrant cards, but it still took five minutes arguing and persuasion to convince the warden to cancel the ticket, which he only did, grudgingly, when they mentioned the attempted murder of Trevor. As they drove away, still irritated, Tom turned to Mel.

'Do you think we've got the right man? He looked gobsmacked when you mentioned attempted murder.'

Mel thought while negotiating a roundabout.

'He's the only suspect we've got, and we know he was at the flat earlier. He's certainly up to something, and we've got him for assaulting Trevor and Kamal. We also need to talk to him about the firearm. I suppose we don't have any direct evidence linking him to the later attack. If only we had the weapon. And what did he mean about Frankie's laptop? Still, it should all come out in the interview, unless the bastard goes "no comment". But it won't be me interviewing him, that's for sure. It's just too bloody personal.'

Tom smiled sympathetically at his wife as they headed back to the station to write up their statements, all thoughts of painting now far from his mind.

Chapter Twenty-Two

THE MOOD at the press conference was sombre. DCI Farlowe, flanked by the force's chief press officer and Emma, opened the proceedings by indicating an image on a screen of a young and smiling Trevor in his freshly pressed uniform.

'This, ladies and gentlemen,' he began, 'is Detective Constable Trevor Blake. Yesterday afternoon he was savagely beaten while investigating a crime scene in central Mexton. He is currently in a coma and is expected to remain in hospital for some time. It is possible that he has suffered permanent brain damage.

'We are anxious to hear from anyone who was in the vicinity of Eddington Street between the hours of one and three pm yesterday. Did they see anyone acting suspiciously near number seventeen? Did they see anyone carrying a baseball bat, or similar item, which could have been used to attack DC Blake? We are particularly keen to see dashcam footage from vehicles driving along the street between those times.

'We would be most grateful for co-operation from the media in this investigation. DC Blake is greatly admired by his colleagues, and we are determined to catch the person or persons responsible. A copy of a press release and DC Blake's photo are in the press pack that you have been given. I'm afraid we cannot take questions at the moment, but please feel free to contact the Press Office for updates as things unfold. Thank you for your attendance.'

'Do you think it'll do any good?' asked Emma, as they returned to their offices.

'We can only hope,' replied Farlowe. There are still a few people who don't like to see the police hurt. But so many wander around in a cloud, stuck to their phones, and wouldn't notice a charging rhinoceros, let alone someone carrying a baseball bat. We'll see.'

Marcus was desperately searching for Crompton's workshop, a gargantuan task since there were hundreds of small workshops scattered around Mexton, some as part of industrial estates and many just single railway arches or converted garages. He asked around in every workshop and garage he found, as well as in pubs and cafes.

By two in the morning, he was exhausted. A few people he had talked to knew Crompton, but no one had heard of his workshop. In desperation, he looked up workshops for hire on the internet and found four companies offering large and small spaces for short- and long-term lets. He would try them in the morning. In the meantime, he would attempt to sleep but he had little expectation of rest. He found a couple of sleeping tablets in a cupboard, left over from when his mum was alive, and swallowed them. After twenty minutes of horrific imaginings, he finally fell asleep.

Chapter Twenty-Three

Day 5

'Quiet please, everyone,' called Emma as she started the morning briefing. 'We have some developments.'

The team settled down expectantly, the clatter of conversations falling away.

'Firstly, Trevor is showing signs of improvement. The swelling in his brain is going down and the doctors hope to bring him out of his coma shortly. They can't predict the eventual outcome, but this does seem like progress.'

A murmur of cautious optimism ran round the briefing room.

'His suspected assailant, Michael Crompton, was arrested by Mel and Tom Ferris yesterday evening and will be interviewed this morning. Apparently, he denied assaulting Trevor and claimed he only pushed him over when he rushed out of the flat earlier in the day. His interview was delayed because he needed medical treatment for the wound on his face.'

A couple of detectives snorted in disbelief.

'We know he was in the flat earlier, so his prints and DNA found there tell us nothing useful. We don't know if Trevor saw him and, of course, he can't tell us at the moment, so it's vital we find the weapon for forensic testing. We're getting help from uniforms to search bins, gardens and anywhere else in the vicinity of the flat where it might have been discarded.'

'How about the car, guv?' asked Kamal.

'Forensics got back to us late yesterday,' replied Emma. 'Crompton's blood was found on the seats and there were also traces of gunshot residue. It's clear he used the vehicle after firing a weapon. They also found some latent partial prints on the firearm that match Crompton's. They may not be good enough for court, but they will be useful to us during the interviews.

'Ballistics reported that the weapon had no rifling, which means bullet-matching is impossible, even if we can find the spent round. Unfortunately, we don't know where the weapon was fired. We'll organise some door-to-doors near where it was dumped, in case someone saw or heard something, but that could be some distance from the site of the offence.'

'But if he was injured, surely he would drop the weapon at once?' suggested Kamal.

'Maybe. If we're lucky.'

Emma didn't seem hopeful.

'We're looking at CCTV and ANPR for the car,' said Jack. 'Nothing yet to pin down where the shooting may have taken place. The techies are interrogating the vehicle's electronics for records of journeys but the car's fairly old so they won't get as much data as they would from a new model. Worth a try, though. More promising is Crompton's phone, which Trevor had in his pocket. Amira Khan is working on it, and we should be able to track his movements, unless he was smart enough to remove the SIM card and power down the battery.'

'OK. Thanks, Jack. That will do for now. You've got plenty to do. I want you all back here at six for a separate briefing on the Eastside shootings. An officer from the NCA will be joining us, as there are some peculiar features about the case. Thanks, everybody.'

'Boss,' called Sally, as the team dispersed, Can I have a word?'

'Of course.'

'I've spoken to Jenny Pike's partner. She's adamant that Jenny would never have indulged in autoerotic asphyxiation. She'd spoken up and written about its dangers. It must be murder, by a very clever individual. Can we open up a formal investigation now?'

Emma pursed her lips and thought.

'I'm inclined to agree with you. You can see we're extremely busy, and the last thing we need is another murder investigation. But I'll discuss it with Mr Farlowe and see what resources we can make available. OK?'

'Yes, thanks, boss.'

'And, Sally, well done for pursuing this.'

Sally smiled to herself at Emma's praise and kept her fingers firmly crossed that the DCI would agree.

Chapter Twenty-Four

GARRETT'S PHONE call jarred Marcus from sleep at half-past eleven, the combination of whisky and sleeping tablets having kept him unconscious for nine hours.

'Fuck,' he swore, reaching for his mobile.

'Report,' Garrett snapped.

'Uh, yes, boss. I'm working on finding Crompton's workshop.'

'Is that it? Really? You are disappointing me, Marcus. You should have found him by now. I'm getting impatient.'

Marcus shuddered.

'It's okay, boss. I'll have the laptop by the end of the day.'

'Do so.' Garrett cut the call.

Why Marcus promised to meet such an unrealistic deadline, he couldn't think. He had to get Garrett off his back somehow. If he couldn't manage it, he would have to either stall Garrett some more or vanish. And Frankie Garrett had a talent for finding people. In desperation Marcus started phoning the workshop hire firms he'd identified the previous night. His spiel was that he needed a small workshop, with electricity, for six weeks, in which to build a sound system for a mobile disco. Whether that would take six weeks, he had no idea, but he didn't think many other people would either. He asked each company whether they had such premises available, saying that Michael Crompton had recommended them. The first two said that they did have some units available, but six months was the minimum term for a let. They denied having heard of Michael Crompton. The third appeared to have gone out of business, but, in the middle of the afternoon, he struck lucky with the fourth.

'Yes,' said the young man in the office of Mexton Property Management, 'Your friend did rent a unit from us, on the Oldmexton Estate. He told us he wouldn't want to renew the rental, so it should be available at the end of the month. Would that suit?'

'Yeah. It would. What number was it, again?'

'Number forty-two. Would you like to view it this afternoon? We have keys and I'm sure Mr Crompton won't mind, as he's a friend of yours.'

'No, you're all right. I'll fix up an appointment later in the week. Cheers, mate.'

'I've got Michael Crompton's phone data, Jack,' said Amira Khan, the IT technician, as she dropped a pile of printouts on the DS's desk. 'There are two locations that he's visited regularly over the past few weeks. A residential area, not far from the Eastside, and a light industrial place on the outskirts of town. He's only been to the residential place a couple of times recently, though.'

'Probably his old address before he shacked up with Josie Lambert,' said Jack. 'That's great stuff, Amira, thanks. How precise can you be about the locations?'

'I've drawn circles on the map but, as you can see, they cover a lot of buildings – fewer in the case of the industrial site. You'll still need boots on the ground.'

'Yeah, sure. We've got some old addresses for Crompton that

we can match with the first site. We've not had time to check them out, yet, so this will save us time. I'm guessing he has some sort of workshop in the industrial area. I'll send a couple of DCs to have a look around.

———

Marcus grabbed a few tools, checked the address of the estate, and wheeled his motorbike out of a garage he rented. No one, including Garrett, he hoped, knew about the garage or the bike so he reasoned that his trip would be unnoticed. If the police had found the laptop already, Frankie's source would know and Marcus would already be dead, so that was some consolation. If Jasper Burnham already had it, he was also dead. So the workshop was his last chance saloon. He took a roundabout route to the estate, checking all the time that he wasn't being followed, and pulled up, relieved, in the half empty car park.

———

In a hospital bed, four miles away, Trevor Blake stirred as the drugs keeping him in a coma wore off. Susie Blake leaned over him, tears dropping on the sheet. Trevor's eyelids flickered, opened. He looked at the face above and heard her whisper.

'You're back with us, my love! You're back!'

Trevor spoke, his voice creaky from the ventilating tube.

'Who are you?'

Chapter Twenty-Five

JACK BEGAN the interview by reminding Crompton that he was still under caution. He noted that the interview was being recorded and named those present.

'Mr Crompton,' he began, 'you have been arrested on suspicion of the attempted murder of Detective Constable Trevor Blake, of assaulting emergency workers in the course of their duties, namely Detective Constables Mel Cotton and Tom Ferris, as well as taking and driving away a vehicle without the owner's consent and the theft of medicines from the vehicle in question. You have received medical treatment for the wound on your face and have spoken to Mrs Paula Delaney, the duty solicitor. Before I and DC Chabra ask you any questions, is there anything you'd like to tell us about these matters?'

Crompton, pasty-faced, sour-smelling and nervous, licked his lips and spat a reply.

'I never tried to kill that copper. I just pushed him, and his mate here, when they came to Josie's flat. He fell over and got up again. How is that attempted murder?'

Mrs Delaney gave him a warning glance.

'We know what happened when you ran from the two officers, and that is something we may address at a later time. But you came back to the flat, didn't you? You found DC Blake there and hit him so hard that he had to be put in a coma to protect his brain. He may still die, in which case you will be looking at a potential murder charge.'

'But I never, I told you. I swear I didn't go...'

'Where did you put the weapon?' asked Kamal. 'A baseball bat, was it?'

'No. I mean, I had no weapon. Why would I go back there when you'd already sussed me?'

'To retrieve the laptop,' said Jack. 'There was a charger there, but no machine.'

All the blood drained from Crompton's face.

'Oh fuck. Oh fucking fuck. I'm dead.'

'What do you mean?' asked Kamal.

Crompton tried to compose himself and failed.

Sobbing, he replied: 'It wasn't mine. I was looking after it for someone.'

'Whose was it?'

'I can't tell you. They'll kill me.'

'Who's Frankie?'

Crompton didn't answer.

'What was on it?'

'I don't know. They told me not to, but I tried to look. It was locked. And if it's lost, I'm dead.'

'So if you didn't go back to the flat, where were you between one and three pm the day before yesterday? If you have an alibi, please tell us,' said Jack.

Crompton sat mutely for a few moments.

'I'd like to talk to my brief now.'

'Okay. We'll take a short break. I must warn you that, in addition to the offences I've mentioned, we want to talk to you about a potential firearms offence. Interview suspended at eleven oh three.'

'What do you think, Kamal?' asked Jack, as they sipped lukewarm coffee from the machine in the custody suite. 'Do you believe him?'

'Well, he's obviously shit-scared about that laptop. I did notice one on a table when we first went round and it wasn't there when Mel found Trevor, so maybe he's telling the truth. They've had half an hour. Let's get him back in and see what he has to say now he's talked to Mrs Delaney.'

Kamal restarted the recording, recited the formalities and asked Crompton if he had anything to add to his previous answers. Paula Delaney spoke in his stead.

'My client has prepared a written statement, which I will now read out to you.' She cleared her throat. 'I, Michael Crompton, admit that I pushed past two police officers outside Josie Lambert's flat, but I did not intend to assault them and knock them down. For this, I apologise. At no time did I return to the flat or attack Detective Constable Blake. At the time of the alleged offence, I was shopping in a Mexton Minimart at least two miles from the flat and I can produce receipts to prove it. CCTV in the minimart will support this. When I was accosted by the officers who arrested me, I did not realise they were police. They claimed to be so but did not produce any identification until after I was handcuffed. I have a number of enemies, and I was in fear of my life, which is why I attempted to defend myself. Also, I was in pain from the cuts on my face, so I probably wasn't thinking clearly. This was why I borrowed the pharmacy van to look for pain killers and antibiotics. I have no further comment to make on these matters.'

'All right, Mr Crompton,' said Jack, inwardly seething. 'If you provide us with those receipts we will speak to the shopkeeper and request access to the CCTV. Can you tell us why someone would wish to kill you over the missing laptop?'

'No comment.'

'I'll ask you again, who did it belong to?'

'No comment.'

'OK,' said Jack. 'Changing the subject, how did you get those cuts on your face?'

'Cut myself on some glass.'

'Where was this?'

'Don't remember.'

'Why didn't you go back to the hospital for treatment instead of "borrowing", as you put it, the pharmacy van?'

'I had stuff to do.'

Kamal took over the questioning.

'In the vehicle, which you crashed into a lamppost three nights ago, we found gunshot residue. Do you own a firearm, Mr Crompton?'

'No comment.'

'Can you suggest how that residue came to be in the vehicle?'

'No comment.'

'Not far from the crash site a 3D-printed firearm, which had apparently exploded, was found. Would that have anything to do with the wounds on your face?'

'No comment.'

'Blood was found on the weapon, Mr Crompton, and is being processed for DNA as we speak. Would you like to amend your answer?'

'No comment.'

Kamal looked at Jack, who nodded and spoke.

'Mr Crompton, you will be returned to the cells while we consult a senior officer over how to proceed. Interview terminated at eleven fifty-three.'

'Can I remind you, Detective Sergeant,' said Paula Delaney,

after Crompton had left, 'that the custody clock is ticking. You have under six hours in which to charge or release my client. I believe the receipts you need are in Mr Crompton's wallet, which you have among his possessions.'

'I'm well aware of the custody clock, Mrs Delaney. The Superintendent has authorised a further twelve hours while we continue our investigations. We will, of course, check Crompton's alibi and act accordingly. But there remains the question of the firearm, which is a much more serious matter than the assault on two officers and the theft. The magistrates are currently hearing our application for a further extension until the DNA results are back. We are also examining your client's clothes for gunshot residue. If you wish to speak to him again, please see the custody sergeant. We will, of course, notify you when we resume questioning.'

Chapter Twenty-Six

'So the bugger's got an alibi!' an incredulous Emma Thorpe snorted, when Jack and Kamal reported the content of the interview.

'Looks like it,' replied Jack. 'The receipts support his story. What do you want to do with him now?'

'Get someone to check the CCTV at the minimart, just to be sure. I think that bollocks about being in fear of his life, hence the attack on Mel and Tom, might get him off the assault charge so the CPS probably won't touch it. That just leaves twocking the van and theft of drugs. Can you check with the pharmacy and find what's missing, Kamal, please? Did he have anything on him?'

'Some painkillers and diazepam. That's all.'

'Well diazepam's Class C, so we can do him for unlawful possession of that, at least. But the thing that worries me is the weapon. We'd bail him on the other charges but we might get a remand on a firearms charge.'

'I'll chase up the lab for the DNA results.'

'Thanks, Jack. The Super's extension expires at five-thirty in the morning. I just hope we've convinced the mags that we've got sufficient grounds to hold him. And we need to look again at the assault on Trevor. They say he's improving but isn't well enough to talk to us yet. He may not remember anything, anyway.'

'One thing, guv,' said Kamal. 'If he made the weapon himself, he must have a 3D printer somewhere. The only address we have for him is Josie Lambert's flat, and they've only been together for a few weeks. He must have another one, and somewhere to operate the printer.'

'You're right Kamal. Amira's identified possible locations for a flat and a workshop. Mel and Sally are taking a look at an industrial estate this afternoon. We need to search his previous address, so check the one on his driving licence, though he may have moved around since it was issued, and the usual sources. Meanwhile, I'll apply for the release of his phone records so we can try to identify who he's been talking to. That might just give us a lead on who his target was. At the moment, we haven't a bloody clue. Get a civilian investigator to help you with this lot. By the way, one bit of good news – Martin Rowse is rejoining us as a CI. Apparently, he missed the job and was bored with stalking husbands who were playing away, and people throwing phoney sickies, for Mexton Investigations. We'll be pleased to see him back. He was devastated when he heard what happened to Trevor.'

Jack smiled at the prospect of working with Martin again.

'And Alice is okay with that?'

'Yes. She realised he was frustrated and, as long as he's not chasing villains and in danger, she's happy. By the way, Mel's going back to Jenny Pike's place later to take another look before tomorrow's briefing. She's bloody determined, isn't she?'

'That's our Mel,' Jack chuckled, and went in search of coffee.

Chapter Twenty-Seven

'So you're OK, back at work then?' queried Mel, as Sally steered the unmarked police car through a maze of low-rise, seventies-built industrial units and workshops.

Sally smiled.

'Yeah, I'm fine. I think. I'm getting counselling, and I still dream about being locked in that burning cellar occasionally. My ribs still hurt a bit. But you've had worse.'

'Maybe,' said Mel, reflecting on several occasions when she'd nearly lost her life in the line of duty.

'Anyway,' continued Sally, 'I'd rather be working than moping. So what exactly are we looking for?'

'Somewhere in this warren we reckon Crompton has a workshop of some kind where he made the printed weapon. It wouldn't need to be very big, as long as it's got power. Once we locate it, we can apply for a warrant. Park up and we'll wander around on foot.'

The two detectives cast their eyes around the site. They quickly discounted larger premises used by vehicle-related firms, as well as a seedy-looking gym, a metal-plating works and a small furniture workshop.'

'How about through there?'

Sally pointed to a covered passage between two larger units.

The passageway led to an open steel door. Either side of a corridor there were doors labelled with their occupant's names. Computer servicing firms, an audio repairer, games designers and companies with impenetrable acronyms hired space there. Several doors bore no names or logos. Outside one of them a bulky individual, in a hoody and trackies, was fiddling with the lock.

'Good afternoon, sir,' called Mel. 'We're with Mexton police. I wonder if you can help us?'

The man looked round, furtively.

'What do you want?'

'Have you seen this man around here? Does he have a workshop?' she asked, showing him a picture of Michael Crompton.

The man started when he saw the picture and looked away.

'Sorry. Never seen him. Look, I gotta go. I brought the wrong keys.'

Before Mel had a chance to ask his name, he pushed past the two officers and rushed down the corridor. A few seconds later, they heard the sound of a motorbike starting up, the noise quickly fading into the distance.

Coppers! And they know about Crompton! Marcus roared off on the bike and parked round the corner. *If the cops get that laptop, I'm fucked. And so is Frankie. He'll get to me, wherever I am. I've got no choice. I'll have to deal with them.* The car park was slowly emptying as people left for the day. Marcus waited in the doorway of an empty unit, concealed from casual glances, from which he could see the passageway to Crompton's workshop.

'He lied, of course,' said Sally. 'And I reckon he was trying to get into Crompton's workshop. We'll knock on a few doors. See if anyone recognises him.'

Three of the units they knocked on were unoccupied. Two people had never seen Crompton, but a third, a website designer, said he recognised him and confirmed he rented the unit that the hooded man was trying to open. He had noticed Crompton coming in as he was leaving, late in the day, on a couple of occasions. He had only exchanged a couple of words with him, and didn't know his name, but he knew which unit he rented. He provided the detectives with details of the managing agents. Mel thanked him and phoned the office.

'Jack, we've found the workshop. Unit 42 on the Oldmexton Industrial Estate. I'm texting you the name and address of the managing agents. Can we serve a search warrant on them? Fortunately, they're local, so they should be able to let us in. Someone rather iffy was trying to open the door when we arrived, so I don't want to leave the premises. Could you get someone to bring us the keys?'

'Sure. Hang on until they get there. I'll get on to the agents and ask the DCI to request a warrant now. Well done.'

Chapter Twenty-Eight

IT WAS four-thirty by the time a youth with the keys turned up on a moped. Most of the premises were packing up for the day or had already done so, and even the burger van in the car park was showing signs of closing.

'My boss was very insistent,' said the youth, attempting to assert his non-existent authority. 'I must stay with you all the time. We have to protect our customers' rights.'

'I'm afraid that's not how it works,' said Mel, kindly. 'Look, why don't you go and get yourself a burger while the van's still serving? You can't come in with us in case the workshop is a crime scene. If we finish quickly, we'll give you the keys back. If not, we'll drop them into the office tomorrow.'

Reluctantly, the lad handed over the keys and hared off to the van. Mel and Sally walked briskly down the corridor to Crompton's workshop and Mel slipped the key into the lock.

When nearly all the tenants appeared to have left, Marcus was about to move from his hiding place. He paused when he saw a youth on a moped drive into the car park. The lad parked, pulled some keys from his pocket and approached the passage. He watched as the young man came out and ran to a burger van that was about to close up. He made his move. He checked that his sawn-off was loaded, ran back to the unit and approached the door, cocking the weapon.

'Booby trap?' queried Sally, as Mel turned the key, recalling a previous search when she'd spotted a bomb set to go off when the door was opened.

'Nah. Crompton's not that bright.'

The door opened smoothly, and Sally found the light switch.

'Holy shit,' exclaimed Mel. 'Look at this lot!'

A 3D printer stood on a table, strips and shavings of plastic strewn around it. A vice was bolted to a small bench that was covered in bits of tubing and metal filings. Beneath a diagram of some kind of firearm, pinned to the wall, an empty box of nine mm ammunition had been dropped on the floor. A small laptop was perched on a stool beside the printer.

Mel and Sally stood in silence, gazing at Crompton's makeshift gun factory, a silence broken by the scuff of a trainer on concrete and the unmistakeable sound of a shotgun being cocked.

Chapter Twenty-Nine

THE TWO DETECTIVES held their breath. Mel motioned to Sally, and they took up position behind the door. Nobody moved. They could hear breathing from the corridor. Then, another footstep. As the twin barrels of a sawn-off shotgun came into view, Mel and Sally threw themselves against the door, smashing it into the gunman's hands. The weapon fired and it fell to the floor. The deafening bang, amplified by the confined space, made their ears ring and the sour tang of gun smoke filled their nostrils.

'Police!' yelled Mel as the two women crashed into the shooter, knocking him to the ground. It made no difference to his struggling. He rammed a fist into Sally's stomach, winding her, brought his knee up, smashing it into Mel's ribs, and headbutted her, causing blood to stream from her nose. Temporarily unrestrained, he crawled over to the dropped shotgun and picked it up by the barrels, flinching as he grabbed the hot metal. Mel staggered to her feet. *One barrel fired or two? I don't fucking know.* She steadied herself as the gunman, still on his knees, reversed his hold on the weapon and aimed it towards Sally, his damaged fingers searching for the second trigger.

'Fuck off or I'll kill...'

Mel kicked him hard in the face, breaking his jaw and knocking him out. The shotgun clattered harmlessly to the floor. Sally groaned as the pain in her ribs flared up.

'Why is it you keep nearly getting me killed, Mel?' she complained, speaking loudly to combat the ringing in their ears. 'This was supposed to be a perfectly safe routine enquiry. Perhaps I should ask to be partnered with Kamal in future.'

'Ah, you'd miss me,' said Mel, putting her arm around her colleague and smiling encouragingly. 'Anyway, he couldn't have shot you.'

She gestured towards the dropped weapon.

'Both hammers are down, so either both barrels fired or only one hammer was cocked. How are you, anyway?'

'My guts and ribs hurt where he hit me, and I'm as nervous as a pig in the Greggs factory. But OK, I suppose.'

'Don't worry about it.'

'But look at you – blood all over your top. You'll be wearing the Grateful Dead T-shirt when you get back to the station.'

Mel grinned and held a tissue over her nose.

'Look, we've got to restrain this bastard before he wakes up. Call for backup and an AFO to deal with the shotgun. Better ask for an ambulance, too. The paramedics will need to check you out, as well as dealing with this arsehole. I'll have a rummage around the workshop for a piece of rope or something.'

A low moan came from the attacker, and he began to stir. Mel grabbed a roll of gaffer tape from the desk, heaved him on to his front and bound his wrists behind him.

'What's your name?' she asked, when the man appeared to be fully conscious.

'Fuck off,' he mumbled, his jaw obviously hurting.

'OK, Mr Fuckoff, I'm Detective Constable Cotton and I'm arresting you on suspicion of possessing a prohibited firearm, namely, a shotgun with a barrel less than twenty-four-inches long.'

She recited the caution.

'I'm now going to search you. Is there anything in your pockets that could harm me?'

'Fuck off.'

Mel pulled on a pair of nitrile gloves and, with Sally's help, went through his clothing. They retrieved two mobile phones, a small plastic bag containing a whitish powder, a folded butterfly knife and three live shotgun cartridges.

Mel and Sally stood either side of the prone, occasionally cursing, suspect, until uniforms arrived. Addy, in full tactical firearms gear, checked the shotgun, tagged it to show it was safe and put it in a clear evidence box. He also collected the cartridges.

'What have you two been up to?' he smiled.

'Oh, the usual. Preserving the King's Peace. Dealing with an armed suspect. Nearly getting shot. Nothing much really,' Mel replied, grinning at her colleague. 'Was the other chamber loaded?'

'Yes, it was. As you noticed, it wasn't cocked. But it was less than a second away from being ready to fire. Knocking him out was a good call.'

'Not exactly the recommended procedure, I know. But reasonable force and all that.'

'Who is he?'

'He wouldn't give his name but there's a driving licence in the name of Marcus Forrest. Looks genuine.'

'OK. I'd better be off. I think I hear an ambulance.'

'Yeah. Thanks for coming, Addy.'

As Forrest was escorted to the ambulance, and Sally had been given the all clear, an anxious Jack appeared in the doorway.

'Are you both OK?'

'A bit of a ruck. Nothing too serious,' replied Mel. 'My ears are still ringing, though.'

Sally nodded her agreement but seemed to tremble slightly.

'It looks very much as though this was where Crompton made the weapon,' Mel continued. 'We didn't have a chance to look closely before the gunman arrived. I know it's a mess in here, but we need forensics to give it a good going over.'

'I agree,' replied Jack. 'We found Crompton's flat and there's a team examining it at the moment. Apparently, it's already been turned over. I'll ask for someone else to come out here. We'll seal the room and take the keys. Now, get yourselves back to the station, get cleaned up and write your statements. Well done, both of you.'

Chapter Thirty

'WHY ARE you wearing a T-shirt featuring a sixties hippie rock band?' asked Kamal, as Mel joined him beside the coffee machine.

'It's a tradition. Anyone who has to change bloodied clothes has to wear it. It was left behind by someone years ago.'

'Oh. What if two people need a change?'

'I think there's one featuring Metallica as a backup, but I've never used it.'

'Blimey, you lot are odd down here. I thought the Met was a bit weird, but this is weirder.'

'Cheeky sod. Now are you going to let me get at the machine?'

Mel carried a drink over to Sally and sat down beside her.

'How are you doing?' she asked.

'Better than expected, actually.' Sally smiled cautiously. 'It happened so quickly I didn't have time to be scared. Ventham's cellar was much worse. But I'll see my counsellor as soon as I can. Come on, the boss is waiting for us.'

'Good evening, everyone,' began Emma. 'Thanks for staying late. I would like to welcome DI Nick Gilmour, from the NCA, to this Operation Athlete briefing. As most of you know, two young males were found shot, execution style, in a flat on the Eastside, four days ago. Forensics sent images of the bullets, recovered from the bodies, to NABIS, who contacted the NCA, which is why DI Gilmour is with us today. Over to you, Nick.'

'Thank you, Emma. The reason we are interested in this case is that the bullets appear to have been adapted for use in converted starting pistols. Now, as you know, these devices are only supposed to fire blanks, and you don't need a firearms certificate to possess them. But, in recent years, underworld armourers have been modifying them to fire live ammunition. Which makes them deadly.'

'How difficult is that?' asked Emma.

'An experienced operator can do it in half an hour,' Gilmour replied. 'Over eight hundred illegally converted blank-firing weapons, of one design, were retrieved between 2021 and 2024, and in 2023 more illegal discharges were reported from converted weapons than from genuine ones. There have been several fatalities.'

'But can't they ban these blank pistols?' asked Mel.

'Four models, from Turkey, were banned in 2024, and there was an amnesty, but we've no idea how many were in the country and not handed in. Some are still smuggled in. Also, there are other models, still legal, that can be converted.'

'Shit,' muttered Jack, under his breath. 'So are you suggesting someone's doing this locally?'

'We've seen a number of similar incidents across the South of England,' replied Gilmour. 'And Hampshire police recovered a converted weapon from a drug dealer in Portsmouth last month. No DNA or fingerprints, and, of course, the owner refused to say where he got it from. So, I'm briefing all teams looking into incidents where converted weapons have been used and asking them to keep their eyes open and let us know of any similar cases. We are particularly interested in finding out who's doing the conversions so any intelligence on that would be gratefully received.'

'We'll certainly do our best,' said Emma. 'Is there anything else we should know about?'

'There is a related issue,' replied Gilmour. 'It's legal to own a conventional firearm, such as a pistol, which has been deactivated. With skill and the proper tools, it's possible to restore such a weapon to its original, lethal, state. Sometimes, it's frighteningly easy. In one case, a Bren gun had been deactivated by welding a rod in the barrel. The owner banged it on the floor, and the rod fell out, leaving him with a functioning machine gun. I don't believe this is happening here, but it's something to watch out for.'

Emma shuddered.

'OK. Thank you, Nick. Will you stay for the rest of the briefing?'

'No, I have to get on. I'm due in Winchester at eight o'clock. Nice to meet you all.'

When Emma had shown Nick out, and the team had refilled their coffee cups, she resumed the briefing.

'So, Jack, where are we with the shootings?'

'Not much further. Dr Durbridge confirmed that each death was a result of a bullet in the brain, travelling upwards from the back of the neck. Powder burns, and the nature of the wounds, indicated that the weapon was in contact with the skin when fired. The bullets remained in the skulls, which indicates a low-powered pistol was used. We now know about the odd ammunition. Both victims tested positive for cocaine and cannabis. He said that the men had been beaten shortly before death – bruising came out later – and, in each case, several fingers had been fractured. There were marks on their wrists suggesting they had been restrained in some way, possibly by plastic or metal ties that were removed before the bodies were found.'

'So they were tortured?'

'Apparently. He wouldn't commit himself to time of death, but said it was likely to be at least a couple of hours before he first saw them and probably not longer than eight hours before.'

'What about forensics?' asked Sally.

'Nothing of use. The flat was a tip, with no surfaces suitable for fingerprinting, and God knows how many people's DNA spread around. No helpful footwear marks or stepped-in blood. No weapons were discovered, but the search team did find a few baggies of heroin and some crack. Samples are being analysed.'

'Anything else? Somebody give me some good news, please,' said Emma, despairingly.

'We've got a phone,' said Mel. 'It was under Tyson Harper's body. It's been stamped on, but the SIM card was still there, and Digital Forensics reckon they can still get something off the memory. Amira says she'll get onto it when she's finished looking at the phone Trevor had in his pocket.'

'I suppose that's better than nothing. But the long and the short of it is two people have been shot dead in the middle of Mexton, and we've got bugger all. What the hell are the media going to make of that? Speaking of the media,' her tone softened, 'Mr Farlowe has agreed to launch a formal investigation into Jenny Pike's death. There will be a briefing tomorrow morning. In the meantime, carry on with these shootings. Contact informants and anyone else who might be prepared to talk to us, either about the weapons or the targets. Jack, have a word with Derek Palmer on the Drugs Squad. His folk may know of the victims. I'm off to the hospital. I gather Trevor is showing signs of waking up.'

The team dispersed, cheered by the news about Trevor but gloomy at the prospects of making progress on the shootings. Emma called Mel and Sally into her office and closed the door. She sighed.

'Another narrow escape for you two. According to Jack, Mel dismissed it as "a bit of a ruck". Come on, now. You could have been killed by that bugger.'

'That's true. I can't speak for Sally, but I didn't think about it at the time. I guess I just reacted. It should have been a routine check on the premises: we never expected there to be any danger otherwise we would have had vests and backup. But, in some forces, uniforms deal with this type of thing almost on a daily basis.'

Sally nodded.

'Yes, I made a bit of a joke about it at the time,' continued Mel. 'That's what we do. Sometimes it's hysterical laughter, like when we were rescued from that cellar. It keeps the shit away for a while. Locks it in a box. But I can tell you that tonight, outside half a bottle of brandy, I'll be sobbing myself to sleep in Tom's arms.'

'How about you, Sally?' asked Emma. 'Did you come back to work too soon?'

'No, guv. I had to get back on the horse. At home I just had Helen – who's brilliant – but I needed to be around coppers who understand what the job's like. The counsellor agreed with me after I explained how I felt. But I will get my ribs looked at again.'

'Do either of you want some time off?'

'No' the DCs said, in unison.

'I agree with Sally,' said Mel. 'We have to keep going. When we've sorted these cases out, perhaps I'll take some leave. I've got plenty owing.'

'Well make sure you do. Both of you.' She smiled. 'Well done, today. It was bloody brilliant work. Now write up your statements, go home and try to relax. I'll see you tomorrow.'

Chapter Thirty-One

Emma found Susie Blake next to her husband's hospital bed, crying her heart out.

'He didn't know me. He opened his eyes and asked who I was. He didn't bloody know me. Then he went back to sleep. What have those bastards done to him?'

Emma pulled a paper towel from a dispenser on the wall and handed it to Susie, putting her arm, awkwardly, round her shoulders.

'He's just come out of a coma, lass. He's got a head injury and he's still full of drugs. He doesn't know cabbage from Christmas. I'm sure he'll recognise you as he improves.'

'You don't know that. And the doctors won't tell me anything. "Just take it hour by hour," they say. A lot of bloody good that is.'

'Look, Susie, I'm not a doctor, but surely it's a good sign that he woke up and is breathing on his own?'

'But we've been married for five years, and he didn't recognise me.'

'All right. I'll tell you a secret. I had a spot of surgery a couple of years ago, under a general anaesthetic called propofol, otherwise known as milk of amnesia. When I came round, Mike was there, but I didn't know who he was. First, I thought he was a lad I went out with in the sixth form, and then I thought he was our local undertaker. It took me several minutes to realise it was Mike, and I've never told him this.'

Susie sniffed and attempted a faint smile.

'Are you sure he'll remember me? Eventually?'

'Course I am. Look, I'll stay by him if you want to nip to the loo or get a coffee. Stretch your legs or something. I'll phone you if he looks like waking up again.'

'Thanks, Emma. I will. I'll try to find a sandwich or something. I haven't eaten since breakfast. Just couldn't face it.'

Emma smiled as Susie left the room and turned to her sleeping colleague. She had exaggerated the story about not recognising Mike slightly, though it was basically true. But she hadn't been bashed over the head, and she worried that she might have given Susie false hope. Looking at Trevor, his head swathed in bandages and his face slack and bloodless, the fury mounted within her. Some low-life bastard had done this, and they would get him for it. She would make bloody sure they did.

Mel, nitrile gloves in place, pushed open the door to Jenny's house, disturbing a pile of mail and circulars that had built up over the past few days. She picked them up, checked to see if there was anything likely to be helpful, and placed them on a small hall table. She noted a card from a courier firm that could be useful. The place smelled stale and unaired. Jenny's partner had been asked to stay away from the premises while the investigation continued, and her fingerprints had been checked against those found. Unsurprisingly, they had matched.

The house was generally clean and tidy, although a few surfaces could have done with dusting, and a small cobweb dangled above the door. Traces of fingerprint powder were visible in places, and the bed had not been made since SOCOs had examined it. Mel resisted the urge to pull the covers back into place and tried to imagine how someone could commit a murder and leave no trace. It's completely contrary to Locard's Principle. The killer must have been not just forensically aware but forensically competent, too. It just didn't make sense to her. She shook her head, baffled. It wasn't often she was completely stumped.

She wandered through the house, trying to imagine the killer's movements, and spent a long time in the bedroom trying to visualise the attack on Jenny. She shuddered and came up with nothing useful. Deciding to call it a day, as Tom was bound to have the dinner on, she was just about to open the front door to leave when something caught her eye.

Mel found a fork in the compact fitted kitchen and heated it for a few seconds in the flame from the gas hob. When it had cooled, she used it, slowly and carefully, to extricate a dead mosquito from the cobweb above the door. Slipping the unfortunate insect into an evidence bag, which she labelled and signed, she closed and locked the door behind her. On her way home she wondered whether she was wasting her time and, more importantly, the force's limited budget – if, of course, she could persuade the powers that be to cough up. But that was for tomorrow. Tonight, she would try to banish the horrors of the day with a vindaloo, a lot of brandy, and a long-promised viewing of the second half of *Dune*.

Chapter Thirty-Two

In a nightclub car park in central Mexton a business meeting was taking place. Absent were notetakers and PAs tapping on laptops. The two negotiating parties contrasted sharply. Francis Garrett, flanked by several stony-faced men with hostile attitudes and bulges under their armpits, wore an immaculate three-piece suit and expensive leather shoes. Jasper Burnham and his companions wore trackies, hoodies and trainers. Both principals radiated menace.

'Jasper,' began Garrett. 'I've invited you onto my turf, with a guarantee of safety, for a chat. I thought we had an understanding about Mexton. We would each have a specific product range, not interfere with each other's markets, and keep out of each other's way. Now, while I have plans for expanding my business, I had always intended to keep to our agreement.'

'Yes, Frankie, but...'

'Don't interrupt.'

Garrett's voice cut through the air like a barbed wire whip.

'It seems, however, that you have not. I entrusted a new recruit with some product only to find that he'd passed it on to one of your low-level employees. He claimed that the police had taken it, but my sources told me that wasn't true. He will be dealt with, and I want my property back.'

There was a brief, tense, silence.

'More serious, and this has upset me considerably, a laptop containing my business plans and other damaging material has been stolen. My information is that the thief, Crompton, who will shortly be dead although he doesn't know it, took it at your behest. You may now speak.'

Burnham shook his head and replied, his strong Bristol accent contrasting with Garretts icy received pronunciation.

'The blow was nothing to do with oi. It was your guy's mistake. Just so's we don't fall out, oi'll 'ave it returned to you, with twice the value of what was sold on top. But oi don't know where your laptop's to.'

'I'm afraid, Jasper, that I don't believe you. With that information you could seriously impede my business. And I won't have it. I guaranteed you safe conduct tonight and that stands. I am a man of my word. But if my laptop isn't returned, free of any signs of hacking, within twenty-four hours, I will visit all kinds of hell on you and your associates. And as I said, I'm a man of my word. Goodnight.'

With that, Garrett turned away and walked unhurriedly to his car while his companions scanned the Bristolians for any aggressive movements. They just managed to hear Jasper mutter, 'Stupid prick. Who does he think he is?' and turned to each other and grinned.

'It's a grand.'

'No fucking way.' Nathan Jones's incredulity left the other man unmoved.

'It's a grand. But I'll give you half back if you return it still working.'

Nathan thought for a moment. He reckoned he really needed a weapon. He'd spent days trying to find one. After all, someone had tried to shoot him, hadn't they? But a grand? He'd have to shift a lot of product to cover that much on top of his other expenses.

'OK.'

Grudgingly he retrieved a selection of notes from various pockets and counted out a thousand pounds.

'Do I get any ammo, too?'

'Yeah. Five rounds. Any more 'll cost you. You need to get in close, and you only get one shot before reloading. There's no rifling, so the bullet can't be matched, but handle everything with plastic gloves. Keep it in this plastic bag so you don't leave DNA or fibres. If you fuck up, don't come back to me.'

Nathan nodded and held out his hand. The other man dropped a plastic bag containing a peculiar-looking pistol into it and drove out of the car park without another word.

Chapter Thirty-Three

'HAVE you heard the one about the bishop, the otter and the yogurt?' asked Terry.

'No, we haven't,' chorused his friends, unenthusiastically, sipping their pints in the Green Man.

'And we don't want to,' said one of them, *sotto voce.*

The trouble with Terry's jokes was that they weren't funny. The only people who laughed at them were Terry himself and his dutiful girlfriend, Marie. Ignoring the response from the naysayer, Terry launched into a rambling tale that was convoluted, anatomically improbable and rather rude. By the time he got to the punchline, most of his listeners had lost track of the story, and one had muttered 'Beam me up, Scotty' under his breath.

Terry was oblivious to his companions' lack of interest and, as he wandered off to the gents, basking in the feeling of a joke well told, he searched his memory for another gem with which to entertain the company. All thoughts of humour evaporated when, as he approached the urinals, a man stumbled out of a cubicle behind him and collapsed on the floor. Stepping carefully over the slowly spreading pool of blood, Terry vomited noisily into a washbasin and staggered back into the bar, wiping his mouth on his sleeve.

'Murder!' he yelled. 'Someone's been murdered!'

'Come off it, Tel,' one of his mates called, 'is this another of your stupid jokes?'

But the sight of Terry's ashen face convinced the bartender collecting glasses that something was wrong. He checked the toilets, called 999 and, within ten minutes, the police had cordoned off the pub and were preventing aggrieved customers from leaving until they had provided their details. Anyone who had been sitting near the gents was asked to remain, but no one spoke to say they had seen anything suspicious. As for Terry, he vowed he would never tell jokes in the Green Man again.

Chapter Thirty-Four

Day 6

'Good morning, ladies and gentlemen,' called DCI Farlowe, as the team settled down. 'I'm taking this briefing as DI Thorpe is dealing with a stabbing in a pub that occurred last night. This is the first briefing of Operation Daffodil, the investigation into the death of Jenny Pike. It was Sally and Mel's perceptive work that led us to believe that Ms Pike's death was non-accidental. Can you tell us what you've found, please.'

'Thanks, boss,' replied Mel. 'As most of you know, Jenny was found in her home, asphyxiated with a bag over her head and pornography running on her laptop. Overhearing officers in the canteen, Sally realised that she would not have been watching that type of porn as she was gay. Furthermore, her partner was adamant that she would never have tried autoerotic asphyxiation, as she was vehemently opposed to the practice.'

Someone sniggered and Farlowe glared at them.

'Jenny died between eleven thirty on the night of the second, when she was seen returning home, and eight the following morning, when a courier needing her signature was unable to get a response and left a card. A friend, who had called to give her a lift to the gym, was concerned about her lack of response to the doorbell and her mobile so she phoned us. She was discovered at ten forty-five by uniformed officers. Dr Durbridge couldn't provide a time of death, other than to say it was sometime during the night, earlier rather than later.'

'Any witnesses?' asked Kamal.

'Apart from the neighbour who saw her getting out of a taxi, no. I managed to get some footage from a doorbell camera, across the road from Jenny's house, which appears to show someone at her door at twelve forty-seven. Digital forensics tried to clean up the blurred image, but it's impossible to see what the person looked like or whether they were coming or going.'

'Thank you, Mel,' said Farlowe. 'I understand that the scene was forensically clean, with no trace evidence at all. The killer was clearly forensically aware and had planned his or her actions down to the last detail. It's probable they knew the layout of the house – perhaps they'd been there before. So, we need to canvass the neighbours for any sightings of suspicious individuals in the area in the days before Jenny died. Someone must talk to her colleagues at the *Messenger* to find out if anyone had a grudge against her and we also need to look at her phone and social media. So far, we have no motive, and I think that's key to identifying a suspect.'

At that point, Sally's phone buzzed, and she glanced at a new text.

'Boss,' she called, 'I've had a message from IT. Amira says the porn was uploaded onto Jenny's machine at twelve thirty-nine. So, the figure outside her door must have been leaving rather than arriving.'

'That's useful, thank you. We now have a more accurate time of death. Right, Jack will organise the tasks. Is there anything else before we finish?'

Mel spoke up, hesitantly.

'There's one thing, guv. I went back to Jenny's yesterday, and I found a mosquito. It could be forensically useful.'

A few officers laughed. One pointed out that Jenny hadn't been killed by malaria, and Farlowe looked thoughtful.

'Go on,' he said.

'I read of a case where someone was identified from blood in the gut of a mosquito that had fed on them. It's an outside chance, I know. But what if the insect had bitten the killer? We may have their DNA.'

'I think I've heard of a similar case,' said Farlowe. 'It's a very long shot, but I'll talk to the lab and find out how feasible, and how expensive, it would be to do the tests. Good idea, though.

'Changing the subject, we've been granted an extra thirty-six hours to question Crompton, but the magistrate made it clear that an additional extension would be highly unlikely, unless we obtain more evidence. So getting DNA results for the firearm and the workshop is vital. OK, everyone. Get to work.'

Chapter Thirty-Five

ROGER BARRETT, the editor of the *Mexton Messenger* was a tall, rather stooped man with a worried expression that looked as though it had been permanently etched on his face. He ushered Mel and Sally into his office and closed the door.

'We were all devastated to hear what happened to Jenny,' he began. 'Some of us thought her death was highly suspicious, even before you started investigating it. We'll help you in any way we can.'

'Thank you, sir,' replied Mel. 'Can we begin by asking how Jenny got on with her colleagues?'

'Pretty well, these days. When she was a normal reporter there was some friction. She was competitive. Always had to get the big story. That eased off when she was promoted to deputy editor, after that unfortunate incident with the poisoner. You saved her life, I believe,' he said, looking at Mel.

'Well, I helped. Do go on, please.'

'Jenny still loved investigating stories and was a passionate believer in local newspapers, at a time when everything is going online and many printed papers are closing. She felt the

Messenger should serve the community and expose wrongdoing. Hence her stint as crime correspondent.'

'So, she must have made enemies,' said Sally. 'Anyone in particular spring to mind?'

The editor looked slightly shamefaced.

'I know she wasn't popular with the police. She could be a bit – how can I put it – over-critical.'

'Scathing and obstructive might be better terms,' muttered Mel.

'How about criminals?' continued Sally, ignoring her colleague's remark.

'She's covered the activities of some serious villains, it's true, and I'm sure she has her own contacts in the underworld. But she's never written a major exposé. She wasn't Woodward or Bernstein. She hadn't had any threats, as far as I know.'

'What was she working on before she died?' asked Mel.

'Rumours of fiddled election expenses relating to our previous MP, and possible backhanders to a couple of members of the Planning Committee. Nothing that could get her killed, I'm sure. Mind you, I think there was something else. She was a bit secretive about it. She often had that focused, hunting look on her face, like a jaguar about to drop on a capybara.'

'And you've no idea what the story was?'

The editor shrugged.

'Fraid not.'

'Thank you, Mr Barrett. You've been most helpful,' said Sally. 'One last thing. Did she have a computer here?'

'No. She used a laptop, which she docked with a workstation when she came in. Most of us do the same. This gave her access to our system without the use of Wi-Fi and the internet.'

'So does she have any files on your server?'

'I can check. I'll talk to our lawyer, but I think you'll need some sort of warrant before I can give you access to them.'

'We'll look into that as well,' said Mel, somewhat frostily. 'In the meantime, we'd like a list of her colleagues. I'm sure you can provide that without a warrant.'

'Yes, of course. I'll email it to you. Feel free to talk to any of the staff in the newsroom on your way out.'

Barrett led the detectives out of his office and called out to his staff.

'Listen up, everyone. These police officers are investigating Jenny's death. Please give them any assistance you can. And please refrain from any smutty speculation about what happened. Thank you.'

He returned to his office after saying goodbye and closed the door.

———

'What do you reckon?' asked Sally, as Mel steered them out of the car park, narrowly missing something dead and furry on the tarmac. A small motorbike with minimal silencing shot past, its exhaust noise ripping through the air.

'Bloody hell!' said Sally. 'That makes more noise than my Dad's old Triumph Bonneville, which had four times the engine size. Sorry. You were saying?'

'I think he was being straight with us, and the staff we spoke to pretty much confirmed what he said. I'd like to know more about this secret investigation she was involved in, though. And I want to see the files on the server. Amira's still looking at Jenny's laptop, so perhaps she'll find something. I wonder what was in that delivery she missed?'

'Probably something from amazon.'

'No. It was another courier. I think we'll swing by their depot and see if they've still got it. You never know, it could be relevant.'

Chapter Thirty-Six

EMMA KNOCKED WEARILY on Colin Farlowe's office door, a fractious, teething, Genevieve, and being called out in the middle of the night to attend a murder scene, having taken their toll.

'You look wretched, Emma,' the DCI said. 'Can I get you some coffee?'

'No thanks, Colin. I've just had one and I'm waiting for the caffeine to kick in. I dropped in to update you on the stabbing at the Green Man.'

'Please, have a seat. How far have you got?'

'Pretty much nowhere. Terry Faraday, the man who found him, said he had just entered the gents to relieve himself when the victim staggered out of a cubicle and collapsed in front of him. He said nothing, according to Terry, and there was no-one else in the toilets at the time. We spoke to everyone still in the pub when uniforms arrived, and nobody saw anything. A few thought they remembered seeing someone dressed like the victim buying a drink at the bar, but no-one else was with him. Obviously, we didn't have photos to show them.'

'CCTV?'

'Nothing showing the area around the toilets. There's some

over the bar and a camera outside. I've asked for the footage and we'll check it for anything suspicious. We'll also run through the customers' names to see if there are any red flags. The killer likely slipped out before we arrived, so it's probably a waste of time. We've identified the victim, one Marvin Staples, and we're tracing relatives and looking for known associates. He had form for assault, minor dealing and various other unpleasantnesses.'

'OK. Thank you, Emma. We'll have a briefing tomorrow morning. Now go home and get some sleep. You need to recharge your batteries and be on form tomorrow.'

'OK. Thanks. I will. I have to say, I'm getting bloody sick of murders with no leads. This is the fourth we've got on our books. And we don't have enough officers to investigate.'

'I agree. But that's the job. I'll try to borrow a few bodies from Highchester. Now off you go.' He smiled.

As Emma left, Farlowe picked up the phone and dialled human resources.

'Do you have any news about that new DI you promised me,' he asked, 'because I really think we need them.'

———

'We've got him!'

Jack put the phone down and jumped up from his desk, attracting enquiring looks from his colleagues.

'Trevor's attacker?' queried Kamal.

'Sadly, no. But the DNA's back on the weapon. Michael Crompton definitely fired it. No prints, but the blood all over it was his. Should be enough for the CPS to authorise a possession charge. They're still processing DNA from the workshop. Have you heard from Sally and Mel?'

'No. D'you want me to call them?'

'Don't worry. I'll give them the good news when they get back. I'd better let the DCI know.'

Colin Farlowe was working his way through a pile of admin when Jack knocked on his half-open door.

'Good news, boss,' said Jack. 'DNA links Crompton to the weapon.'

'Excellent,' replied Farlowe. 'Of course, what we don't know is who he was firing at. If we did, we could charge him with attempted murder. As it is, he could claim the weapon went off by accident, or he was aiming at a squirrel or something. Nonsense, I know, but we've no way of proving otherwise. Have we had any luck finding the bullet?'

'Not yet. We've looked around the area where the gun was dumped but no luck so far. We haven't got the resources to look very far, given that no-one seems to have been hit by it.'

'Right. Let's interview Crompton again and put the DNA results to him. Whether or not he changes his story, we'll seek authority to charge and put him before the court. We'll ask for a remand as he's obviously dangerous. Good progress! Thanks, Jack.'

Trevor Blake opened his eyes, as he had done, briefly, several times previously before relapsing into sleep. *Where the fuck am I?*' he thought. *Why's my head hurting? What's wrong with my throat? Am I dead? Is that an angel looking at me?* His head began to clear. *I know that angel. She's...* He attempted to raise himself on the bed, only managing a couple of centimetres. He tried to clear his throat.

'Suse?' He croaked. 'Is that you?'

Careless of the leads and tubes projecting from her husband, Susie Blake threw her arms around him.

'Of course it is, you soft sod,' she cried. 'Of course it is. Welcome back, my love. Welcome back.'

Chapter Thirty-Seven

'Emma's looking a bit rough these days,' said Sally, unwrapping a bar of chocolate. 'Want some?'

Mel shook her head.

'No, thanks. But you're right. I think she's trying to do too much. She's working more hours than she's supposed to and misses Genevieve. I hope things are OK at home.'

'No sign of her job share then?'

'Apparently not. I heard Jack mutter something about HR not getting their fingers out but he wouldn't elaborate. But, let's face it, we've all had a pretty rough time of it the past few months.'

'True. But we're still functioning,' said Sally. 'It's Trevor I'm worried about. Head injuries can be bloody nasty and he could be pemanently affected.'

'Ah.' Mel brightened up. 'Some good news there. Susie phoned Jack from the hospital. Apparently, he's conscious and more coherent. He recognised her and has taken a small amount of food. It'll be a while before he can talk to us, but the doctors say there are no signs of permanent brain damage. Whether he'll remember anything is, of course, another matter.'

'That's a relief. I don't suppose we're any closer to finding out who hit him?'

'I haven't heard anything.'

'You know,' Sally mused, 'I think that laptop is the key to it. If we knew what was on it, and who it belonged to – this Frankie, presumably, we'd have a better idea about who took it.'

'I don't see Crompton telling us, though. He's shit-scared of someone. I saw the recordings of his interviews.'

'He's about to be interviewed about the firearm – fancy watching?'

'You bet.'

'Mr Crompton,' began Jack, starting the recording. 'May I remind you that you are still under caution. Present are myself, Detective Sergeant Jack Vaughan, Detective Constable Kamal Chabra and your solicitor, Mrs Paula Delaney. Now, when we interviewed you previously you denied owning a firearm. Is that correct?'

'Yeah. I never had one.'

'OK. I am now informing you that we found your blood, confirmed by DNA analysis, on the remains of a 3D-printed firearm, discarded not far from the site of your collision with a lamppost. Would you like to comment on that?'

Crompton paled and looked at Paula Delaney, who shook her head.

'Er... no comment.'

'We believe that you fired the weapon at someone and that it exploded, causing the injuries to your face. Who were you aiming at?'

'No comment.'

'Do you rent Unit 42 on the Oldmexton Industrial Estate?'

'No comment.'

'Would it surprise you to hear that we found your fingerprints on numerous surfaces and pieces of equipment inside that lockup?'

'No comment.'

'Furthermore, there is evidence to suggest that those premises were being used for the manufacture of an illegal firearm. Would you like to respond to that information?'

'No comment.'

'Do you know someone called Marcus Forrest?

Crompton paled.

'No comment.'

'Is there anything at all you would like to say about these matters, or the matters we questioned you about during your previous interview?'

'No comment.'

'Then I must inform you that we have authorisation from the Crown Prosecution Service to charge you with the unlawful possession of a firearm and the illegal manufacture of a weapon. Other charges may well follow, pending the results of our investigations. You will appear in court tomorrow morning, when we will ask that you be remanded in custody. Interview terminated at sixteen thirty.'

A downcast Crompton was escorted back to his cell, accompanied by his solicitor.

'Did he really think "No comment" would do him any good?' asked Kamal, when the interview room was clear.

Jack shrugged.

'It's a default advised by the solicitor. He can't challenge the evidence here. He'll leave that to his barrister at trial. I didn't really expect anything different. It was bloody close to the wire, though – it's a good job we had the extension from the magistrates. I'd love to know who his target was. Can you look again at his background for possible enemies? He did react to Forrest's name. Can you check for a connection?'

'No problem. By the way, did you see this morning's *Messenger*? There was a letter in it that made me laugh.'

Jack shook his head.

'Come on, I'll show it to you back in the office.'

———

Sally joined Jack and Kamal as they pored over the letters page of the paper.

'This one,' said Kamal. It read:

Dear Sir,

I am becoming increasingly disgusted at the police's refusal to clamp down on antisocial behaviour. Any vertical surface in the town appears to be covered by graffiti, drunken youths carouse through the streets at all hours, accompanied by barely dressed young women with foul vocabularies, and the other night someone shot one of my treasured garden gnomes. I still have the bullet on my desk.

There seems to be no point in reporting these things to the police. I tried several times, and they said they would make a note, but they don't have the resources to investigate. Too busy enforcing point-less speed limits, I'll be bound.

Where will it all end? In total anarchy? I will be writing to the Chief Constable to demand that firm action be taken and I urge your readers to join me.

Yours faithfully,

J. M. Braithwaite

Mexton

'What's that, then, Jack?' asked Kamal. 'Gnomicide? Gnome-slaughter? Assaulting a gnome in the execution of its fishing duties?'

Jack laughed.

'Horrible things. They can shoot the lot of 'em. Not that I said that, of course.'

'Hang on,' said Sally. 'We're looking for a stray bullet, aren't we? Perhaps it was Crompton's.'

'Good point,' replied Jack. 'OK. Contact the letters editor and get the writer's address first thing tomorrow, then go and have a chat with the irascible Mr Braithwaite. Collect the bullet, if he still has it, and send it to ballistics. You never know, it might give us a lead on who Crompton was firing at. It's about bloody time we had one. Now, I must be off. It's pub quiz night and I'm cooking the dinner.'

Chapter Thirty-Eight

Day 7

'At last!' exclaimed Jeremy Braithwaite, opening the door to Sally and scrutinising her warrant card. 'A real policewoman. Do come in, my dear. Have a seat in the lounge. I've got a dossier here listing all the problems that your chaps have been ignoring over the years. Shall I start with the graffiti in the town centre?'

'Just a minute, please, Mr Braithwaite. I think many of your concerns are best dealt with by the community policing team. I'm a detective and I'm here about a more serious matter. The gunshot.'

'Ah yes. I was having a snifter before going to bed when I heard a bang. I thought it was some drunk banging on my fence, so I ignored it. Imagine my shock when I went out to collect my *Telegraph* the following morning – I always take a constitutional before breakfast – and found Nigel with his head blown off.'

'And Nigel is a gnome?'

'That's right. He's the one with the fishing rod. Look.'

Braithwaite drew back the lace curtain and pointed to a congregation of stone figures arranged over half the front garden.

'There he is, between Richard and Donald.'

The decapitated Nigel, still fishing, was perched at the edge of a small pond with his companions, his head a short distance away.

'And you said in the paper that you still have the bullet?'

'Yes, I do.'

He handed Sally a distorted lump of metal, which she dropped into an evidence bag, signing and sealing it.

'Can your boffins tell which gun fired it?'

'I think it's unlikely, Mr Braithwaite. It does seem badly damaged. I'm sure they'll try. Did the bullet come through your fence, do you know?'

'It certainly did. I'll show you.'

Braithwaite led Sally into his garden and, stepping carefully around the collection of concrete homunculi, he pointed to a hole in a wooden fence panel. Mel took a photo of it on her phone.

'That's very helpful, Mr Braithwaite. We have been trying to find out where a firearm was discharged illegally six nights ago, and you may have given us the answer. What time was it when you heard the bang?'

'About eleven,' he replied, clearly pleased with himself.

'OK. We'll send a scene of crimes officer round to work out the trajectory of the bullet. Please don't move Nigel until they've been. We're most grateful for your help.'

'Jolly good. And the other matters?'

'I'll have a word back at the station and see what they can do. Thank you again, and good morning.'

Sally scanned the neighbourhood for doorbell cameras and CCTV. Finding nothing, she returned to her car and drove back to the station.

'You won't believe it,' said Emma, chucking a pile of papers on the table at the start of the morning briefing. 'The bugger's got bail. And his brief didn't even argue against a remand.'

'Go on,' said an incredulous Jack. 'Firearms charges, a strong suggestion that he tried to shoot someone, and the mags let him out? They must be doolally.'

'The chair of the bench said that it was important not to remand people to prison unless absolutely necessary, given the overcrowding.'

'Well, that's bloody great.'

'The funny thing is,' said Emma, 'when bail was granted, he looked upset.'

'Perhaps he was looking forward to prison cuisine,' joked Sally.

'Probably better than the canteen,' said Mel, to murmurs of agreement.

'OK, OK, let's get on with the briefing. How did you get on with Mr Braithwaite, Sally?'

'I collected the bullet, boss, but it's badly damaged. Nigel had a hard head.'

'Nigel?' queried Kamal.

'The garden gnome. The bullet knocked his head off. Mr Braithwaite was quite upset.'

'Should we have a minute's silence?' asked Mel, grinning.

'Don't be silly,' frowned Emma. 'Is the bullet likely to be any use, Sally?'

'I phoned the ballistics lab to say it was coming. They said we might get the calibre but not much more. Crompton's weapon didn't have a rifled barrel, so an absence of rifling marks on the bullet, if they can determine that, would be significant.'

'Thanks, Sally. Turning now to Operation Daffodil, you'll be pleased to hear, that the DSup has agreed to pay for DNA testing on the mosquito Mel found at Jenny Pike's. As it's our only lead, I suppose he didn't have much choice. Anyway, it will be some time before we get any results. How about the missed delivery at Jenny's?'

'The depot manager was unwilling to hand the package over, even though I explained it was a murder enquiry,' replied Sally. 'However, he did agree to get it redelivered and left in Jenny's safe place. It should arrive today.'

'A bit risky, isn't it? Somebody might pinch it,' suggested Kamal.

'Well, we can't have someone sitting there all day,' said Jack, tetchily.

Mel looked thoughtful.

'I could ask Dr Mowlem to keep an eye open for the delivery van and to call us when the package is dropped off. Are you OK with that, boss?'

'All right,' said Emma. 'I suppose so. But tell her not to touch it. Where are we with Jenny's colleagues?'

'Mel and I've spoken to them all,' said Sally. 'They couldn't think of anyone who'd have wanted to kill her. They acknowledged that she could be driven and a bit difficult to work with sometimes, but they were used to it. Apparently, she stood her round in the pub, so there was no real animosity. Two of the reporters thought she was keeping schtum about something she was working on, but they didn't know what. I mentioned we were trying to get hold of her files on the paper's server.'

'We haven't heard back from the editor about gaining access,' said Emma, 'and the DCI is looking into that as well. So, basically, we're no forrader.'

Kamal looked puzzled at the unfamiliar expression.

'Right,' said Emma, 'refill your mugs and we'll resume with the stabbing and shootings in ten minutes.'

Chapter Thirty-Nine

MICHAEL CROMPTON WAS SCARED. He was sure he was being followed. *That bloke in the beanie. Isn't he one of Frankie's men? Who's that, hiding in the doorway when I turned and looked at him? Fuck, isn't that Jerome's car? I recognise the dent in the wing. Why the fucking fuck didn't they remand me? I told that stupid cow not to ask for bail but she was as much use as a Kleenex condom.*

Crompton zig-zagged through the traffic, prompting angry hoots from drivers and more than a few hurled insults. He doubled back, running along the pavement, heedless of collisions with pedestrians. Traffic was stalled at a set of roadworks and, in the middle of the queue, he spotted a marked police car. He'd never been so pleased to see the coppers in all his life. Dashing up to the vehicle, he wrenched one of the windscreen wipers off, dropped his trousers and pants, and mooned the car's occupants.

If that doesn't get me arrested, he thought, *I don't know what the fuck will.*

Across the street, a shaven-headed man with steroidal biceps and the absent teeth of a seasoned streetfighter spoke urgently into his phone.

'We've missed him, boss. He's got 'imself nicked again. Prob'ly thinks he's safe inside.'

'Well make fucking sure he isn't.'

'Michael Crompton wants to talk to you,' said the custody sergeant, when Emma picked up her phone.

'Why? What's happened?'

'He's got himself arrested for criminal damage to a police car and insulting behaviour. He said he wanted to speak to whoever's in charge of the attack on DC Blake.'

'All right. I'm running a briefing at the moment, but I'll come along to talk to him later on. Thanks, Tim.'

Emma carried her coffee back to the briefing room and called everyone to order.

'The stabbing in the Green Man,' she began. 'What do we know about the victim?'

'His name was Marvin Staples, he lived on the Eastside, and he'd been known to us since he was fourteen for various minor offences,' replied Kamal. 'Theft, twocking, possession of Class B, going equipped. He did a few months for assault and ABH a couple of years ago, but he seems to have kept out of trouble since then. He'd had a number of temporary jobs and, for the past three months, worked in a warehouse for a mail order retailer.'

'Amazing!' joked Mel.

'No, Goodsflight,' said Kamal, looking irritated.

'Any relationships?' asked Jack.

'He was unmarried, but he had a sister. She's been asked to identify his body in the mortuary at three this afternoon.'

'Can you go with her, Sally, and have a chat?' requested Emma.

'Sure, boss.'

'We've been through the CCTV,' said Jack. 'There's a figure

in a hoodie picked up entering the pub and leaving it, before and after the stabbing. He wasn't on the recording from the camera above the bar, so he didn't buy a drink. The uniforms who attended are certain they didn't see him, so he must have slipped out before they arrived. Street CCTV didn't pick him up, so he either got into a vehicle or changed his appearance.'

'So, bugger all, then.' Emma ran her hands through her hair. 'Let's focus on Marvin's known associates. His sister might know who some of them are. Has he had a partner? Was he convicted alongside anyone else? Was he part of a local Eastside gang. You know what to do.

'One piece of good news, though,' she continued. 'The search team turned over Marcus Forrest's place and found more cocaine than he could reasonably claim was for personal use. We've got him on intent to supply.

'Now, the shootings. Tyson's phone was mainly used to call other burners, some of which, we believe, were used by other drug dealers before being discarded. Amira and her colleagues are attempting to plot the phone's movements in the hours up to Tyson's death, but it's taking a while. Given that drugs seem to be involved, I've asked DS Derek Palmer, of the drug squad, to brief us on current activities, hopefully tomorrow. I think most of you know him.

'We're looking at known associates, but we don't have much to go on. Both victims seem to have been loners, with no real family connections. Both fathers are inside, and we don't know where the mothers are. Tragic, really. So, basically, that's all we've got. With no forensics, witnesses or CCTV, we're going to have to rely on intel to solve this one. So, please carry on. I'm off to interview Michael Crompton. Not a DI's job, but he did ask for the SIO.'

As Emma walked to the interview room, collecting Kamal on the way, she reflected on her own upbringing. She was raised in a loving family, decently housed and properly fed, with plenty of opportunities in front of her. She would ensure it was the same for Genevieve. But what chances did people like Tyson Harper and Shane Hopton have, growing up in the squalor of the Eastside, with a disintegrating and indifferent family, the only opportunity available being crime? She shook her head and opened the interview room door.

Chapter Forty

'So what's this all about, Michael?' Emma asked, after the formalities had been concluded. 'You deliberately got yourself arrested and I'm told you looked upset when you were granted bail. Why's that?'

'Before I say anything, I need protection. What can you do for me?'

'Protection from whom?'

'I'll tell you in a minute. So? Can you get me remanded?'

'Probably, if we explain to the bench that it is for your own protection. You reckon you'll be safer in prison?'

'Hope so. Out here, they're definitely gonna get me. Inside, there may be a chance.'

'We can certainly talk to the prison governor. I can't promise you'll be safe, but I'll try. So what did you want to tell us?'

Crompton took a deep breath, his fingers tapping nervously on the table. He looked as though Death was about to tap him on the shoulder.

'Look, I aint a grass. But when they said the laptop was gone, I started shitting myself. I was looking after it for Frankie Garrett, a heavy bastard from Portsmouth way. He's been moving into

Mexton to take over the drugs now the Albanians have gone. He's already got most of the blow and gear tied up. Forrest is one of his boys.'

'Yes, I've heard of Garrett. What was on the laptop? And why did he leave it with you?'

'I don't know. And if he knew I'd tried to unlock it he'd've chopped my fingers off. Not sure why he chose me to look after it. Perhaps a test of loyalty before recruiting me?'

He dropped his gaze.

'Could've been he didn't trust someone in his own organisation, or he was expecting to be raided. I dunno. But I was fucking lumbered with it. I couldn't say no.'

'Do you know anyone else in his gang?'

Crompton paused, reluctant to answer.

'There's a bloke they call Speedy. Built like a brick shithouse and very slow moving. But fucking lethal. Saw him once and don't want to again. He often works with a tall, thin guy known as Max the Plank. There's a driver called Jerome and a couple of kids – I didn't get their names. That's all I know.'

'All right, but who would want to take the laptop?'

'I dunno. An enemy of Frankie's, maybe? I thought it might've been you lot, but obviously not. But if Frankie doesn't get it back, I'm dead.'

'OK. Thank you, Michael,' said Emma. 'We'll do all we can to ensure your safety. Now, is there anything you'd like to tell us about manufacturing that firearm?'

'No comment. It's personal.'

'OK.' Emma noted the time, concluded the interview and switched off the recording equipment.

A lead at last! thought Emma, returning to her office. *Not a very big one, but something. I'll ask Derek if he can give us anything on*

Frankie Garrett for tomorrow's briefing. But I'm uneasy about this loyalty test. It sounds like bollocks. But why is he lying? Her thoughts were interrupted by Mel.

'I've had a call from Dr Mowlem. The courier van's just pulled up outside Jenny's place and left a package.'

'Excellent. Nip over there would you, lass, and pick it up?'

'Sure.'

Half an hour later, Mel dropped a bulky, padded envelope on Emma's desk. The DI was just about to open it when Mel shouted 'Stop!'

Emma froze.

'Are you thinking *bomb*?' she asked.

'Could be. Someone obviously hated Jenny. Is there a return address?'

Emma turned the envelope over.

'Yes. Mexton Investigations. It's printed here in small letters.'

'Let me check,' said Mel, pulling out her phone.

She pressed a saved number and was answered within a few seconds.

'Hi Martin, it's Mel. Has anyone in your office sent a package to Jenny Pike?'

There was a short pause.

'OK, thank you. We may need to talk to someone about the contents. When are you joining us, by the way? Oh, that's great. Many thanks.'

She turned to Emma.

'Martin Rowse confirmed that it came from them, so you can open it without blowing yourself to bits.'

Emma slit open the envelope and a wad of documents slid onto her desk.

'So, what's all this?' asked Mel, peering over her boss's shoulder as she shuffled through the papers.

'Newspaper cuttings, printouts from websites, the latest report from the Forensic Science Regulator, transcripts of TV and radio programmes – a whole load of stuff relating to the police use of forensic science.'

'So, what was Jenny doing? Pitching a script for *Silent Witness*?'

'Look more closely,' said Emma, examining them carefully. 'Every one of these deals with errors: either lab cockups, misuse of evidence, police mistakes, or corruption somewhere in the system.'

'Anything local?'

'Most of them, all covering disputed or abandoned cases.'

'Shit! Was she trying to find another way of getting at us?'

'I don't know. Could be. Look, you'd better have a word with Mexton Investigations. Why did Jenny ask them to do what looks like quite a lot of research. It must have cost her. If they claim client confidentiality, remind them that she's dead.'

'OK. I'll talk to Martin. He knows the score. And he'll be one of us again soon.'

'Do that. We'll discuss these documents at tomorrow's briefing. Now, we've got a possible lead on Trevor's attacker, an enemy of this Frankie Garrett, so I need to make a few phone calls and write up the policy book. Thanks, Mel.'

Chapter Forty-One

CHLOE STAPLES STARED at her brother's corpse, white faced. She swallowed hard and just managed to squeeze out the words.

'Yes. That's him. That's my brother Marvin.'

As the attendant recovered Marvin's face with a sheet, Sally showed Chloe into a private room and handed her a tissue, although the woman's eyes remained dry.

'How did the poor sod end up like this?' Chloe asked, bitterly. 'Was he in a fight? He always had a temper.'

'We don't think so. It looks as though someone simply went up to him and stabbed him in the gents' toilets in the Green Man.'

Chloe grimaced at the image.

'Was it some random maniac? Was anyone else hurt?'

'No. We have to assume he was targeted, and we need to know why. What do you know about his friends and his activities? Did he have any enemies? I'm really sorry to press you at such an awful time, but the more we know, the better our chances of catching who did this to him.'

Chloe shrugged.

'I didn't see that much of him since our parents died, to be honest. We'd have a coffee or a drink once in a while, if we bumped into each other, but nothing regular. I knew he had a warehouse job.'

'How about his friends?'

'He used to be good mates with Nathan Jones. I don't know if he was still in touch with him. Last time we met he was going out with a girl called Natalie. Natalie Viner, I think. Worked in a burger joint in the shopping centre. Don't know if he was still seeing her.'

'I have to ask you this. Was he involved in anything criminal?'

Chloe dropped her eyes.

'Well I think he did a bit of dealing a while back, but then he stopped. He looked scared. Said it had all gone wrong. I think it was after those Albanians got done. Don't know if he started again, but he began getting proper jobs, so maybe not.'

'Thank you, Chloe,' said Sally. 'If you remember anything else, please get in touch. Here's my card. I'll show you out.'

Chloe turned at the door.

'How about the funeral? I s'pose I'll have to arrange it.'

'I'm afraid that may not be for some time. If we get someone for his murder, the accused's defence team can request a second post-mortem. I'm sorry, but we'll let you know when his body can be released.'

'Oh, I see. Yes. Please do.'

She straightened up and left the building without looking back. The further she got from the door, the more her erect bearing crumpled. Eventually, above the whisper of the gentle breeze that blew across the car park, Chloe Staples could be heard crying.

Chapter Forty-Two

Day 8

'Guv! I've got a couple of possibles for Crompton's target.'

DCI Farlowe looked up from his desk as Mel appeared in the doorway.

'Go on.'

'I looked into his assault conviction. He claimed that two dealers sold his daughter, Kerry, heroin contaminated with nitazenes, which killed her. One of those dealers was a low life called Nathan Jones. The other was Marvin Staples.'

'So, he shot at one of them and missed. Presumably he wants to finish the job at some point.'

'Yes. Addy's wife said he mentioned "unfinished business" at the hospital.'

'But he couldn't have killed Staples. He was in custody. Are you suggesting that two separate people wanted to kill a minor, possibly reformed, drug dealer?'

'Well, it looks that way. I suppose Crompton could have paid the bloke who stabbed Staples to do it. I don't think he's well-off enough to hire a hitman, but I suppose he could have found some way to pay him. A favour or something.'

'OK. We can't ask Staples if anyone's shot at him recently but get hold of Nathan Jones and have a chat with him. Also, find out more about Kerry's death. Was there anyone else involved?'

'Will do. And DS Palmer may know about other nitazene-related deaths. I'll ask him at the briefing today.'

'Good. I'll be running the briefing as DI Thorpe's off today. Nice work, Mel.'

'Fancy a trip to the beautiful, downtown Eastside?' asked Mel.

'OK,' replied Kamal, 'but don't you normally partner Sally?'

'Yes, but she's got an appointment. We've got a couple of hours before the briefing, so I thought we'd use it to find out if Crompton shot at Nathan Jones.'

'Lead on. Will I need a vest?'

'Do fish swim?'

Kamal grinned and followed Mel to the car park.

Nathan Jones's flat was on the ground floor of Dalton House, in the heart of the Eastside. As Mel droved the marked police car slowly along the narrow roads, curtains fluttered, the odd missile was hurled at the vehicle and the occasional shout of 'cops' or 'five-oh' could be heard. On a blank wall adjacent to Jones's front door, a would-be entrant for the Turner prize had executed a multicoloured mural involving the slogan 'Fuck Off Pigs'.

'Nice to feel welcome,' said Kamal, knocking on the door. 'Nathan Jones? Are you in there? We'd like to talk to you. It's the...'

Bang!

A small hole appeared in the front of the door. Mel gasped and stumbled backwards, holding her chest. Kamal eased her to the floor as another bullet whistled past his head.

'His name is Nathan Jones,' Frankie Garrett said. 'He's annoyed me. He did things he shouldn't have, and I'm displeased.'

Despite his mild language, the two men in front of him shivered slightly.

'So what do you want us to do, boss?' the tall, thin man asked.

'I want you to send a message to his stupid little friends who think they can disrespect me. Something public but untraceable to us. He's surplus to requirements, so you can get rid of him. I'm sure you can work something out, Max. That's what I pay you for.'

'No problem at all, boss. We know where he lives. Me and Speedy'll pay him a visit.'

'Good. If he's on the move, ask Gary to track his phone. He's got the number. Now off you go.'

The two men breathed sighs of relief when they stepped out into the fresh air. Despite the fact that they were both bigger than their boss, they remained scared of him. He had a reputation, and the general consensus was that you didn't mess with Mr Francis Garrett.

Chapter Forty-Three

'FUCK! ARE YOU OK,' Kamal shouted.

When Mel nodded, he reached for his Airwave.

'Ambulance and armed response needed. Dalton House, Eastside. Officer shot. Urgent.'

The two detectives crawled away from Nathan's door, keeping low, and found a place to sit, out of the line of fire, while they waited for backup.

'How bad is it?' asked Kamal, looking scared. 'I've never been shot.'

'I'm OK. The vest stopped the bullet. I'll just have a sore tit for a while. Ballistics will want it. The bullet, that is.' She managed a laugh. 'Fucking hurts though.'

Ten minutes later, an ambulance, two police cars and an armed response unit were blocking the narrow roads. Local residents were keeping a low profile, unwilling to challenge such a show of force.

'Put the door in and send in the dog,' ordered the Tactical Firearms Commander.

'Armed police,' shouted Addy, as his colleague wielded the Big Door Key. 'Come out with your hands where I can see them.'

There was no reply. A few minutes later, the firearms dog trotted out, wagging his tail. The two armed officers entered the flat and cries of 'Clear' could be heard as they checked each room.'

'Flat's empty,' said Addy, reporting to the TFC. 'He got out of a back window. No weapon found.'

'OK. I'll notify the Super. We'll put out an alert for an armed suspect and warn the public not to approach him. OK, guys. We're done here.'

The armed officers piled back into the ARV, leaving uniformed officers to guard the scene until SOCOs arrived. A paramedic checked Mel out and pronounced her unharmed, apart from an emerging bruise.

'Back to the station then.' She threw the car keys to Kamal. 'You know what I need? A very large brandy. But somehow I don't think that Mr Farlowe would approve.'

'Well you shouldn't get yourself shot in the morning, should you?' grinned Kamal, 'Wait till knocking-off time in future.'

Mel laughed and climbed into the passenger seat, gingerly putting on her seatbelt and wondering how she would tell Tom that she'd nearly been killed again. Forty centimetres higher and the bullet would have hit her in the head. And that would have meant much more than a bruise. She didn't start shaking until she got back to the station, spending half an hour in the toilets to compose herself. She knew she wouldn't sleep easily tonight.

'Settle down, everyone, please,' called DCI Farlowe, at the start of an afternoon briefing.

'First off, Mel and Kamal went to interview Nathan Jones, who we suspect may have been Michael Crompton's target, this morning. They were shot at and Jones fled. He is now being sought as a priority, and I must urge extreme caution when approaching him. You will be pleased to know that Mel and Kamal are unharmed, although Mel was hit, her vest saving her from serious injury. Ballistics are working on the bullet.

'Now, as drug dealing appears to feature in the pub stabbing, the Eastside shootings and, peripherally, in Crompton's case, DS Derek Palmer is here to bring us up to date on the Mexton drug scene. Over to you, Derek.'

'Thank you. As you know, the destruction of the OCG led to something of a vacuum in the supply system. Small- and medium-level dealers moved in, and we were able to pick quite a few of them up. New faces stood out and didn't know the turf. So either we, or rival dealers, dealt with them. A&E was kept busy for a while. A few months ago, things began to quieten down, and a major player has moved in, recruiting locals for street-level dealing and crushing any competition.'

Derek fiddled with a laptop and an image of a tall, smartly suited man of about fifty, with a smooth, suntanned face and eyes like flints, appeared on the screen behind Farlowe.

'This is him. Frankie Garrett.'

Emma nodded her recognition.

'He prefers to be called Francis to his face. DI Thorpe asked me about him. He's ex-Royal Navy, is normally based in Portsmouth, and, we believe, has links with Colombian, Dutch and Turkish wholesalers. He has a fearsome reputation, according to my counterparts in Hants Police, and has been linked to several murders and a number of savage beatings. His speciality is torture sessions, which he calls discussions.'

'Nasty piece of work, then,' commented Jack.

Derek nodded and continued.

'He is reported to treat his crimes like any other commercial enterprise, with business plans, spreadsheets and project management software. Portsmouth Drug Squad told me this: an accountant was tricked into working for Garrett and went to them, hoping they'd be able to protect her. She ended up in the Solent, minus her tongue, before they could put together a case. Garrett is not good news. We're sure he's developing a network of street dealers in Mexton. He owns a strip club, The Golden Thong, and also an amusement arcade, The Crazy Diamond. We think the latter is just used for money laundering.'

'Is there anyone else significant on the scene?' asked the DCI.

'Possibly. A crew from Bristol seems to be supplying a lot of cannabis and a good few pills. They don't seem to be doing much heroin or cocaine, which is Garrett's speciality.'

'Any likelihood of gang warfare?' asked Mel, absent-mindedly rubbing her chest.

'Not sure,' Derek replied. 'Maybe a few skirmishes so far, but their markets don't overlap too much. Though, given Garrett's reputation, I wouldn't be surprised if he tried to put the Bristol mob out of business. One way or the other.'

A feeling of foreboding settled over the team.

'Are there any more questions?' asked Derek.

'Changing the subject a bit,' said Sally, 'what are nitazenes?'

'Horrible chemicals. They are turning up in heroin to boost its effects, like fentanyl is. There've been numerous accidental over-doses as a result – they are many times more powerful than heroin and more dangerous than fentanyl. Why do you ask?'

'The daughter of one of our customers on remand was killed by nitazene-contaminated heroin a few months ago. Her father beat up a couple of dealers and, we think, tried to shoot one of them a few days ago.'

'Yes, there was a nasty batch of heroin going around for a few weeks. Haven't seen any recently, thank goodness.'

'Thank you, Derek, for a very informative briefing,' said Farlowe. 'We believe that a laptop belonging to Frankie Garrett has gone missing and he's anxious to retrieve it. Obviously, we need to get it first. We'll share it with you when we do.'

On that optimistic note, Farlowe closed the briefing, and the team went off in search of coffee.

Chapter Forty-Four

'Fancy a burger, Mel?' asked Sally.

Her colleague wrinkled her nose.

'Not my thing, really. Why do you ask?'

'I've found out where Natalie Viner works. A place in the shopping centre. Shall we go and chat to her?'

'OK, as long as she doesn't shoot at us.' Mel smiled. 'But I suppose the cholesterol is just as deadly in the long run.'

'Well, if you want to stay healthy and protect the planet, we'll walk.'

———

Few people were patronising Mexton Burgers Deluxe when the two detectives arrived, and Natalie had no problem leaving her post to talk to them. They found seats in a corner of the food court and Sally ordered them coffees from a stall.

'We'd like to talk to you about Marvin Staples, Natalie,' began Mel. 'We understand you were together at one point.'

'Yeah, that's right. About four months, I reckon. I was sorry to hear he'd been stabbed.'

'Can you think of anyone who would want to do that? Any enemies or rivals?'

'Not really. He got on with most people, unless they took the piss. He got beat up by some nutter who said he killed his daughter. Absolute bollocks. He helped people out with a bit of gear sometimes, but he would never hurt anyone unless they went for him. At least, that's how he used to be.'

'What do you mean?'

'After the attack, he gave up dealing 'cos your lot came sniffing around. It wasn't a big thing for him anyway. He got moody and took to drinking too much. That's what led to us splitting.'

'What do you mean?' asked Mel.

'He came home pissed one night and slapped me. Only the once, but that was enough. I saw what my bastard dad did to my mum, and I wasn't having any of it. So I chucked him. Of course, he said he was sorry. That it wouldn't happen again. But that's what my dad said. And it did.'

'I'm sorry,' said Sally.

'Yeah, it's a pity. He was a nice bloke when we met. Bit of a lad, I suppose, but he'd been getting proper jobs, although they were temporary and zero hours, most of them. Thought we had a future,' she said, wistfully.

'Well thanks for talking to us, Natalie,' said Mel. 'You've given us a better picture of Marvin. We'll let you get back to work.'

'No problem. And thanks for the coffee.'

'How's the counselling going?' asked Mel, as they walked back to the station.

'I think it's useful,' replied Sally. 'I was sceptical at first. I've seen those American TV programmes, where they seem to need psychotherapy for an ingrowing toenail or whatever, and never gave it much credence. I know it's not strictly psychotherapy, but this morning's session did help to clarify things. I'll keep on going.'

'I should. It's helped with my PTSD. I won't say I'm completely happy going up against people with blades, but I don't freeze like I used to.'

'Yeah. I suppose nearly getting your head chopped off with a sword will do that to you. I'm kind of glad I wasn't with you this morning though. Sorry, was that insensitive?'

'No, you're all right. We're mates. Now let's go and type this lot up.'

Chapter Forty-Five

Day 9

'Has your mate Robbie been busy again, Mel?' asked Jack, sternly, before the morning briefing started.

It was known, but not acknowledged, that Robbie's hacking skills had provided, illegally, vital information on more than one occasion.

'Not as far as I know, Jack. Why? What's happened?'

'Yesterday afternoon a courier dropped off a memory stick. Amira scanned it for viruses and declared it safe, so I took a look before I went home. It contained dozens of files from the *Messenger*'s server that Jenny Pike had been working on. Their lawyers had been blocking our requests for access, so I wondered whether you'd had a word with Robbie.'

'No. Not at all. In fact, he's been on his honeymoon with Ollie this past couple of weeks.'

'Perhaps someone on the paper helped us out then.'

'Could be. We mentioned we needed access when we interviewed the reporters, and most were keen to help. So, what was in the files?'

'I was hoping you'd take a look. I had a quick scan but didn't see anything useful. It needs a detailed examination. A deep dive, if you like. You're almost as good as Trevor at that. And you'd better not mention this to the DCI.'

Mel grinned. 'Jack, I'll dive so deep I'll need a bloody oxygen tank. Speaking of Trevor, is there any news?'

'I popped in to see him in the way home. He's making progress, but they'll not let him out until it's safe to do so. He'd like to see you, though.'

'I'll visit him this evening. Take him some biscuits, if the nurses will let him have them.'

'Good plan.'

Their conversation was interrupted by DCI Farlowe calling the team together for the briefing.

***

I can't believe I was so fucking stupid, Nathan Jones berated himself. *Shooting at bleedin' coppers. I thought they was Frankie's boys. Shouldn't have smoked so much weed. Now everyone's after me, and I can't carry the shooter on the street. Ok. I'll lie low. Hope it blows over and Frankie'll be cool again. Gotta hide the gun where I can get it again. And I know just where.*

An hour later, smartened up slightly, in contrast to his usual wear, Nathan presented himself at the door of a well-kept semi in the Mexton suburbs.

'Hello, Gran,' he said, proffering a bunch of the petrol station's finest carnations. 'Thought I'd pop in and say hello.'

'Nathan!' exclaimed the white-haired septuagenarian. 'Lovely to see you, dear. You've not been round for weeks. I do wish you visited more often. Come in and I'll put the kettle on. She hugged him and kissed his forehead.

Looking round to check that he hadn't been followed, Nathan

breathed a sigh of relief and followed his grandmother into the house.

'The thing is, Gran,' he began, drinking tea and helping himself to biscuits at the kitchen table, 'I've got a bit of a problem. A pipe burst in the flat above mine and everything's soaking wet. I need somewhere to stay while the insurance company sorts everything out and gets it redecorated. I wondered whether I could stay here? It's just for a few days.'

'That would be lovely, Nathan,' she replied. 'You can sleep in your old room. It'll be just like old times.'

'Aw, thanks Gran. You're a diamond. I'll bring some of my stuff over later. Can I make you another cuppa?'

Chapter Forty-Six

'First off,' began DCI Farlowe, 'is there any progress on the Staples stabbing? You talked to his ex-partner, didn't you, Mel?'

'Yes, guv. Sally and I met her. She can't think of anyone with a motive for killing him. She hasn't seen him for a while, so she wouldn't know whether or not he was Crompton's target. They split up because he hit her once, when he was drunk. Apparently, he'd been moody since Crompton's assault. She said he wasn't a major dealer, and he stopped when we investigated the attack.'

'Thank you, Mel. Anything to add, Sally?'

'Only that he didn't seem to be a total villain. He had a temper, hence the ABH conviction, but he didn't go out looking to hurt people. I've had a thought, though. This moodiness after he was assaulted. That wouldn't normally affect people like him. He'd have been thumped many times. Could he have felt guilty about Kerry Crompton's death?'

'Possibly. Stranger things have happened,' replied Farlowe. 'Can we look a bit further into this girl's death? And find out exactly what Crompton said, when interviewed and in court.'

'On, it, boss,' said Kamal. 'I've been doing some digging into Nathan Jones,' he continued. 'His mother died when he was three. His father had a series of girlfriends after that and was in and out of jail. The women never seemed to want to look after Nathan, so he spent periods with both sets of grandparents, depending on who was able to care for him at the time. He still went to school, until he started bunking off at thirteen. Eventually, he was taken into care, when his grandparents couldn't cope, and was left to his own devices at eighteen. His current address is the flat on the Eastside. He built up a stack of minor convictions from about fourteen onwards but never got a custodial sentence.'

'Sad case,' commented Sally.

'One of many,' said Mel, 'but don't forget he shot me and...'

'Have we had any sightings?' interrupted Farlowe.

'His bank card was used at a petrol station, early this morning,' said Nick Waters, one of the civilian investigators. 'Someone needs to check the CCTV footage to make sure it was him.'

Jack nodded.

'Do that, please,' said Farlowe. 'I think that's the only one. His photo's been circulated to the media and put on our website, with warnings not to approach. We can only hope someone spots him. We also need to trace his grandparents in case he's been in touch with them.'

Farlowe looked defeated.

'On top of Jones's disappearance, I'm afraid we're getting nowhere with the Eastside shootings,' he said. 'We've had no solid intelligence, although someone suggested that they might have fallen foul of "a big dealer". No name was mentioned.'

'Garrett?' suggested Mel.

'Possibly. I've booked a Zoom with someone at the NCA to find out what they know about him. Do we have any good news on the Pike case?'

'I've been going through the documents from Mexton Investigations. Apparently, she asked them to dig up whatever they could about police incompetence, failed trials, mishandled evidence – anything that could put us and our colleagues in a bad light.'

'Shit, she wasn't still doing that, was she?' said Sally.

'Apparently,' Mel replied. 'But Martin Rowse told me she said she was following a specific angle, not just a general rubbishing of the police. He couldn't say what it was. I'll keep digging.'

'Please do that,' said the DCI. 'One other thing. Marcus Forrest is out of hospital and in custody. He's given a "no comment" interview and will be in court tomorrow morning. Given that the CPS has authorised us to charge him with attempting to murder Mel and Sally, as well as firearms offences, I'm confident he'll be remanded. Right, you've all got jobs to do. DI Thorpe will be back tomorrow, but please let me know of any significant developments in the meantime.'

Mel sat at her desk going through the files captured from the *Messenger*'s server. Most of them related to stories already published, going back to Jenny Pike's time as the newspaper's crime correspondent. More recent files covered her investigations into the planning committee members and the election expenses. Both seemed to have stalled.

The remaining files were in a separate folder, marked 'X', and proved more interesting. They covered a number of cases that Mexton police had investigated, going back several years. In each case, the prosecution had collapsed, either in court or during the investigation stages. A spreadsheet summarised Jenny's probing, each row listing the basic details of the case, the SIO, why the case collapsed and, in the final column headed 'X?', a tick or a cross. *So who or what is X?* she wondered. *And what is the significance of a tick?* She printed off the spreadsheet, resolving to show it to Jack when she could get him on his own. Perhaps he would recognise the cases and provide some kind of explanation.

Chapter Forty-Seven

Day 10

NATHAN JONES HAD to get out. His gran was driving him mad with constant questions about what he was doing, how he was looking after himself and what happened to his various, temporary, girlfriends. She reminisced at length about events he couldn't remember and insisted on updating him on the activities of people he'd never heard of. Must be her age, he thought, as he struggled to remember the picture of his life he'd painted for her.

Staring at the childish wallpaper in the room he'd often slept in, years ago, he reasoned that the police would be unlikely to find him in this part of Mexton. They'd be watching the Eastside and the town centre, not a respectable suburb. And no one else would know he was here. So it would be safe to nip out to the local park, get a few cans from the offie, and maybe smoke a spliff or two. That would do wonders for his nerves. But he'd better hide the gun somewhere his gran wouldn't find it. He wouldn't need it here, and carrying it was always a risk.

'I'm going out for a bit, Gran,' he called. 'Back for dinner. I'll bring fish and chips.'

He pulled on his hoodie, closed the door behind him, and quickly scanned the street for signs of police or other threats. Nothing. The only unusual sight was a large van, bearing the name Mexton Removals, negotiating its way through the parked cars. He'd thought about getting a job with a removal firm once. It was a good way of checking out homes for some illegal removals later. He'd had a trial with one firm, but it had been too much like hard work and he'd packed it in after three days. Stepping briskly down the road, his mind occupied with thoughts of intoxicants, he didn't notice the van pulling in outside his grandmother's house.

'Police emergency. How can I help?'

'Yes, er, I've found a gun.'

'Yes, sir. What sort of gun?'

'A handgun. It was in the piano. It looks real.'

'OK, sir. Can you give me your details and the address, and we'll send someone round immediately. Please don't touch the item in the meantime. Thank you for contacting us.'

Ten minutes later, Mel and Addy pulled up behind the removals van and walked up the path.

'I'll check the weapon,' said Addy, 'while you find out how it got there.'

Mel nodded and knocked on the door. A burly removal man, in a brown coat, opened it and showed them into a chintz-bedecked sitting room. He lifted the lid of the piano and pointed to the unmistakeable shape of a pistol nestling among the hammers. Wearing gloves, Addy retrieved it, ensuring that it was pointed away from the others in the room, and checked it was unloaded. He also removed a plastic bag with three cartridges from the depths of the instrument. He tagged the weapon and put it in a clear box.

'Looks like a converted blank-firing pistol,' he said. 'We've been told there's some about. Thanks for calling this in Mr...?'

'Chalmers. Fred Chalmers,' replied the removal man. 'It was my mate Charlie what found it but he's making a cup of tea for the old lady.'

'Did either of you touch it?'

'No. Don't like the things. I wasn't sure it was real, but I didn't want to find out by accidentally shooting myself, and neither did Charlie.'

'You did the right thing,' said Mel. 'Does the homeowner know about it?'

'I said we'd found something that the police needed to see. She seemed a bit confused.'

'OK. I'll go and talk to her.'

'Right. Can we move the piano now?'

'I'm afraid not. We'll need to get fingerprints and so on. It could take a while.'

'Better have another cuppa, then.'

Mel nodded and went to talk to Nathan's grandmother, who was sitting in the kitchen with the other removal man.

Chapter Forty-Eight

'Good morning, madam,' Mel began. 'I'm Detective Constable Mel Cotton. I'd like to talk to you about something Charlie, here, found in your piano. First, though, can I ask your name?'

'Wright. Mrs Emily Wright.'

'Thank you, Mrs Wright. Do you have any idea why there would be a firearm – a handgun – inside your piano?'

'No, dear, I don't. What would I be doing with a gun? Horrible things. They frighten me.'

'Has anyone in your family ever owned a gun?'

'My father brought one home from the war. Got it from a German officer he captured. But he handed it in to the police after that dreadful business in Scotland. Good riddance, too.'

'OK. Have you had any visitors recently?'

'Only young Nathan. He's staying here for a bit while his flat's being redecorated. He's out at the moment, but he's bringing fish and chips for dinner.' She smiled. 'My Syd always liked his fish and chips.'

A tingle ran down Mel's spine.

'Syd was your husband?'

'That's right, dear.' She pointed to a framed photo on the kitchen dresser.

'And do you know where Nathan went?'

'He just said he was going out. He's bringing back fish and chips for dinner.'

I don't think she'll be getting her fish and chips, Mel thought. *Not if we nail the little bastard first.* She stepped out of the room and called Jack.

'We've found where Nathan's been staying – his grandma's – and Addy's retrieved a pistol from her piano. Can we have a SOCO to dust for prints? And some uniforms? He may still be in the area.'

'Great, Mel. Give me the address and we'll get the troops out looking for him. I think we'd better assume he's still armed, in case the weapon from the piano isn't his. We'll have someone watching the premises for when he comes back.'

Mel returned to the kitchen and continued her conversation with Mrs Wright. She managed to establish that Nathan had turned up on her doorstep the previous day, with a bunch of flowers. She hadn't seen him for weeks but was happy for him to stay for a while. He'd told her that he was working for the Council and that he had good prospects. She didn't know the address of his flat. She didn't think the weapon was Nathan's.

'Why would he need a gun to work for the Council?' she asked.

She explained that she was giving the piano to the vicar at St Stephens as she hadn't played it in years and the one in the church hall had been vandalised.

'Well thank you very much, Mrs Wright,' said Mel. 'Someone will be along shortly to look for fingerprints. Then the men can take the piano away. If Nathan comes back or phones you, can you give me a call? We'd like a word with him. And please don't mention we've been.'

She left her card and said her goodbyes.

By four o'clock the SOCO still hadn't arrived, so Fred and Charlie had another cup of tea and went home, promising to return in the morning.

Chapter Forty-Nine

'Are you doing anything for lunch, Jack?' asked Mel.

'Er... no. I've brought sandwiches. Why?'

'Can you meet me in the canteen? The back corner where we won't be overheard. I've got something to show you.'

Half an hour later, Mel pushed aside a half-eaten salad and spread a printout on the table.

'I got this from Jenny's files, in a folder marked "X". It lists failed cases. Can you take a look, see if you recognise them.'

Jack perused the spreadsheet, frowning and nodding from time to time. Then he looked up at Mel.

'I don't recall all of these. Some were the responsibility of other teams. But those I do know all pissed me off at the time. We were certain we'd got the right people, but either they never got to court, or the case collapsed for various reasons. For instance, evidence went missing, the chain of custody was broken, or forensics were equivocal.'

'Could X be a dodgy police officer?'

'Makes a change from H, I suppose,' he smiled grimly. 'No, there were several different SIOs leading the investigations. I know most of them and they are, or were, competent and straight.

The idea of DCI Farlowe, DCI Morgan or DI Gale deliberately throwing a case is absurd. So, X must refer to another officer, or some other factor, common to the cases with a tick beside them.'

'Great. So, I've got to go through the whole sodding lot to find a link. When the fuck am I going to get the time to do that, with everything else that's going on?'

'Christ knows. You can't do it officially and ask for help, as the legality of our having the files is questionable. For the same reason you can't do it as official overtime. And you're too honest to throw a phoney sickie and do it then. I'm happy for you to leave a bit early some days and do it at home, if you like. I'll tell anyone who asks, and they probably won't, that you're looking through some files for me. Will that do?'

'I suppose so. I'll probably be able to enlist Tom's help, which would make it a bit quicker.'

'Thanks, Mel. I appreciate it. Because I'm sure that somewhere in those files is the reason Jenny Pike was murdered.'

Nathan Jones felt considerably happier as he turned into his grandmother's street. He'd chilled out in the park with some decent weed and a couple of cans and, when a thin drizzle started, he'd found a quiet pub to have a few lagers and try his hand, with no particular success, at the puzzles in a free newspaper. He didn't dare use his phone, which was switched off with the SIM removed. But no one disturbed him, and he stayed there until the chippie opened.

He felt the comforting warmth of double cod and chips under his hoodie. She was putting him up, so buying her dinner was the least he could do. But he stopped short, a hundred metres from the house. *There is no way that scruffy Astra, belongs there. They aint millionaires on this street, but they've all got better motors than that. And what about the two heavy-looking blokes in it, pretending to look at their phones? It's either the cops or Frankie's boys – and Frankie has better cars, too. Fuck! The filth must have tracked me from school records or something.*

He turned on his heels and ran back around the corner. He needed to find out what had happened, but he couldn't ring his gran from his phone. But perhaps one quick call wouldn't matter? On the telly it always took ages for them to trace a call, so he decided to risk it.

'Gran,' he said, when she picked up the phone. 'It's Nathan. Did you have any visitors today?'

'Oh, yes. A police lady and a Black policeman came and, do you know what? They found a gun in the piano. A real gun! I was so scared and I can't think how it got there. It must have been the tuner who left it although it's years since he's been and I don't see why he would have one. Thank goodness they've taken it away.'

'Oh, fuck, Gran…'

'Please don't swear, Nathan. You know how it upsets me.'

'Sorry. Why were they there?'

'Well, I said the church could have the piano, and the removal men came to collect it. Then the police arrived. They asked if I knew about the gun and whether I'd had any visitors. "Only you", I said. They want to talk to you. I wasn't supposed to say, but I had to tell you about the gun. I hope I won't get into trouble. They said to ring them if you called or came back.'

'No, please don't do that, Gran,' he said, panic building in his voice. 'I've got to go somewhere, so I won't be back for a bit.'

'But what about my fish and chips?'

Nathan hung up.

Chapter Fifty

'JONES'S PHONE HAS JUST PINGED,' said Jack, muting a call from Technical Support. 'It's not far from his gran's place.'

'There's a car there,' said Mel. 'Haven't they seen him? Are they bloody asleep?'

'We'll call them and get them some backup. You know that we only get an approximate position.'

'Yeah. Well, I'll go out and lend a hand. Coming, Sally?'

'Be careful, You two. Assume he's still armed. And if you find him, wait for the AFOs.'

'OK, OK,' she snapped, grabbing her car keys and almost dragging Sally out of the door, completely unaware that it wasn't only the police who were tracking Nathan's phone.

After an hour's driving through the leafy suburbs of outer Mexton, Mel and Sally were on the verge of giving up when Sally suddenly shouted.

'That's him. By the bus stop. I'm sure of it.'

Mel pulled the car in on the opposite side of the road, a few metres from the stop.

'D'you think he's catching a bus? Doesn't the idiot realise they have CCTV?'

'He could be waiting for someone,' replied Mel, 'or just lurking. I think I'll go over and have a chat. There's no one else there.'

'Don't be daft. We're supposed to wait for backup.'

'I know, but I don't want the little shit escaping. He doesn't look as though he's carrying a firearm, anyway. He's in jeans and a T-shirt, with no bulges in his pockets that I can see. I suppose he could have a knife, though. Look, call it in and when I get out, shift over to my seat and keep the engine running in case he legs it. OK?'

'All right, but you're bloody mad, Mel Cotton. Bloody mad.'

Mel had just started to open the door, baton in hand, when a large, white van roared past, swerved across the road, mounted the pavement and knocked Nathan Jones into the air. He flew over a low wall, smashed into a stone bird bath on a pedestal and lay inert in a bed of petunias, blood streaming down his face and his legs at physiologically improbable angles. The bus stop was wrecked.

'Fuck!' shouted Sally, leaping out of the car. 'Follow the van. I'll see to him and call it in.'

Mel slammed the car into gear and shot after the van that had regained the carriageway and was heading off into the distance, strange noises coming from the front end where steel had been bent by the impact with Nathan and the bus stop. She caught up with it as it halted at a crossroads, waiting for a car transporter to inch its way across the junction. Before she could call in the van's registration, its reversing lights flashed. It shot backwards, crashing into Mel's car.

The impact was drowned out by the bang of the airbags inflating. By the time she had cleared them out of the way, the van was long gone. Her ears were ringing from the noise of the explosion, and she had a headache. She suspected her face would be bruised, too. She climbed unsteadily out of the car to inspect the damage. The bonnet had been pushed upwards, a wing had been bent back against a wheel, jamming it, and an ominous pool of liquid was forming beneath the radiator.

A fucking write-off! And it won't bloody move. At least it's a police vehicle and not mine. But the Super's gonna be royally pissed off.

With help from a couple of passers-by she managed to push the car into the kerb. She called the police garage for a recovery vehicle and walked disconsolately back to the bus stop. By the time she got there, paramedics were stretchering Nathan into an ambulance. Mel's spirits were lifted slightly when she saw he had an oxygen mask over his face instead of a sheet.

'What happened to you?' asked Sally, gazing at Mel's unkempt appearance.

'Bastard backed into me at a junction and wrecked the car. My ears are still ringing from the bloody air bags, and I've got to explain how a police vehicle came to be trashed. What are they saying about Nathan?'

'Not a lot. He's alive, just. He's had a bang on the head, loads of bones damaged and they don't know what's going on internally. He'll not be selling gear for a while and will probably need loads of the nice, clean, NHS version for the pain.'

'Was he armed?'

'Nope.'

'Pity we didn't get to him five minutes earlier, then. We'd better get this area cordoned off and let the bus company know the stop's out of use, and probably unrepairable. We'll hitch a lift back to the station,' she pointed at a couple of marked cars that had attended the scene, 'and collect our stuff from the car on the way. Then it's statements to complete and a load of bloody paperwork.'

In a room above a 'gentleman's club' near the centre of Mexton, three men sat around a table. Two were drinking whisky while the third was drinking tonic water.

'Is it done?' asked Frankie Garrett, the water drinker.

'Yes, boss, replied Max the Plank. He wasn't at his flat, but we clobbered him hard in the street with a van. If he aint dead, he'll be in hospital for ages. Might need a wheelchair.'

'I suppose that will do. A message sent. He won't steal from me again. Or talk to the police. Any problems?'

The third man, Speedy, shifted uneasily in his seat.

'There was this bird followed us after the hit. I had to ram her to stop her.'

'Why should she do that?' Garrett asked.

'I think she was a cop, unless she was some stupid do-gooder. They've been looking for the little shit as well. Apparently, he shot at one of them.'

'That's... distressing.'

Both whisky drinkers looked uneasy and gulped at their drinks.

'Did she see you?'

'No, boss,' they chorused.

'We torched the van,' said the thin one. 'Probably still hot. No evidence.'

'You'd better be right, or I'll be upset. Keep an eye on things. If you're wrong, we may have to deal with the policewoman. And have a discussion with her. Now go.'

Chapter Fifty-One

Day 11

'Morning, all.'

Emma greeted the team, receiving a number of muted replies, the lack of progress in the various cases clearly taking its toll.

'I'd like to begin with an update on Trevor. He's recovering pretty well, although they still can't say when he'll be able to go home. I've had a brief chat with him. He's reasonably coherent but he can't remember a thing about the attack, which is only to be expected. The brain protects itself by blocking out bad memories, the doctor said. Anyway, he did say he was very pleased that so many of you had visited, and Susie was also grateful. Keep the biscuits coming, he said.'

Several officers chuckled at that.

'So, to business. Where are we with the Jenny Pike murder?'

'The mosquito's still being tested, guv,' replied Mel. 'They're fast-tracking it, but it will still be a day or so before we get a report.'

'Door-to-doors and interviews with her colleagues have

yielded absolutely sod all,' said Jack. 'Mel's been through the material from Mexton Investigations and found nothing of use – it was all publicly available stuff on police incompetence, failed investigations and so on. There is one thing of interest. The Chief Constable's PA called me yesterday. Apparently, Jenny emailed him requesting a meeting to discuss "a matter of enormous public importance". She copied the email to me, and it doesn't hint at what the matter might be. But it does suggest that Jenny was on to something significant. I asked her partner, but she had no idea what it was.'

'Did the Chief agree to speak to her?' asked Emma.

'He hadn't decided by the time Jenny died,' replied Jack.

'So we've still got bugger all.'

''Fraid so. We're still looking at CCTV and ANPR in the area, in case there were any suspicious vehicles about. There aren't many cameras in that residential area, so I'm not optimistic.'

Emma snorted her frustration.

'OK. The Staples stabbing?'

'Nothing new, guv,' replied Mel, 'although I did look into Crompton's assault case. He didn't say much when arrested, only that "they had it coming". In court he said he attacked them because they were responsible for his daughter's death. The defence called a toxicologist who explained how lethal nitazenes are, and that must have swayed the judge. Derek's guys arrested Jones and Staples and searched their premises but found nothing. They were probably expecting a pull and got rid of everything. One other thing. Kerry's mother, Abbie Jackson, had a breakdown when her daughter died. She was sectioned and taken to a psychiatric hospital. Crompton never mentioned that. All he said when interviewed was that he'd lost touch with her.'

'Poor lass,' said Emma, wondering how she would feel if anything like that happened to Genevieve when she was older. She shuddered.

'So we've got nothing on Staples, either. Somebody give me some good news, please.'

'Nathan Jones is still alive,' said Sally, 'but he'll need months of treatment and rehabilitation. His legs were wrecked, so 'he won't be signing for Mexton Rovers any time soon.'

A couple of detectives laughed.

'When can he be interviewed?' asked Jack.

'Probably not for a day or two, according to the doctor. She'll let us know. Oh, the stolen van the attackers used was found torched in the woods. The twats could've started a forest fire. No CCTV of any use.'

'Bollocks!' said Emma, becoming increasingly frustrated.

'Ballistics rang,' said Jack. 'The bullet that knocked the gnome's head off showed no traces of rifling, which is consistent with it coming from Crompton's weapon. Neither did the bullet retrieved from Mel's vest. The pistol found in Nathan's gran's piano was an unrifled converted blank-firer, which means it was probably what he fired through the door when Mel and Kamal called to interview him.'

'Useful information, I suppose, but nothing we didn't think we already knew. We need to find out where he got the weapon from, not that I expect him to tell us. I don't like the idea of an underworld armourer on our patch, but we haven't the resources to mount an investigation.'

'Perhaps the NCA could help?' suggested Kamal.

'Aye, possibly.' Emma ran her hands through her hair. 'Look, we're getting nowhere. Can I suggest a session in The Cat and Cushion after work? We may come up with some ideas.'

The detectives nodded and dispersed, in better spirits than when the briefing started.

'It's no good, Jack,' moaned Mel, when she'd managed to get him alone. 'Tom and I were up half the bloody night going through those cases. There were no officers common to all of them. A few were involved in four of the six cases ticked and several more in three, but there's no consistent pattern. It's a sodding dead end. I've had a chat with Kate Bartlett, a SOCO I know, and she couldn't shed any light on it, either.'

Jack thought for a moment.

'It's a big ask, but how about other personnel. Civilian investigators, admin staff, perhaps. Maybe civilian contractors? Remember we had a bent security guard who tipped off the OCG about our movements.'

'You're bloody kidding! That's loads more people. We'd never get it done in a month of Sundays.'

'Hold on, hold on.' Jack held up his hands in a pacifying gesture. 'Start with the people most able to have compromised the cases, then move outwards. Once you've eliminated the impossible...'

'You're not going to quote Sherlock Bloody Holmes at me, are you?'

'Wouldn't dream of it,' said Jack, smiling and eliciting a faint grin from Mel. 'You seem a bit tense, though. Anything specific wrong?'

'Apart from frustration at the lack of progress and getting shot, you mean?' Her shoulders slumped and she looked gloomy. 'Actually, there is. I believe Tom's drinking more. I think he needs his prosthesis adjusting. He hasn't said anything, but sometimes it seems to be hurting him. I reckon it's getting him down.'

'Best not invite him to the pub, then.'

'No, no. I will. I'll make sure he's the designated driver. I'm sure he'd love to see everyone. And we'll have another go at those cases.'

'Thanks. You're a star.'

'Listen up, everyone,' called Emma, rushing into the office. 'I've had a call from the governor at HMP Grazely. Michael Crompton's been shanked. He's on his way to hospital under guard. He may not live.'

'OK, FOLKS,' said Emma, bringing a tray of drinks to the table. 'Ideas, please. You've got to earn your beer.'

'Kicking off, then,' said Jack, 'Why would anyone want to stab Crompton in Grazeley?'

'He hasn't been there long enough to piss anyone off sufficiently to merit a shanking,' said Sally. 'He thought he'd be safe on remand.'

'So it's back to Frankie Garrett,' said Kamal, sipping his pint.

'And that bloody laptop,' added Mel.

'But if Garrett wants his laptop back, what's the point of killing Crompton. Surely he'd lean on him to return it? Make him find out who took it.' said Jack.

'That assumes that Crompton knows,' said Emma. 'All we know is someone, not Crompton, bashed Trevor over the head and grabbed it. If it was one of Garrett's people, he would have it back and wouldn't be worried about it.'

'So Crompton's stabbing could be a punishment for losing it,' said Kamal. 'A bit extreme, don't you think?'

'Not impossible,' replied Emma. 'Garrett's a really nasty

bastard. Mr Farlowe's got some intel about him from the NCA. He'll brief us tomorrow.'

'Hang on,' said Tom, nursing an orange juice and gazing wistfully at the beers on the table, 'Mel's told me a bit about the case and something's bothering me.'

'Go on.'

'Why would a serious player like Garrett give a low-level scrote like Crompton the laptop with all his business on it, just to look after it? Surely he could find someone more reliable to hide it, if he was expecting to be raided?'

There was a moment's silence.

'That makes sense, Tom,' said Emma. 'I thought the suggestion of a loyalty test was nonsense and I'm sure Crompton was lying about it. So what was he doing with it?'

'Perhaps he stole it.'

'What?' said Mel. 'To ransom it back to Garrett? He must have been tired of living.'

'Perhaps the bugger was planning to take over some of Garrett's trade,' suggested Emma.'

'Well, I wouldn't sell him a life insurance policy if he tried,' said Kamal.

'The obvious explanation,' said Tom, 'is that he stole it on behalf of someone else and they collected it. And Garrett had him stabbed out of revenge.'

'Possible,' said Emma. 'But he won't be in a position to confirm or deny for a while, if ever. Some food for thought, though. Time for another round, and some crisps.'

'I'll get these,' said Jack.

He'd just stood up when a familiar face appeared behind him.

'Mind if I join you?' asked DS Derek Palmer.

'Please do,' said Jack. 'What're you having? And what brings you to The Cat and Cushion?'

'Theakston's, please. My wife's late-night shopping, and I

fancied a quiet pint. I didn't expect to find you lot here.' He smiled.

'I'm glad you came,' said Emma, once the drinks had been dispensed. 'We were wondering why Michael Crompton had Frankie Garrett's laptop.'

Derek whistled. 'That's about as sensible as keeping a lump of plutonium under your pillow. What are your thoughts?'

'Either he's planning to move in on some of Frankie's territory, or he had it on behalf of someone else. We presume he stole it.'

Derek thought for a while.

'I can look into the idea of him expanding, but I think it unlikely. He's only ever been a low-level dealer and that kind of ambition would inevitably get him killed. He's pretty much a lone operator. As to the other idea, the only people I can think of who would want the machine, apart from us, that is, are the Bristol gang. There hasn't been any conflict so far, but they might want to expand. I'll have a chat with Avon and Somerset. See if they've heard anything.'

'Thanks, Derek. Look, someone's waving at you.' She pointed to a woman just inside the door of the pub.

'Oh, that's Alison,' he said, draining his pint. 'Good to see you, and thanks for the drink. Cheers!'

As Derek left, Emma finished her own drink.

'I'd better be off. I want to say goodnight to Genevieve. Thanks, guys. I think it's been productive. G'night.'

'That was really useful, love,' said Mel as Tom pulled up outside their home. 'It's obvious that Crompton was lying about minding the laptop for Garrett.'

Tom winced as he pulled on the handbrake.

'I'm not as immersed in things as you guys. I could stand back a bit. See them from a different perspective.'

'Well, it worked. Changing the subject, your hand seems to be troubling you and you've been pretty low recently. Is something wrong?'

'No, I'm absolutely... well, actually, yes.' He looked miserable. 'You know I had a friendly competition bout at Tae Kwan Do a few weeks back?'

'Yes. You didn't say much about it, only that you lost.'

'Well, I got a bit ambitious and I think I've damaged something. My hand's hurting, and using a keyboard is painful, so I'm back to one-handed typing. It's not exactly helpful in cybercrime. I'm trying to get an appointment at the prosthetics department but they're snowed under.'

'Why the bloody hell didn't you tell me?' she demanded. 'You've not said a word about it. Honestly, Tom, for someone who works with computers and all that technological shit you can be bloody useless at communicating.'

'I know. I'm sorry. I didn't want to worry you, what with all you've had to deal with.'

'Sod that. I'm your wife. It's my job to worry about you. For fuck's sake, don't keep me in the dark like this.'

Her tone softened slightly.

'What about painkillers?'

'Paracetamol isn't strong enough and codeine makes me sleepy. Anyway, it's addictive. Ibuprofen gives me mouth ulcers if I take it too often. So, I'm rather fucked.'

'Hence the Scotch?' said Mel, sternly.

Tom's face set in a mutinous expression, then relaxed.

'You've noticed.'

'Hard not to, given that we live together.' She smiled. 'Look, I can't do anything about your hand, but I'd rather you talked to me than to a whisky bottle. And, yes, I know I like brandy when I'm stressed, but not all the time. Maybe we could do something to cheer you up occasionally.'

'What did you have in mind? A country walk? A cream tea courtesy of the National Trust? Not quite doing it for me, I have to say.' He smiled slightly.

'Well, we could have a ready meal and go to bed early.'

'That,' said Tom, grinning, 'is a very good idea.'

Chapter Fifty-Three

Day 12

I WONDER IF ANYONE CHECKED, thought Mel as she drove into work. *It's bloody obvious, but we could have missed it. I'll make a couple of calls before the briefing.*

It took her nearly an hour of searching, being passed around a switchboard and arguing with an unhelpful administrator before she got the information she needed. She sat back at her desk, sipped her coffee and pondered. *It's possible. Not very likely. But definitely possible.*

'First up,' said Emma as she started a slightly delayed briefing, 'we've had the DNA results back on Mel's mosquito. No match with anyone who's been arrested, or with Jenny or her partner, I'm afraid. A good idea, though, Mel.'

'Shit!' said Mel, obviously disappointed. 'I suppose it could have bitten someone outside and flown into Jenny's place. But the profile could still be useful if we arrest a suspect without a record.'

She threw a screwed-up piece of paper at a waste bin and missed.

'I've found out something else, though. Not to do with Jenny. It's Abbie Jackson.'

The name was greeted with blank looks from the team.

'Who?' asked Kamal.

'Abbie Jackson. Kerry Crompton's mother. We know she was sectioned after Kerry died, but I eventually managed to speak to someone at the hospital. Abbie was discharged two weeks ago. I've got an address in Mexton and I think we should talk to her. She might know something about Marvin Staples's murder.'

'Good thinking, Mel,' replied Emma. 'Go and see her. I suppose there's a chance she persuaded someone to stab Staples. Be gentle with her, though. She's obviously fragile.'

'Of course, boss.'

'Now, Nathan Jones. He's had loads of surgery, and it looks like he'll recover, at least to some extent. The hospital wouldn't give me any more details than Sally had and couldn't say when he would be fit enough to answer questions. He'll be with them for quite some time, though. But the question in my mind is, apart from Michael Crompton, who would want to kill him? He's such a minor player. And how did they know where to find him? He was well away from his usual haunts.'

'Another vengeful parent?' suggested Sally.

'Improbable. And Kerry's was the only nitazene-related death we've had, although there were plenty of overdoses that responded to treatment.'

'So it looks like he pissed off someone pretty serious, then,' said Jack. 'Someone able to track his phone. It was only on for a minute or so. They must have been watching for it. Just as we were.'

No one wanted to voice the thought that someone in the police had tipped the would-be killers off.

'Are we thinking Frankie Garrett again?' asked Mel?'

'Could be,' said Emma. 'The larger gangs often have a tame hacker who can do that sort of thing for them. There's the Bristol lot, of course, but I'm still waiting to hear from Derek Palmer. When we finally get to talk to Nathan, we may be able to persuade him to give us something.'

'Do you really think so, boss?' said Kamal. 'He's looking at a long sentence for firearms charges. He won't consider us his friends.'

'True, but if he's in fear for his life he may ask for some form of protection. He's no supergrass, though.'

'We're still nowhere with the Eastside shootings,' Emma continued. 'We've traced the movements of Tyson Harper's phone. He stayed mainly in the Eastside, presumably supplying local customers, but he also made a few longer trips. We're looking at the locations but, so far, nothing of interest has turned up.'

'Do you think, guv,' asked Mel, 'that we could go at it from the firearms angle? If we can trace the weapon, we could maybe find out who it was sold to.'

'A good idea, but I don't think we have the resources. Tracking down an underworld armourer is a major job and, anyway, they don't issue receipts. I'll have another word with the NCA. On a positive note, Martin Rowse is joining us tomorrow as a civilian investigator. Perhaps we could task him to look at recent firearms offences to see if there's a pattern.'

Several officers smiled at the prospect of Martin's return.

'OK people. That's all for now. Please keep me informed.'

Chapter Fifty-Four

SALLY PARKED the unmarked car outside the address the hospital had provided for Abbie Jackson, in a rundown area of town. Once a prosperous district, its Victorian houses had largely been converted into flats and bedsits, with walls, gardens and exterior decoration frequently neglected and in urgent need of maintenance. Abbie's building was no exception, with an ill-fitting, half-open, badly painted front door opening onto a hallway piled with uncollected letters and junk mail. Six bell pushes, half of them with illegible names, were fixed to the wall outside and Mel managed to pick out the initials AJ on the lowest one, Flat 1. Persistent ringing produced no response, so the detectives pushed the door wide open and knocked on the door of Flat 1.

'Oh shit,' said Mel. 'I know that smell. We need to get in.'

The cheap rim latch was easily defeated with a credit card, and a flood of foul air greeted the detectives when the door swung open. The buzz of hundreds of flies ripped the air like an electric saw. Mel and Sally stepped cautiously over a filthy carpet towards a doorway leading to a bedroom. A corpse lay on the bed, pulsating with a carpet of black insects and small white maggots.

Where skin was exposed, it was greenish and marbled, indicating the early stages of decomposition.

'Abbie, I presume,' said Sally, choking back her nausea.

'Reckon so. I'll call it in. We'd better not go any closer but I can see an empty gin bottle and several pill boxes.'

Mel sighed.

'Poor woman. I guess she never got over the death of her daughter. We'll wait in the hallway until the others turn up. But close the bedroom door to keep those fucking flies in.'

The detectives waited in the hall. None of Abbie's neighbours came in or out. Clearly the smell hadn't disturbed them. Within half an hour, paramedics and Jack arrived.

'Looks like suicide,' said Jack, 'so I don't think this is a crime scene. There'll be a PM, obviously, but there's no need to call Dr Durbridge out. We'd better get a SOCO to photograph the body, just in case.'

'That was a smelly one,' said Kate Bartlett, putting away her camera. 'I'll send over the images in the morning. Is there anything else? I'm just about to knock off, but I'll hang on if needed.'

'No, that's it,' replied Jack. 'Thanks, Kate. Can you wait here until the mortuary van arrives?' he asked Sally and Mel.

'OK,' said Sally, 'but we'll be outside in the fresh air. I won't be able to eat my lunch if I stay inside much longer.'

Jack smiled and returned to his car.

As Mel watched the departing forensics van her brow furrowed. *Have we missed something? Why would Abbie kill herself if she'd been considered well enough to leave the hospital? I wonder...*

Chapter Fifty-Five

'Sorry to do this to you, Sally,' said Mel, 'but I think we need to search the flat.'

Sally grimaced.

'What are we looking for?'

'Not sure, but I've got a hunch. Anything that looks out of place, really.'

They put on gloves and overshoes in the hall and re-entered the flat. Opening the windows to let some of the stench of death out, they started working their way through the flat's squalor. Mel suddenly stopped, listened carefully and dashed out of the room leaving a puzzled Sally sorting through a pile of dirty clothing heaped in a corner.

'Stop! Police!' she yelled at the refuse collector who was about to empty a wheely bin into the back of the collection vehicle.

'Put it back. I need to check the bins.'

'Do what you like, luv,' the man said, 'but we can't wait for you. We've got a schedule. We'll have to collect them next time.'

He signalled to his mate and the vehicle continued slowly along the road, the compactor munching noisily on its malodorous load.

'Sally,' she called, poking her head round the flat's front door. 'Come and get some fresher air. We've got bins to sort through.'

'Lovely. My favourite,' Sally replied, sourly.

'The bins are numbered, so give me a hand with Flat 1. Then we'll move on to Flat 2. I suspect what I'm looking for will be in one of the bins normally nearest the door.'

'Why are you being so bloody enigmatic? For God's sake, tell me what we're after.'

'Humour me. Think of it as a test of your detective abilities.'

'Bollocks,' Sally muttered, as she helped Mel tip the bin's contents onto a plastic sheet retrieved from the car. 'Ah. Is this what you wanted?'

Sally pointed to a kitchen knife with a dark stain on the white plastic handle.

'Bingo!' Mel almost whooped. 'Pity Kate's gone off duty. We'll get a SOCO back to retrieve it properly, as well as these clothes and trainers. I had a hunch that Abbie could have been involved in Marvin Staples's stabbing.'

'But he was killed by a bloke. In the gents. So you think the killer came here to report back to Abbie and dump the knife? A hitman doing her a favour?'

'Improbable, but not impossible. But I have another idea which will depend on what the lab finds. Did you come across a phone?'

'Yes, I put it in an evidence bag. If she did get someone to do the job, there may be an electronic trail.'

'Right. I can't wait to get back to the station for a change of clothes and a shower. It takes ages to get this stink out of my hair. Perhaps I should shave it all off.'

'I don't think the Sinéad O'Connor look would suit you. And Tom might have an opinion, too.'

'Yeah, he would,' laughed Mel. 'Look, here's the SOCO.'

A grumpy woman of about thirty, in a forensic suit, slammed the van's door behind her and stamped up to the detectives.'

'What's this all about? A knife? I've just come from a murder and I've seen enough sharp implements for one day, thank you very much.'

Mel smiled sweetly.

'There's a knife that needs to go in a tube and some clothing and trainers that need bagging up. We don't have the proper containment, and we couldn't just chuck it in the back of the car, could we?'

'I suppose not,' the SOCO acknowledged, grudgingly. 'OK, show me the items. Is there a crime scene?'

'Probably not, but we'll seal the premises anyway. It's the stuff in the bins we're interested in.'

While the SOCO did her job, Mel and Sally closed the windows and doors of the flat and fixed police tape over the doorway. Five minutes later they were heading back to the station with all the car windows wide open.

'She was in a bit of a strop, wasn't she?' said Sally. 'I mean, I know she'd just come from a murder, but this was hardly a big job.'

'Yes but she... oh fuck.'

'What is it, Mel?'

'Oh sodding fuck.'

Mel remained silent for the rest of the journey.

Chapter Fifty-Six

'Jack, do you mind if I knock off early,' asked Mel. 'I still stink, and I'd like a long bath. I've written up my statement and there's something I want to do on the Jenny Pike murder.'

'No, go ahead. How's it coming along?'

'I've got an idea. Could you do something for me?'

'What is it? Nothing dodgy, I hope.'

'Can you ask the lab to run the DNA profile from the mosquito against the elimination database? And can you find out which SOCO attended the scene?'

'Sure. Are you going to share your suspicions?'

'Not yet. I don't want to look a tit. But I may have something tomorrow. Thanks, Jack.'

Mel and Tom spent much of the evening going through the files from the *Messenger* server, occasionally logging on to court reports and other databases. At half past ten, Mel leaned back in her chair, poured the last drops of wine into her glass and punched the air.

'Result! I know who killed Jenny Pike. At least, I'm ninety percent certain. I just need some information from Jack, and we're ready to make an arrest.'

She explained her reasoning to Tom who nodded his agreement.

'You could be a detective,' he joked.

'Well, it was both of us grinding our way through this lot. And something someone said today pointed me in the right direction. The trouble is, we can't use this in court. We didn't get the files legitimately. I'll have to find a way round that, which is where Jack's info comes in. Now, let's say good night to the parrots and go to bed. I really need some sleep.'

'Have they appointed your jobshare DI yet?' Mike Thorpe asked Emma, pouring glasses of wine while Emma changed Genevieve.

'They've had the interviews, and the selection panel is supposed to be deciding tomorrow, I believe. It shouldn't be long now.'

'Good.' Mike sounded relieved.

'Is something worrying you?'

'No. Well, yes, a bit. You're supposed to be half time, but you've been putting in many more hours than that. I love being with Genevieve. Don't get me wrong. But the university asked me to take on some more lecturing and I didn't know what to tell them.'

'OK. But you know my job's not nine to five. I can't ask murderers to fit in with your lecturing timetable.'

There was an awkward silence.

'Sorry, Mike. I didn't mean to get mardy. I'm sure things will get easier when the new DI starts. Find out exactly what this new commitment involves, and we'll try to work round it. Now pass me that bloody wine. It's shit at work at the moment, and I need to relax. And can you please order a pizza?'

Chapter Fifty-Seven

Day 13

Taking advantage of a bright, dry morning, Mel decided to cycle to work as she'd missed the gym of late and felt she needed the exercise. She'd received an early morning text from Jack that confirmed her suspicions, and she was looking forward to presenting her findings to Emma at the briefing. She'd barely reached the end of her street when she spotted a forensics van parked by the roadside, its hazard lights flashing and the back doors open. Puzzled, she leant her bike against a lamppost, approached the van and called out.

'Hi. It's DC Cotton. Is anything wrong?'

A muffled reply came from the back of the van. All she could make out was the word 'stuck'. She leant in and saw a figure in a forensic suit crouched on the floor. She started to climb in when the figure swung round and something hard and heavy struck her on the side of her head. Dazed, she felt herself dragged into the van and thrown face down onto a steel floor. Gaffer tape was plastered over her mouth, and she felt her hands and feet being cable tied. She kicked ineffectually at her attacker, who climbed over her, elbowing her in the back. The van doors slammed and, as the vehicle lurched away, Mel castigated herself with one thought. *Should've remembered The Silence of the fucking Lambs.'*

'Any idea where Mel is?' asked Tom, anxiously, when Jack answered his call. 'Only she was supposed to be cycling in, and I've just spotted a bike like hers left in the road. Did someone give her a lift? If so, why did she leave the bike? She's not answering her phone, either.'

'Sorry, Tom. She's not here and we're waiting for her so we can start the briefing. Hang on, I'll check.'

He asked around the office.

'No one's seen her and it's not like her to be late without telling someone. Should we be worried?

'I don't know. I'll drive along the route she usually takes and look out for her. I'll get back to you. Call me if she appears, won't you?'

'Of course. Good luck.'

When Mel hadn't arrived after half an hour, and there was no word from Tom, Jack knocked on the DI's office door.

'Emma,' he said. 'Mel's missing.'

After a bumpy and nausea-inducing ride the van stopped. Mel heard what she guessed was a garage door opening, the van was backed into an enclosed space and the door rattled again. The driver switched off the engine, pulled open the back doors and hauled Mel out of the van feet first. Mel managed to get her hands in front of her, breaking the fall with her forearms and reducing the impact of her face with the concrete. Pain flared through her elbows and the rough surface tore at her cheek as she was dragged along. Her captor propped her up against a wall alongside the van, tore off the gaffer tape and removed her own mask. It was the SOCO who had collected the knife and clothing from Abbie Jackson's the previous day.

For a moment, nobody spoke.

'I gave myself away, yesterday, didn't I?'

'Of course you fucking did. No competent SOCO would go from one scene to another without a complete change of clothes. I saw the blood from the murder on your suit, which should have gone in a bag as you left the premises. But I know who you are. Clare Miller. You're a crap SOCO, you're possibly corrupt and you killed Jenny Pike.'

'Well you're the clever one, aren't you? Yes, I'm not much good at the job. I thought it would be glamorous, like on the TV, but it's boring, smelly and bloody hard work. No wonder I made mistakes. But I've never been on the take or been paid to lose evidence.'

'Then why not leave, for fuck's sake?'

'Because I've got a book deal for my memoirs and it's been optioned by Channel 4. They can't get enough on forensics these days, and I'll be somebody, not just a basic grade SOCO who never got a commendation or promotion. But Jenny Pike was about to destroy everything. She had to bloody meddle. She'd been looking at cases I'd fucked up and was coming close to identifying me.

'You know what's funny? Pike interviewed a SOCO who'd been persuaded to retire early because of poor performance. He was my partner, which she didn't realise, and I'd persuaded him to admit to some of my mistakes. Of course, he said nothing but told me what was going on. I had to deal with the meddling journalist. And I guarantee you won't find any trace that I'd been at the scene. I didn't even work it.'

'Locard,' spat Mel.

'Yes, I know. Locard's principle. Every contact leaves a trace. But I didn't.'

'You did.'

Clare looked uneasy for the first time.

'A mosquito bit you and I found it in a spider's web. The lab ran DNA on the blood in its gut. Results came back today.'

'You fucking bitch,' Clare screamed, kicking Mel in the chest, still sore from Nathan Jones's bullet.

'I knew someone was looking at old cases and talking to people. Your name came up in the canteen, but I didn't think you would get anywhere.'

Miller paced around the garage, radiating fury.

'Your sodding mosquito's changed everything. You've made me look incompetent. I can't have it. I'll have to disappear. You've fucking ruined everything.'

A pillar of ice formed in Mel's spine.

'So what about me?'

'Do you think for one fucking moment I'll let you live? After what you've done?'

'For fuck's sake. You really are a shit SOCO. They'll look for you when you don't turn up at work, they'll trace the van, my DNA's inside it and also in this garage. My colleagues will already be looking for me and guess who's top of the list to talk to. The search for you will be relentless. Christ! A teenager watching *Dexter*, or even *Midsomer Murders*, could do a better job of getting rid of me.'

Clare gasped at the insult and kicked Mel in the ribs.

'We know everything,' said Mel, panicking. 'You won't get as far as the airport, if you try to leave the country. Stop being a twat. Give yourself up. Killing a copper will get you a whole life tariff. You know how it works.'

'I don't fucking care anymore. Everthing's gone. My job, my reputation and my chances to prove to the world I'm someone. The SOCO who couldn't even get away with murder. Now there's a title for a documentary.' Her face contorted with hate. 'And it's all fucking down to you.'

Clare picked up a wicked-looking machete from a shelf. Images of sweeping blades flashed through Mel's head and she shivered.

'I found this at a crime scene a few years ago. There'd been some kind of shootout between drug dealers on the Eastside. I didn't book it into evidence and kept it as a souvenir. And I will take considerable pleasure in using it to cut off your fucking head.'

Chapter Fifty-Eight

'Have you any idea where she could be?' Emma asked Jack.

'None at all. We have a prime suspect for the Jenny Pike murder, and she was looking forward to presenting the evidence at the briefing. She wouldn't voluntarily miss it.'

'She wouldn't have gone off to interview the suspect on her own, would she?'

'She knows better than that. She would have told me where she was going and taken someone with her. She can be impetuous but she's not stupid.'

'Tom said her bike was dumped on her route to work. Could she have been kidnapped?'

'That,' said Jack, grimly, 'is the most likely explanation.'

'OK,' said Emma. 'Let's not piss around. Alert all patrols to be on the lookout for her. Check A&E in case she's been injured. Track her phone. Get hold of the bike, if Tom hasn't collected it. Get someone to walk the route she normally takes – a patrol car could miss something. Now tell me about this prime suspect.'

'Mel and Tom have been looking at links between cases where investigations or prosecutions have failed. This was what Jenny Pike was working on. There were no police officers who worked on all the cases and the SIOs were all competent. But she looked further and found a SOCO had worked on every case. And I asked the lab to run the DNA from the mosquito against the elimination database. The results came back this morning. It matched the SOCO, and she didn't work Jenny's scene. So she's definitely someone we need to speak to. Her name's Clare Miller.'

'Right. Contact her team leader. Find out where she's working and invite her for interview when she finishes at the scene. Arrest her if need be. And let's get a bloody move on.'

Jack called the team together, distributed jobs and called the forensic unit. His face paled and he rushed back to Emma's office.

'Clare Miller didn't sign in this morning, and one of their vans is missing. I'll get it tagged in case it shows up on ANPR. I've got her address. I'm going round there.'

'Take a couple of uniforms with you. Do you want armed response?'

'Shouldn't think so. She may have suffocated Jenny, but I doubt she's armed. Maybe put them on standby.'

'Well, be careful.'

Jack, hurtling out of the office, didn't answer.

'This is the address,' said Jack. 'But there's no sign of the van.'

'Probably in the garage,' said PC Halligan, pulling up at the kerb. 'Some of those plants alongside the drive have been damaged, as if a large vehicle has pushed past them.'

'Well spotted. OK. You and I will take the garage. Can you two,' he turned to the officers in the back of the car, 'take the house. One at the front and one at the back. Give it fifteen seconds and we'll knock simultaneously.'

The four officers took up their positions quietly, keeping an eye on their watches.

'What's that noise?' whispered Jack, listening at the garage door. 'Someone's speaking. Sod fifteen seconds. On a count of three, lift the door. We're going in.'

I mustn't freeze. I mustn't freeze. Mel screamed inside. She leant back against the wall, drew up her knees and kicked at her captor with her bound feet, catching her on the shins. Clare swore, stumbled and dropped the machete. As she picked it up again the two women heard the shout.

'Three!'

With a grinding noise, the garage door was hauled upwards, and two silhouettes were visible at the entrance. Clare made a last attempt to cut Mel. PC Halligan's Taser cracked, and fifteen hundred volts coursed through her body as the electrodes lodged in her thigh. She fell to the floor, twitching, and the machete clanged against the side of the van.

'Oh good,' said Mel. 'It's the fucking cavalry. Nice to see you, Jack. Glad you dropped by. Now please get these cable ties off me. I need the loo. Urgently.'

Chapter Fifty-Nine

AFTER A TEDIOUS COUPLE of hours in A&E, getting her scraped face dressed and being checked out for concussion, Mel returned to the station to write up her statement. Tom hugged her in reception and the team cheered when she entered the incident room at the start of a delayed briefing.

'Well done, Mel,' said Emma. 'Jack's briefed me, but can you summarise for the rest of us how you got on to Clare Miller?'

'Yes, guv. Jenny Pike was investigating police foul-ups and a group of them involved evidence going missing, forensic failures and so on. There were no officers in common, so Tom and I looked at other groups of people, starting with SOCOs. We found that Clare was a common denominator. She gave herself away when she turned up to collect evidence from Abbie Jackson's place in clothing she'd worn at a murder scene.'

Several officers groaned at this blatant stupidity.

'Anyway, she realised Jenny was getting close, so she got rid of her, using her forensic training to avoid leaving traces. But she didn't notice a mosquito biting her, though how it found some exposed skin beats me. Jack told me the blood matched this morning.'

Jack nodded.

'She also heard that I'd been nosing around her old cases – talking to people and looking at files – so she went for me. I saw this, apparently broken-down, forensics van on my way to work and went to offer help. She dragged me into it, knocked me on the head and tied me up. She got me into her garage and admitted what she'd done. When I told her about the mosquito, she went ballistic and was going to cut my head off with this bloody great machete. I'd put an end to a book and TV deal she's got which would have made her a celebrity. She must have an inferiority complex, or whatever they call it now. I was fucking terrified. I managed to kick her, and she dropped the weapon. Then Jack and the others turned up and Tasered her. So, ta, Jack.'

She made a mock curtsey in his direction. Her colleagues looked on in horror.

'You'll be pleased to know,' said Emma, 'that Clare has made a full confession, and the CPS is reviewing the charges as we speak. She will go down for a long time. Jenny's body can be released for burial and, although she was a pain in the bum, I think some of us should attend her funeral.'

There were murmurs of agreement.

'Now, to other matters. Michael Crompton reached the hospital just in time and is likely to live, although he'll have to manage on just one kidney. He has asked to speak to us, so we'll visit him when the doctors say it's OK. He's being guarded by a prison officer. I'll check whether he wants a solicitor present. Nathan Jones is still in hospital and, surprisingly, has also asked to speak to us. We'll arrest him in due course. There's still no progress on the Eastside shootings or on the Staples stabbing, unless any of you have something to add?'

'Actually, guv, I have,' said Mel. 'I know the DNA on the knife we found at Abbie's hasn't come back yet but I'll bet the blood is Marvin Staples.'

'So you think the killer dumped it there to incriminate her?' asked Kamal.

'No, I don't, not least because we weren't supposed to find it. It would've ended up in a landfill if I hadn't heard the rubbish truck. I think it was Abbie herself.'

'But it was a male who did the stabbing, in the gents toilets. Abbie was a skinny lass. It couldn't have been her,' said Emma.

'That's where the clothing comes in,' said Mel. 'We found a puffer jacket and a large-sized hoodie in Abbie's bin. She was quite tall and, if she wore the hoodie over the jacket, and kept the hood up to conceal her face and hair, she would have looked like a man, at least on CCTV. No one would have taken much notice of her in the pub unless they were looking for someone suspicious. I'll bet Marvin's blood is on the hoodie and Abbie's DNA is all over both items of clothing. If I'm wrong, I'll pay for all the drinks next time we're in The Cat and Cushion.'

At that point, Amira Khan entered the incident room.

'Thought you might like to see this, Emma,' she said. 'I've had a quick look at Abbie Jackson's phone. There's nothing much on it, apart from a strange text. Just a few letters. UMSMNJ. I've no idea what it means, but it came from a burner found in Michael Crompton's flat.'

'Shit,' said Sally. 'I know what that means, or at least what it could mean. "You Marvin Staples Me Nathan Jones." It's conspiracy to murder. Kerry's parents took one dealer each.'

'So, we really would like to talk to Crompton,' said Emma. 'And the bugger will bloody well need a solicitor, whether he thinks so or not. So that's two murders solved, which will please Mr Farlowe and the DSup no end. All we need do now is prevent open warfare between a couple of drug gangs, solve a double shooting and find an underworld armourer.'

'No problem at all,' joked Mel. 'Just a lunchtime job, really.'

The team laughed.

'Before you all head for the coffee machine,' said Emma, 'I'd like to introduce a new member of the team.' She waved at the door, and a familiar face appeared, to smiles from the other officers. 'Most of you know Martin Rowse, but, for those who don't, he did a sterling job as a DC with us and then moved to Mexton Investigations. Bored with the private sector, he's rejoining us as a Civilian Investigator. Welcome back, Martin!'

Chapter Sixty

'WE GOT a message that you'd like to talk to us,' said Mel, sitting down beside Nathan Jones's hospital bed. 'I'm DC Mel Cotton and my colleague is DC Sally Erskine.'

'Yeah, that's right. Thing is, I'm fucking scared. Someone's tried to kill me twice in the fast few days and I need protection. I can tell you stuff.'

'OK, Nathan. I must caution you, and I'll record what you say on my phone. I'll write it up as a statement and you can sign it later. Do you want a solicitor?'

'No. Let's just get on with it.'

He licked his lips nervously as Mel recited the caution.

'I did something totally fucking stupid. Frankie Garrett has been recruiting dealers and is taking over the Eastside for gear and the posher bits of town for blow. He's doing it gradually and if he makes you an offer, you daren't refuse. I joined his mob and then this bloke from Bristol turns up and offers a better deal. A bit more commission. He said he could protect anyone who went over to his side, so like a twat, I did. And I gave him some of Frankie's product.'

Nathan trembled at the memory.

'So they came after you.'

'Yeah. I don't know how they found me. I thought I was safe around me gran's.'

'Maybe the same way we did. Your phone pinged in the area. They must have someone who can track them. Some kind of hacker. Do you think they were trying to kill you?'

'What do you fucking think?'

'OK. I'll take that as a yes. And the other time?'

'Someone took a shot at me. It missed and I didn't recognise the shooter. I think something went wrong 'cos I heard him scream.'

'I believe we know who that was. Is that why you got the gun?'

'Yeah. I needed something for self-defence in case he came back. I didn't mean to shoot at coppers. I'm really sorry. I thought it was Frankie's boys come for me. Honest.'

'We'll come back to that at a later date,' said Mel, stiffly. 'Where did you get the weapon?'

Nathan looked shifty.

'Do I have to say?'

'It will help you in court if you do.'

'I got this number from someone in the pub. I called it at seven o'clock, like the bloke told me, and said what I needed.'

'Do you remember the number?' asked Sally.

'No, but it ended in three nines.'

'That's OK. We've got your phone, so we'll find it. Which pub?'

'The Fife and Drum.'

'What happened then?' asked Mel.

'I met this bloke in the rugby club car park at midnight on the eighth. He told me how much — a grand, can you believe it? Anyway, I paid up and he gave me the shooter. His motor was a dark Range Rover, if that helps.'

'Yes, thank you,' said Mel. 'And you've no idea why someone would shoot at you?'

'No. The only person I've seriously pissed off, as far as I know, is Frankie. And his guys wouldn't miss. In fact, they would've grabbed me and tortured me.'

Nathan looked sick.

'Is there anything else you want to tell us, Nathan?' asked Mel, gently.

'No, I don't think...'

'How about the Eastside shootings?' interjected Sally. 'Shane Hopton and Tyson Harper. Do you know anything about that?'

Nathan shrugged.

'I didn't really know them, but the word is they turned down Frankie's offer. No one'll do that in future.'

'OK, Nathan. Thank you. Interview concluded at ten forty-two. Your co-operation will be mentioned to the judge when you go to trial, and it should get you a reduced sentence. We may have some more questions later. I don't know what you'll be charged with. That's up to the Crown Prosecution Service.'

She stood up.

'What about my protection?'

'We can't put a guard on your room, I'm afraid. We don't have the resources. But I'll tell the hospital staff to watch out for anyone suspicious, and there is a prison officer guarding someone else. We'll also alert the governor when you're remanded to prison pending trial.'

'Is that all you can do? Fucking hell, I might just as well have a target tattooed on me face.'

'If the person who shot at you is who we think it is,' said Sally, 'You needn't worry. He's out of action. As to Frankie, he may think he's done enough damage to you already. He might reckon seeing your injuries would put other people off from crossing him. Good luck, anyway.'

Mel and Sally left a distraught Nathan Jones and went in search of the hospital canteen.

———

'What do you reckon, Sally?' asked Mel as the two detectives compared notes over coffees and cakes. 'Was he telling the truth?'

'He was obviously dead scared,' Sally replied, cautiously. 'What he said rang true. He was clearly reluctant to say how he got the firearm, but I don't think he lied.'

'I agree. We'll get the techies to track the number he called. It was probably a burner, but we may get some idea of where it's been. There's also CCTV. I doubt the rugby club will have cameras in the car park, but you never know. Otherwise some poor sod will have to check ANPR for dark Range Rovers in the area, around the time concerned. Perhaps we could ask Martin,' she grinned mischievously. 'Right. Drink up. We'd better get back to the station and type up our reports.'

They walked back past Nathan's room and peered in, noticing he was asleep. What they didn't notice was the name on the adjacent room. 'Crompton. M.'

Chapter Sixty-One

'How DID you get on with the Range Rovers, Martin?' asked Mel, when she had finished her reports.

Martin Rowse grimaced.

'That was a job and a half. There were seventeen vehicles, matching the description Nathan gave, picked up by ANPR in the area before and after he bought the weapon. Twelve were just passing through and picked up only once, so I've eliminated them for the time being. One, a top-of-the-range model, was reported stolen the following morning. I've looked into that one. It triggered a number of speed cameras along the M4 and the M25 and was picked up by ANPR cameras in Essex, where it apparently disappeared.'

'So do we think the armourer is in Essex? It's a bloody long way to go to sell a pistol and, surely, there are plenty of local customers.'

Martin smiled.

'It's stranger than that. The Environment Agency's international waste shipments people got a tip-off that a container of waste being exported for recycling was a bit iffy. Apparently, a helluva lot of waste ends up dumped in developing countries rather than being processed properly. They intercepted a container bound for the Far East, via the UAE, at Harwich Docks and found the car, hidden behind a load of waste plastic. It had been stolen to order and put in the container at a recycling plant near Basildon. Essex police have made arrests and more should follow. The plates were false, and the owner's identity has been confirmed by the VIN.'

'Nice! But what about the others?'

'Two of them seem clean. They're registered to a consultant surgeon and the owner of a chain of estate agents. The fifth is the interesting one. It was picked up by ANPR on the Highchester Road heading north about an hour before Nathan met the gun supplier. An hour and three quarters later, it was picked up again, heading south. So wherever it went, the destination was most probably in a band between that camera and the next one along the road.'

'That's a pretty big area.'

'Yeah, I know. But I've eliminated some of the side roads with ANPR and I'm contacting places likely to have CCTV. There are no buses running at that time of night, though, and we can't put out a call for dashcam footage with only this evidence.'

'That's great, Martin. We can tag the car and get patrols to watch for it. If it turns up again, we'll follow it and grab the bastard. Then I'll buy you a pint!'

Chapter Sixty-Two

23.30

PC Dave Jordan pulled the patrol car into a lay-by on the Highchester Road, switched off the engine and lights, and reached for his flask of tea.

'Fancy a cuppa, Joe?' he asked his colleague.

'No, you're all right. I'll only need to stop for a piss if I do.'

'Blimey. Can't you hold it anymore? I would have thought...'

The discussion about Joe's bladder ended abruptly when Dave handed him the flask, started the car and swung back on to the main road.

'What are you playing at? You nearly soaked my bloody uniform. And this was a clean shirt this morning.'

'Did you see the Range Rover that just went past?' asked Dave, accelerating smoothly. 'The dark one?'

'No. I was listening to you taking the piss out of me.'

'It's the one we're looking for, in this area. A suspected firearms dealer.'

'We're not gonna stop it are we?' Joe's anxiety was obvious.

'No, you idiot. Call it in.' Dave recited the reg number. 'We'll follow at a distance until an ARU arrives. They can have the pleasure of getting shot at.'

'Sounds fair,' said Joe, mollified.

Ten minutes later, the Range Rover slowed down and turned into a side road.

'I know where that leads,' said Joe. 'There's a patch of woodland on a nature reserve a couple of miles up the road, where people go dogging.'

'How do you know that, then? Something you're not telling me?'

'Sod off. We've had complaints from the volunteers that the shaggers were disturbing nesting owls or bats or something. They put up a CCTV camera to deter them, but it just produced loads of footage on the internet of people mooning at it.'

Dave laughed.

'Is there anything else along that road?'

'A couple of holiday cottages, I think. Can we turn the lights off? The driver'll see us otherwise.'

Dave frowned and did so, cautiously navigating the narrow road by intermittent moonlight.

'I don't reckon gun dealers go dogging,' he said, 'so I guess it's one of the cottages.'

They passed the first cottage, which was clearly unoccupied. The gate leading to it was padlocked and the windows were boarded up. Further on, the road rose, and a glimmer of light was visible through the trees. Dave parked the car off the road, beside a farm gate, and the two officers approached the second cottage on foot.

The building was set back from the road and two cars, one of which was a Range Rover, were parked outside. There was no noise from the cottage. Only the bark of a fox, and the call-and-response from a pair of tawny owls, disturbed the night. Joe, whispering, updated the station on their position, and the pair crouched behind thick bushes to await their armed colleagues.

Ten minutes later, a dark van moved quietly up the lane and stopped just short of the cottage. The doors were eased open and four armed officers stepped out, one carrying a Big Door Key and one holding a German shepherd dog on a lead. They formed a huddle around the Tactical Firearms Commander, receiving whispered instructions. Then they moved towards the cottage, communicating mainly with signs. One made his way towards the back of the cottage, and, after precisely two minutes, the door was smashed in with cries of: 'Armed police. Stay exactly where you are. Do not move.'

A few moments later the dog trotted out, wagging its tail, and officers entered. They found a man and a woman, both stark naked, standing obediently immobile. The man, looking to be in his thirties, was holding a whisky bottle and the woman, apparently somewhere in her forties, was holding a pillow over her face and sobbing.

'What the fucking hell do you think you are doing?' snarled the man. 'This is my property and you've no bloody business storming in and terrifying us. Do you know who I am?'

'No, sir,' replied the TFC, who had just entered. 'But I suggest you and your companion get dressed and tell us. We entered your premises lawfully as we were in receipt of information suggesting that firearms may have been present and there was a possible threat to life. As this does not appear to be the case, since the dog found nothing, we will, of course repair the damage. But we still need to talk to you.'

The officers stepped outside to allow the cottage's occupants to dress, and the ARU departed, leaving Dave and Joe to take their statements.

'First, I need your names, please,' began Dave.

'Alan Burston,' said the man, sullenly, 'and my friend is Caroline Clarke.'

The woman nodded mutely, terror in her eyes.

'Why don't you take Ms Clarke to the kitchen and make a cup of tea, Joe? I'll interview Mr Burston, and we'll have a chat with her afterwards.'

Joe guided the trembling woman out of the room while the two men sat down, and Dave cautioned Burston.

'Before I say anything, I want to know why the hell you're here. Otherwise you can piss off and wait till my solicitor arrives.'

'You can, of course, ask for a solicitor, but you're not under arrest. I'm not at liberty to give you the full details, but I can say that your vehicle was seen in close proximity to a suspected firearms offence on the eighth of this month.'

'That's bollocks. I've never owned a firearm or even handled one.'

'Then can you explain what your car was doing between eleven and one that night?'

'Yes. I drove from my home to this cottage, and back again an hour or so later.'

'Can anyone corroborate that?'

'Ms Clarke.' He paused. 'Look officer,' he said, modifying his manner in an attempt to be charming, 'the fact is, we are both married. But not to each other. We would both be very grateful if you could keep this incident out of the papers. For both our sakes.'

Dave wasn't sure if 'both' included Burston's companion or was some kind of veiled threat.

'Rather late for an assignation, wasn't it?'

'Caroline's husband was at a golf club dinner that went on until two in the morning. I waited for my wife to go to bed and told her I had to go into the office, as there was an emergency.'

'And what do you do, Mr Burston?'

'I'm the owner of Civet-AI. The fastest growing AI company

in Europe. We're challenging the Americans, which doesn't make us popular over there.'

Dave shrugged.

'I don't see why this incident should be made public, as you don't appear to have committed an offence. Apart from the false number plates. Would you care to explain?'

'Ah. Yes. Sorry about that. I think my wife is suspicious and I was worried she could trace my car through those number plate cameras. She has a friend in the police. That's why I used false plates – but only for our meetings.'

'Well, any officer using our systems for the purpose of checking up on someone like that would be dismissed and be likely to end up charged with misconduct in public office.'

Burston did not seem reassured.

'I think that will do, sir,' said Dave, standing up. 'You will be reported over the false plates, and I suggest you remove them immediately. I'll talk to Ms Clarke now.'

Burston slunk out of the room and Caroline entered. She had nothing significant to add to her friend's statement and also implored Dave to try to keep the incident out of the press.

As the two PCs walked back to their car, Joe chuckled.

'You know who she is, don't you?'

'Caroline Clarke, she said.'

'Caroline Clarke, my arse. She's Caroline Collins. The ACC's wife.'

Chapter Sixty-Three

Day 14

'Well that was a complete foul-up,' said DCI Farlowe, when the laughter at PC Jordan's report had died down. 'I think we can take it that Mr Collins will not be contacting us about the incident, but woe betide anyone who leaks it on social media. Understood?'

Everyone nodded their heads, some more readily than others.

'So, of the four likely vehicles, two are definitely discounted,' Farlowe continued. 'We'd better interview the owners of the other two, in case someone was using one of them without the owner's knowledge. Could Martin Rowse have missed one?'

'Not a chance, boss,' said Mel, concealing her annoyance. 'If it was there, he'd have found it. He's extremely meticulous.'

'OK. Fair enough. We do have some further information, though. I've asked Amira Khan to present it. Go ahead, Amira.'

The IT specialist stood up and projected a map onto the screen.

'The burner phone Nathan dialled,' she said, 'was only in use occasionally. It was mainly switched on between seven and seven-thirty in the evening and, during that period, it was always on the move. It was last used yesterday. There were a few calls to and from the phone – see the red dots on the map for the approximate locations. They're all in the south of Mexton, as you'll have noticed, and most, but not all, coincide with the evening active period. It would be nice if they formed a clear circle around the suspect's home but, as you can see, they don't.'

'But it's reasonable to assume the suspect's base is in the south, isn't it?' asked Kamal.

'Probably, unless they're being especially clever.'

Jack grimaced.

'Can we link the calls to a particular vehicle?' asked Mel.

'If you have the reg, we can match locations from CCTV and ANPR to the places where the calls were made. Even better would be the log on the car's onboard computer. That would give much more accurate locations and timings.'

'First catch your car,' muttered Sally.

'Right,' said the DCI. 'Let's focus on the cars. Interview the surgeon and the estate agent. If there's nothing of use there, check some of the vehicles Martin only saw once. They may have returned by a different route, although they should have been picked up somewhere. That's the best we can do at the moment. Thank you, everyone.'

———

'Neptune! Titan! Miranda! Oberon! Sit!'

At their owner's command, the four massive rottweilers sat obediently at the end of Charles Boyle's drive.

'Police, sir,' called Mel, waving her warrant card at the athletic-looking, middle-aged man approaching the electronically controlled gate. 'DC Cotton and DC Erskine.'

'Yes, you said, over the intercom. How can I help?'

'It's about your car. The Range Rover. Can we have a chat?'

'Of course. Can we do it through the gate? I'd invite you in, but the dogs are a bit frisky at the moment. What do you want to know?'

'That's OK, sir. Can you tell me where your car was on the night of the eighth of this month, between eleven and one?'

'That's easy. It was in the dealer's workshop, where it had been for three days, waiting for a spare part. Renfrew's in High-chester.'

'Could it have been taken out of the garage?'

'Not without a clutch. I can assure you it was off the road between the sixth and the tenth. Why do you ask?'

'I can't give you all the details,' replied Mel, 'but a Range Rover with your registration number was seen in the vicinity of an incident on the night of the eighth. I'm afraid it looks like your number has been cloned.'

'Well that would explain why I got a speeding ticket on a road I've never driven on. Bloody cheek.'

'When and where was that, sir?' asked Sally.

Boyle provided the details.

'Is there anything else I can help you with?'

'No, that's fine Mr Boyle. Thank you for your time. You should definitely appeal against that speeding ticket – feel free to give the office my name.'

'Thanks, DC Erskine. I will.'

'He's doing alright for himself,' murmured Sally as they watched Boyle striding back to his house, followed by the dogs. 'There must be a lot of money in estate agency. It would cost half my salary to feed the four rottweilers of the apocalypse, I reckon.'

Mel chuckled.

'Not a dog fan, then?'

'Yes, I am. It's just that those four seemed a bit intimidating *en masse*. I'm rather glad we didn't go in. Still, we got what we came for: the number of the car the armourer was using. I'll check with

Renfrew's to make sure it was in their workshop when he said. There's no need to interview the surgeon, I reckon.'

'Good. I'll let Jack know. We can concentrate on tracing that number through ANPR, assuming the plates haven't been switched, that is. And maybe Amira can link its movements to the phone.'

'Yeah. But we still won't know who's bloody driving it.'

'Cheerful, aren't you! Haven't you heard? Every little helps.'

'Yes, but we're not looking for ten pence off bleeding bananas, are we? Sorry. I'm just a bit gloomy at the moment.'

'The PTSD?'

Sally shrugged.

'No, not so much, although Forrest's shotgun didn't help. Helen and I are trying to buy a flat and we're having trouble getting a mortgage. The building society's surveyor found a crack in the wall and we're having to pay for a structural engineer to look at it. It's been dragging on for bloody ages.'

'I sympathise. Tom and I were lucky when we bought our place. No problems. Perhaps the body in the garden helped.'

Sally smiled.

'We'd better get back to the nick. There's a briefing in half an hour and I'm desperate for coffee.'

Chapter Sixty-Four

MICHAEL CROMPTON KNEW he was going to die. Not from the shanking, although he'd lost a kidney and the doctor had warned of a possible infection, but from Frankie's vengeance. He felt reasonably safe in the hospital, with a bored prison officer sitting beside his bed, but he knew Frankie would get to him once he was returned to prison. So he had nothing to lose. He turned to the officer.

'Could you get in touch with Detective Inspector Thorpe again, please. I'm ready to make a statement.'

Half an hour later, Emma and Jack appeared in the doorway. They asked the prison officer to wait outside the door.

'I believe you wanted to talk to us,' said Emma. 'I'll have to caution you again and record the interview on my phone. Do you want a solicitor.'

'Do what you like. No brief. I'll never see the inside of a court. Frankie'll get me one way or the other. The thing is, I haven't been completely honest with you.'

Jack raised his eyebrows in mock surprise.

'I wasn't looking after that laptop for Frankie. I'd nicked it from him. Or, rather, from his accountant. A bloke called Billy offered me ten grand, from this guy in Bristol, to get it. I was supposed to deliver it the day after my gun blew up.'

'Do you know the name of the Bristol man?'

'Jason, Jasper, Jacob? Something like that. Anyway, he must have sent someone to get it from Josie's flat. Or Frankie did, though I don't know how he knew I had it. So whoever took it must have hit your mate.'

Emma nodded.

'How did you get the laptop?'

'I followed Frankie's accountant and Marcus Forrest from the health spa. I got a waiter to put something in Forrest's coffee that made him pee, so when they got to the services he ran off to the bog and I held up the accountant. Poor sod nearly shat himself.'

'OK. Can you remember the address where you were supposed to deliver it?'

'Yeah.' Crompton recited it.

'Is there anything else you would like to tell us?'

'It was me what shot at Nathan Jones. I printed the gun and did something wrong, I guess.'

'And this was because you blamed him for the death of your daughter?'

'Yeah. The bastard. Him and Marvin Staples. I'm glad he got done.'

'You may not be so glad to know that it was your ex stabbed him. Then she took her own life.'

Crompton half smiled.

'Good girl. I knew she would. We decided on one each. Sad that she topped herself, though. Ever since Kerry died, she said she had nothing left to live for. But we was both determined to make those arseholes pay. We split up after the funeral but kept in touch over this.'

'Thank you for clearing a few things up, Michael,' Emma said. 'We suspected you and Abbie were acting together. We'll certainly chase up that address in Bristol. I'll get this interview transcribed from my phone, so you can sign a formal statement. The CPS will undoubtedly be considering further charges against you, and I strongly advise you to consult a solicitor.'

Crompton shrugged.

'You should be safe enough here, under guard,' said Jack. 'We'll liaise with the prison service to protect you from Frankie.'

'Yeah, like that worked last time. I'll sign your statement, and the CPS can do what the fuck they like. I'm gone. I know it.'

'I'm sure the prison staff will do their best. Someone will be back tomorrow with the statement,' said Emma. 'I hope you recover soon.'

As Jack opened the door to summon the prison officer, Michael heard a nurse and a doctor emerging from the room next door, discussing a patient. When he heard the name, he froze. *Nathan Jones. The fucker's here. Next door.* He hardly noticed Emma and Jack leaving, preoccupied as he was with the knowledge. He resolved that somehow, whatever it took, he would finish the job he'd started with that stupid plastic gun.

Chapter Sixty-Five

'Settle down, folks,' said Emma, at the start of the briefing. 'We've made a small amount of progress on the armourer. Martin and Amira have worked on correlating ANPR and CCTV sightings of the car with hits from the phone. What did you find, Amira?'

'A link, boss,' replied the IT specialist. 'In over half the pings from the phone, the Range Rover with the cloned plates was in the area. There may have been other instances, not covered by cameras. Most were in the south of Mexton.'

'Do we think there's more than one vehicle involved?' aske Kamal.

'Very possibly,' said Martin. 'I looked at camera locations and there were quite a few calls made near cameras where the Range Rover was absent. Of course, the user could have been on foot or on a bike, but I think another car's more likely. I checked the weather in a few instances, and it was pouring with rain.'

'OK. Thank you both,' said Emma. 'Some confirmation that this is the car involved, anyway. Anything else?'

'I'm working on tracing the Range Rover's movements over the past few weeks. It's a big job but I'm making progress,' replied

Martin. 'Sally told me about the speeding ticket – the driver was doing fifty-two in a forty miles-per-hour zone, also in the south of town, seven days ago. The plate's tagged now, so we should get any new sightings. With a bit of luck, we should be able to narrow down the location of the workshop where the weapons are converted.'

'Good stuff, Martin. Now, does anyone have any further thoughts about our armourer?'

'How about a sting?' suggested Sally. 'One of us poses as a buyer. Then we nick him when he drops off the weapon?'

'Hmm,' said Jack. 'Didn't work so well the last time, did it? I suppose it's worth a try. What do you think, Emma?'

'I'll run it past the DCI. As long as no one's put at risk, he should be OK with it. What I'd like to know is how closely Frankie Garrett is linked to the armourer. Is he just a customer for converted weapons or is the armourer part of his outfit? I'll have a word with the NCA. See if they know of any connection. Now, where are we with the Eastside shootings?'

'Not much further, I'm afraid,' replied Jack. 'We're pretty sure they were killed because they refused to work for Frankie. We've still not found anyone who's prepared to say they saw or heard anything. Par for the course down there, especially as they're all terrified of Frankie.'

'How can he take over in Mexton when he's based in Portsmouth?' asked Kamal.

'He establishes a presence here, gets things up and running and leaves things at home to his most trusted advisers who keep things going from day-to-day. He'll return to Portsmouth when it's all cushti and pop back from time to time to keep the fear going. It's a common business model. For drug dealers, anyway.'

'Have we found out anything more about the Bristol mob?' asked Emma.

'Avon and Somerset have sent us a list of vehicles they believe the gang uses. We're keeping an eye open for them, but there've been no sightings yet. I've had a thought, though. When you were on maternity leave, your stand-in came from Bristol, a DI Chidgey. He worked drugs and it may be worth having an informal chat with him. He might be able to tell us a few things, unofficially, about the Bristol drug scene.'

'Good idea. Give him a ring and see if he's prepared to come to us, or whether he wants us to go over there.'

'Will do,' said Jack. 'I suspect he'd be more than happy to spend an evening in The Cat and Cushion with us.'

'OK. That's it for now,' said Emma, wrapping up the briefing. 'You've all got things to do. Thank you.'

Chapter Sixty-Six

'I'VE HEARD you can get me a shooter.' Martin Rowse spoke tentatively to the man with the burner phone, at five minutes past seven.

'I've no idea what you're talking about. What gives you that idea?'

'A bloke in the pub said to call this number after seven. Said you could help.'

'Which pub?'

'The Fife and Drum.'

'And you're a regular there, are you? The landlord would recognise you?'

'Prob'ly not. I only went there the once. My cousin said it was the place to ask.'

'And what would you want with a shooter, anyway? They're expensive. And dangerous.'

'Some bastard's fucking my missus, and I want to warn him off. He's usually tooled up with something. I want to be safe.'

There was a silence. Sweat coated Martin's hands and he nearly dropped his burner.

'OK. I might be able to arrange a pistol. It'll cost you a grand. You got that much?'

'I can get it in a couple of days.'

'All right. Call this number in three days' time, at seven. I'll arrange a meet. What's your name?'

'Tony. Tony Martin.'

'OK. Tony. Just to let you know, if I see anything iffy about the meet, or if you mention our arrangement to anyone, the deal's off. And then there will be repercussions.'

'Yeah. Sure. Ta.'

The line went dead.

'Well done, Martin,' said Emma, beaming. 'You sounded really convincing. D'you think he bought it?'

'It sounded like it. Actually, I enjoyed that. I won't be going to the meet, I presume?'

'Not a chance. But you can watch from the command vehicle, I'm sure. Right. I'll alert firearms that we'll need a unit in a few days' time. Great stuff!'

Chapter Sixty-Seven

Day 15

MICHAEL CROMPTON COMPLAINED to the hospital staff that he needed some exercise. He assured them that he was feeling better, despite the surgery he'd just undergone, and he persuaded them to provide him with a walking frame with which he could make a slow perambulation along the corridor, accompanied by Prison Officer Markham. He hid the fact that he was still in pain and assured the nurses that it was his own responsibility. He appeared to find walking difficult, often stumbling and taking short rests every few metres. In truth, his strength was better than he expected. The work he had put in at the gym was paying off, but he made sure that no one realised this. Despite the pain, desperation drove him, as he realised that he would only get one opportunity to finish his mission.

Finally, it was time to act. He paused for a rest outside Nathan's room, apparently exhausted. Markham looked irritated, but his eye was caught by an attractive young nurse who smiled as she passed him by. He watched her backside until she turned into a side room. For a brief moment, the corridor was almost empty.

Michael straightened up and kicked Markham hard in the groin, catching him behind the ear with his elbow as the man fell. He threw the walking frame on top of him and staggered into Nathan's room. He scanned it quickly, saw that Nathan was immobile on the bed, with his legs and right arm in casts, and was alone. Nathan looked at him with a complete lack of recognition but, as Michael struggled to pick up a bedside chair, his expression turned to terror. He screamed, but his cry was cut short by the impact of the chair leg on his head. He jerked, silently, and a second blow stilled him completely.

'For Kerry,' yelled Michael. But Nathan was well beyond hearing.

Prison Officer Markham staggered to his feet and vomited. He lurched into Nathan's room, saw Michael stumbling away from Nathan's bloody corpse, and reached into his pocket for the pair of surgical scissors he'd stolen from a trolley earlier. Michael turned as he approached. Markham swung his arm upwards. The blades of the scissors easily penetrated the flimsy hospital robe, slipped between Michael's ribs and sliced into his heart.

As Michael slumped to the floor, dying, Markham wiped the scissors to remove his own fingerprints, placed them in Nathan's dead left hand and called for help. The whole episode had taken less than twelve seconds, and Markham's balls were still throbbing agonisingly. But he was satisfied. The hospital would be blamed for leaving a dangerous implement where a known criminal could get hold of it, he would get through any disciplinary hearing without any serious consequences, and Frankie would pay him well for fulfilling his mission. All in all, a good result.

Chapter Sixty-Eight

THE SMALL, rectangular parcel sat on Emma's desk, exuding a faint acrid smell and making her furious. It wasn't the contents that angered her – she hadn't opened it yet – but the addressee:

Mr Tony Martin
c/o The SIO
CID
Mexton Police Station
Mexton

'What's up, Emma?' asked Jack, standing in the doorway. 'You look seriously pissed off.'

'Aye. The bugger's rumbled us. Look.'

Jack read the address and sniffed.

'What's in it? D'you reckon it's safe to open?'

'Probably. This lot don't go in for bombs, and I had a firearms dog take a sniff at it.'

Taking a pair of scissors from a drawer, Emma carefully removed the brown paper encasing the box and opened the lid. Resting on a layer of bubble wrap was a child's pink water pistol containing an orange-looking fluid. There was also a message. A square of cardboard bearing, in capital letters, the words 'DON'T TAKE THE PISS.'

'The cheeky bastard!' said Jack. 'And I don't need three guesses to work out what that liquid is. Can we get DNA from it?'

'Possibly,' replied Emma. 'There should be a few cells with DNA in them, but I'll bet the the person who donated the sample isn't on the database.'

'So Martin wasn't as convincing as we thought. Perhaps he shouldn't have used the name of that bloke who shot a burglar, as an alias. He'll be disappointed.'

'Not half as bloody disappointed as I am. I can't stand the thought of someone arming up every minor criminal on our patch with lethal firearms. It's getting like bloody America. We've got to stop these buggers, we really have.'

'I agree. And the sting was worth a try. But...'

Jack was interrupted by Kamal appearing in the doorway, clearly distressed.

'Guv! Nathan Jones and Michael Crompton. They're both dead.'

'What? How? Crompton was under guard at the hospital.'

'Seems like he knocked the officer over, got into Jones's room and beat him to death with a chair. Jones managed to stab him with some scissors as he attacked. It's a bloody mess.'

'Oh shit. Crompton was determined to finish the job. And it looks as though it cost him his life. I'll go to the hospital myself. Can you let forensics know? You'd better come along and take witness statements.'

'Yes, guv.'

———

'Good morning, DI Thorpe.'

Dr Durbridge greeted the two detectives as they approached Nathan Jones's sealed-off room.

'Morning, doctor. What brings you here?'

'I'd just given a lecture to some med students and was passing. I thought I'd take an early look at my customers. I'll start the PMs straight away but, given the unusual circumstances, it seemed a good idea to see them *in situ*.'

'Any thoughts?'

'I have a few concerns, I must admit. All I'll say at the moment, is don't jump to conclusions. Things may not be as simple as they seem.'

With those enigmatic remarks, the pathologist left, leaving Kamal and Emma looking perplexed.

'We can't go in there until the CSIs have finished,' said Emma, peering through the small window set in the door. 'We need to talk to the ward manager, any staff in the area, and the prison officer. I'll take him. Can you find out who else was around?'

'Will do. Just basic statements?'

'Yes, for now. I might caution the PO as there could be an issue of negligence. I'll see.'

While Kamal went to talk to nursing staff, Emma found a nervous Roy Markham sitting in a side room, an undrunk cup of coffee on a table beside him. Emma introduced herself and sat on a chair opposite.

'It must have been pretty unpleasant for you, from what I've heard,' she began, after reciting the caution.

Markham shrugged.

'I've seen worse on the wing. It's part of the job.'

'OK. Tell me what happened.'

'Crompton tricked us. Asking for exercise and pretending he was really weak. He claimed he had to use both hands on a walking frame, which is why I didn't handcuff him. I honestly didn't think he was a risk.'

'I see. Go on.'

'He was a lot fitter than he looked. As we passed Jones's room he suddenly attacked me and knocked me over. I was out of it for a few seconds and when I went into the room, I saw Jones with his head bashed in and a pair of scissors in his hand. Crompton was on the floor with blood on his chest. I went over to him and felt for a pulse. I called for help, but by the time anyone got there, he had died.'

'OK. Seems straightforward.' Emma thought for a moment. 'Do you have any spare clothes in your car, Roy?'

'Yes, I do. I was going to change before I went home after my shift. Why?'

'We'll need your uniform for forensics, I'm afraid. If you give me the car keys, I'll get DC Chabra to fetch them.'

'Sure. But you know there'll be blood on the uniform. Crompton's and maybe Jones's as well.'

'I know. It's only routine. We just want to get as full a picture as possible of what happened in the room.'

'Suit yourself.'

Markham handed over his keys. Five minutes later, a CSI arrived, and Emma asked her for an evidence bag.

'If you'd just wait there for a moment, Mr Markham, my colleague will be back shortly. We'll need a signed statement from you at some point, but what you've said is helpful. Crompton blamed Jones for the death of his daughter, which is why he tried to shoot him and has now finished the job. But I wonder why Jones had the scissors.'

Markham shrugged.

'Perhaps he heard that Crompton was in the hospital and feared he'd be attacked. And he was right, wasn't he?'

Emma nodded, stepping out of the room to wait for Kamal.

Chapter Sixty-Nine

'Why did you want his clothes, boss?' asked Kamal, while Markham changed. 'Do you suspect him of something?'

'I'm not sure. His story didn't quite ring true. If Jones stabbed Crompton in the chest with a pair of scissors, why didn't he stagger to the door and call for help? Even if the blades went straight into his heart, he wouldn't have died instantly. No, it doesn't feel right. I'll get the lab to examine the blood on Markham's uniform and I'll certainly be interested in what Dr Durbridge has to say. We'll get a coffee when Markham's changed and wait for the CSI to finish.'

It didn't take long for the CSI to finish photographing the bodies and the footwear marks where Crompton's blood had been walked in.

'I've not done tape lifts or wiped for DNA,' she told Emma. 'There's no point. Too many people have been in here, and I gather you know who was in the room at the time, anyway. I've retrieved the murder weapon.'

She showed Emma the scissors, sealed in a transparent knife tube.

'May I see?'

Emma rotated the tube, examining the scissors from all angles.

'That's not right, either. Can you see?'

The CSI peered at the scissors where Emma indicated.

'The handles. There's not much blood on them. Is that what you mean?'

'Exactly. It looks as though they've been wiped. Can I have detailed photos of the scissors and a report on the distribution of the blood?'

'Sure. I'll tell the lab. Do you want to see the crime scene, now?'

Emma nodded and followed the CSI into the room. She spent several minutes examining the position of the bodies from different angles and, at one point, crouched down beside Nathan's bed.

'Did you spray the floor with Luminol or Bluestar?'

'I did,' replied the CSI. 'I have photos, but most of the blood was close to Mr Crompton's body or had been walked in and transferred between his body and the door. I also did the walls beside and behind Mr Jones's bed. There was some spatter there. There was blood on the chair, notably on the legs and underside.'

'Yes, it looks like Crompton used it to kill Jones. Look, I'm not ready to release the scene at the moment. I may want you to come back and do some more work on the blood. Maybe bring in a spatter expert. Thanks for all you've done so far.'

The CSI smiled, packed up her gear, and left while a hospital porter transported Nathan's body, in a body bag, to the mortuary. Emma posted a uniformed officer outside Nathan's room and followed the porter. Dr Durbridge had agreed to do the post-mortem immediately and she wanted to be there.

'Come on Kamal,' she called. 'You're the exhibits officer.'

'Can't wait,' he muttered, and followed his boss down into the bowels of the hospital.

Chapter Seventy

Emma watched from the viewing gallery as Dr Durbridge stepped away from the post-mortem table, leaving the anatomical pathology technologist to sew up Michael Crompton's cadaver. Once he had changed out of his scrubs and washed, he invited the detectives to join him for coffee in his office.

'I gather we've both got reservations about the prison officer's account,' he began. 'Would you like to go first?'

'OK,' replied Emma. 'My first thought was why didn't Crompton try to get to the door and call for help? He was found on the floor two metres from Jones's bed. I assume that death wouldn't be instantaneous. Am I right?'

'Yes, you are. He could certainly have taken a few steps, judging by the wound he'd suffered, although he was weak because of the surgery and his injuries. Anything else?'

'There was no visible blood on the floor immediately next to the bed, which I would have expected if he'd been stabbed there. There was blood on the walls, I assume from Crompton's attack on Jones, but that part of the floor was clean. I'm thinking of getting a much more detailed analysis of blood distribution, with DNA identification, if the budget will run to it. I also wondered whether Jones's bed was too high up for him to have inflicted Crompton's stab wound, though I didn't have any measurements. Finally, it looked as though the handles of the scissors had been wiped. I'm waiting for a report from the lab on that.'

'That's pretty impressive and ties in with what I've found. The wound to Mr Crompton's chest was most probably caused by the scissors moving inwards with an upward component. The position of marks on his ribs, among other things, indicate this. It's most unlikely they would have been caused by a horizontal blow from the bed. Furthermore, when I examined Mr Jones, and consulted his hospital notes, I found that his left shoulder was severely sprained, presumably from the incident that brought him into hospital. In my opinion, he wouldn't have had the strength to stab Mr Crompton in the heart.'

'So the prison officer was lying. A more credible scenario, then, is that he stabbed Crompton, swinging the scissors upwards into his chest, after he had stepped away from Jones's bed. He then wiped the scissor handles and placed them in Jones's hands, all the while preventing Crompton from reaching the door.'

'Of course, it's up to you to prove it. But it's entirely consistent with my findings and your observations. I will attend to Mr Jones in the morning, but it does look as though death was the result of head trauma. Have a pleasant evening.'

'Thank you very much Doctor. I'll look forward to receiving your reports.'

Chapter Seventy-One

Day 16

THE FIRST THING Emma did the following morning was phone the forensic lab.

'You know that uniform we sent you yesterday,' she began, having identified herself.

'Yes,' replied the lab manager, cautiously. 'It's on our job list for later today. Maybe tomorrow if other jobs run over.'

'Could you possibly take a quick look at it for bloodstains, for me, particularly the front. I'd be really grateful.'

'Hold on. A quick look wouldn't stand up in court. It will take several hours to examine it properly, collect samples for DNA and write a report We don't do slipshod jobs. You should know that.'

'Of course not. Your work is exemplary,' Emma replied, desperate to mollify the manager. 'I'm not asking you to be anything less than thorough for the full examination. It's just that I have a theory, and if you can tell me something about the distribution of blood on the clothing it could confirm or negate my suspicions. All I need is a quick phone call, nothing in writing. I wouldn't ask if it wasn't important. It is a murder inquiry, after all.'

'That's the trouble. Everyone's job's important to them. Never mind anyone else's. And I've got to make the decisions.' He sighed. 'OK. I'll ask someone to take a look at it and give you a ring in an hour or so. It'll only be a preliminary opinion, mind, not for quoting. And don't do this again.'

'Thanks very much. You're a star,' she said, ending the call.

'Awkward bugger,' she muttered and headed for DCI Farlowe's office to brief him. On the way, she called to Mel.

'Can you find out if Roy Markham reported for work at the prison this morning? And tell the troops there'll be a briefing at eleven.'

The lab called just before the briefing was due to start and Emma smiled when she heard what the scientist had to say.

'OK, folks,' she began. 'We're about to arrest a murderer.'

The team looked at her in surprise.

'As most of you know, Michael Crompton killed Nathan Jones in Mexton General Hospital yesterday. It was originally assumed that Jones killed Crompton, by stabbing him with a pair of scissors, before he died. In fact, it was a crude attempt to shift the blame onto Jones.'

Emma outlined her reasoning and the pathologist's opinion.

'So, the scenario related to us by the prison officer, Roy Markham was false,' she continued. 'Apart from his lies, we had no firm evidence that Markham was responsible. But I've just heard from the lab. There was blood on his jumper, particularly the sleeves, which was to be expected, given that he claimed he felt for Crompton's pulse. But there were also two tiny spots on his trousers, consistent with him pulling the scissors out of

Crompton's chest while standing in front of him. He'll have trouble explaining that!'

'Nice one, guv,' called a detective at the back of the room. Several others chuckled.

'Did he turn up to work this morning, Mel?'

'No, boss. He called in sick.'

'Right. We need a team to go round to his home in case he really is ill. Get his car tagged for ANPR and circulate his photo. Alert the airports and ferries in case he tries to leave the country. Check the railway station CCTV. We'll get the bugger before he knows what's hit him!'

Earlier that morning

Roy Markham shaved off his beard, filled a holdall with essentials and picked up his wife's car keys. Easing open the garage door, he went straight to a box labelled rat poison and removed the stash of notes he'd been adding to, ever since Frankie Garrett started employing him. How he would receive the latest payment, he didn't know, but what he had now was enough for him to disappear for a while. If he'd really thought about the situation, he would have realised that he would be caught eventually. He didn't have a carefully crafted alternative identity to adopt, or a secret bolthole to hide in. But surging adrenaline on top of a sleepless night propelled him to flee. He phoned the prison explaining he was unwell following Crompton's assault, and drove slowly out the drive, heading for the nearest airport.

Chapter Seventy-Two

Tina Markham looked with puzzlement at the two uniformed PCs standing on her doorstep.

'Sorry to bother you, Mrs Markham. I'm PC Halligan and this is PC Mahmoud. We'd like a word with your husband.'

'But he's at work. At the prison.'

'I'm afraid he called in sick.'

'Sick? That's the first I've heard of it. I know someone hit him at the hospital, but he was fine yesterday evening.'

'Well it looks like he's disappeared.'

Tina looked confused.

'Why would he disappear? Is he in any trouble?'

A flicker of anxiety crossed her face.

'We'd just like to talk to him. Is that his car?' Halligan asked, pointing to a BMW parked in the road.

'Yes. Just a minute.' She looked over the PC's shoulder. 'The garage door's open and my car's missing. Why would he have taken that?'

'OK, Mrs Markham. Can you give me the registration number, please? We may need to search the premises in due course but, in the meantime, could you take a look to see if there are any signs of him going off somewhere?'

'I suppose so,' she grumbled. 'I wish you'd tell me why you want to speak to him. You'd better come in.'

She showed the two officers into an expensively fitted kitchen and invited them to sit. Ten minutes later she reappeared with a worried expression.

'His passport's missing, and some clothes. Also, a holdall that's usually in a cupboard isn't there. He must have gone somewhere, but he never said anything.' She paused. 'Has something happened to him?'

'Why would you think that, Mrs Markham?' PC Mahmoud asked.

She dropped her eyes and fiddled with a button on her cardigan.

'He's been a bit edgy lately, and he's had a couple of phone calls that seemed to worry him. He wouldn't say who they were from. I assumed it was something to do with work. I know that prison officers are sometimes targeted at home, but he assured me there was nothing wrong.'

'I see. OK, Mrs Markham. I think someone from CID will want to speak to you later. In the meantime, could you stay at home, please, and let us know if Roy contacts you? I'm sure you've nothing to worry about.'

'If you say so,' she replied, unconvinced.

PC Mahmoud called in the registration number of Tina Markham's car as they sat in the patrol car, a dozen metres from the house.

'Let's just wait here a bit,' said Halligan, reaching for a flask. 'Just in case she knows where he is and nips out to meet him. Fancy some tea?'

Half an hour later, with no sign of movement from Tina Markham, the officers returned to base.

Chapter Seventy-Three

'HE'S IN THE WIND, GUV,' said Mel, when PC Mahmoud's report came through to the incident room. 'It looks like he's taken his wife's car, and his passport's missing. We've tagged the car and circulated the number. His wife's no idea why he's done a runner, but we'll need to talk to her again later.'

'Thanks, Mel. Unless he changes cars, we'll have him,' said Emma.

'Why would he kill Crompton, anyway?' asked Kamal.

'There's only two reasons, really. Either he had some massive personal grudge, or he was doing it for someone else. Presumably Frankie Garrett. I'll get authorisation to look at his finances, and his wife's. In the meantime, can you contact the prison governor, Kamal, and find out if there's been a problem between him and Crompton, or any disciplinary issues?'

'Yes, boss.'

'Mel,' continued Emma, 'find out how much his car cost and how much he paid for his house. See if there's any mismatch with his salary. And go and see Mrs Markham and find out whether she has an income of her own, any useful background, you know the drill.'

'Will do.'

Roy Markham resisted the urge to put his foot down. The last thing he needed was to get pulled for speeding. But sticking to the limit was increasingly frustrating as time ticked by. *Surely they'd be looking for me by now? Good job I've got Tina's car, though they'll find out it's missing soon enough. Tina knows nothing, of course. She'll have to find out eventually. But not yet. If I can just get out of the country, I'll work out a plan. Perhaps Frankie can help. I did what he wanted, after all. But maybe I'm disposable. No more use to him if I'm not in the job. Oh shit. Oh fucking shit.* His reverie was interrupted by a lorry blaring its horn as he wandered across the lanes, and he resolved to concentrate on his driving. The future would have to wait.

He pulled into the car park at Southampton airport, nervously scanning the site for police cars. None was evident, and he walked into the building with increasing confidence, inspecting the departure boards for the next flight out of the UK. Palma? Faro? He decided on the latter and approached the booking desk. But he didn't reach it. A man and a woman blocked his path and brandished warrant cards.

'Roy Markham? Hampshire Police. Come with us, please,' said the woman. 'Our colleagues in Mexton want to talk to you.'

Markham all but collapsed on the spot and accompanied them, resignedly, to a waiting unmarked police car. *I could have hit them and run. But what was the point? What was the fucking point?*

'Boss,' said Sally, knocking on Emma's door. 'Markham's on his way back to us. Hantspol picked him up at Southampton airport trying to book a flight. We suspected he was heading that way, from ANPR hits, and they had some plain clothes guys waiting.'

'Good stuff, lass. OK, work up an interview strategy with Mel. Press him on motivation. Let him know we're looking into his finances. If we can prove Garrett hired him that'd be a brilliant result. I'll watch on the monitor.'

'Sure, boss. I'll let the duty brief know. Markham'll be at least an hour getting here, and he'll need to be processed, so I'll set it up for two o'clock.'

'Thanks, Sally. Now go and get some lunch.'

Chapter Seventy-Four

A DEJECTED Roy Markham sat in the interview room, facing Sally and Mel, and listened listlessly to the caution and the introductions. He had declined the services of a solicitor and wanted to get the whole business over with as soon as possible.

'Mr Markham,' began Sally. 'You have been arrested on suspicion of the murder of Michael Crompton. Would you like to tell us anything about that?'

'I stick by my original statement. Nathan Jones must have stabbed him before Crompton beat him to death.'

'Then I must advise you that the opinion of the forensic pathologist is that Nathan Jones was physically incapable of inflicting the fatal wound on Michael Crompton, owing to the injuries he had received to his shoulder.'

Markham shrugged.

'Furthermore, the angle of the wound is inconsistent with Mr Jones's position on the hospital bed,' continued Sally.

'So what? It doesn't prove I killed him.'

'Don't you agree that this evidence doesn't fit with your statement?'

Markham shrugged again.

'For the benefit of the recording, I am showing Mr Markham exhibit MC 31. Please look at this photograph. It shows blood spots on the trousers of your uniform.'

'Sure. I approached Crompton and checked for a pulse. I crouched on the floor beside him. Of course there's blood.'

'That accounts for the blood on your sleeve. But the advice from the forensic scientist is that these bloodstains are more likely to have come from the scissors, as you withdrew them from Mr Crompton's chest while he was standing up. Would you like to say anything about that?'

Markham stared at the ceiling and said nothing for a few moments. He sighed noisily and looked at the detectives.

'OK. If I admit it, what can you do for me? If I go inside my life'll be hell.'

'We'll obviously liaise with the prison authorities to ensure you get as much protection as possible,' said Mel. 'But you know how it works. Your best bet is to co-operate in return for a reduced sentence.'

'All right. Yes, I killed Michael Crompton in Mexton General Hospital, with a pair of scissors I'd stolen from a trolley. I hated him. I will plead guilty in court. That's all I'm saying.'

'Why did you hate him?' asked Mel. 'We spoke to the governor. He said that you got on well with the inmates and had no particular problems with any of them.'

'No comment.'

'We will be looking into your finances in detail, but we note that you have an expensive car and live in a valuable property. They would seem to have cost rather more than a prison officer would normally be able to afford.'

'No comment.'

'Mr Markham. Did you kill Michael Crompton on behalf of someone else? Frankie Garrett, for instance.'

A brief shadow of fear crossed Markham's face.

'No comment. I told you I've nothing more to say. Now can I

go back to my cell, please?'

Mel looked at Sally who nodded.

'OK. Interview terminated at fourteen twenty-seven.'

Once the recording was switched off, Markham stood up and addressed the detectives in a whisper.

'I'm not admitting anything. But if anyone so much as mentions Garrett's name in a police interview, they're dead. Just so you know.'

'Nice work, guys,' said Emma, as Mel and Sally returned to the incident room. 'What did he say to you, just before he was taken to the cells?'

'That anyone who mentioned Garrett was dead.'

'Hmm. I suppose we can't blame him for not admitting Frankie paid him. Pity. But we'll still look at his finances and see if there's any link between them. For now, I'll contact the CPS for authority to charge him with murder and get him remanded. We can put one crime, at least, to bed.'

Istvan, terrified and naked, sat tied to a chair, while Frankie Garrett put on a set of overalls. He stared at the array of gleaming steel implements, laid out on a table, and nearly vomited.

'What you want? Why am I here? I haven't done anything.'

'Relax,' said Frankie, testing the sharpness of a scalpel on a piece of cloth. 'We're gonna have a discussion and, one way or another, you will tell me what part you played in the theft of my property.'

'What theft? I know nothing about theft. Or property.'

'But you put something in my employee's coffee. Something that made him piss. Now what do you think I should do to someone who made my employee piss so my property could be stolen?'

He waved the shiny scalpel in the direction of Istvan's groin.

'No!' screamed Istvan, pulling futilely at the cable ties that secured him.

'It was ecstasy. His friend said to make him happy. Said he was grumpy bastard. Needed cheering up. A joke. Nothing about stealing.'

Istvan sobbed, tears leaving tracks down his bare chest.

'And who was this friend?'

'I don't know. He said Billy sent him. He gave me the powder and fifty pounds. Said to put it in coffee before man leaves. That's all. I swear. On my mother's life.'

'Who's Billy?'

'Kid from Eastside. He gets me cocaine sometimes.'

'Do we know a Billy?' asked Garrett, addressing Max and receiving a nod in return.

'What did this friend look like?'

'Ordinary man. Older than me but not old. Not fat. Not thin. Tall. Tattoos. Short hair. Ordinary.'

'Did he say his name?'

'No. Just he was friend of Billy.'

'Is there anything else you'd like to tell me?'

The scalpel gleamed in a shaft of sunlight that forced its way through a grimy roof light.

'No. No. I swear. I'm sorry about your property. I didn't know. Honest.'

'All right. I can accept that. But I can't accept the consequences of what you did. Since you've told me what you know. I suppose you've earned a certain amount of mercy.'

Hope rose in Istvan's eyes, extinguished when Frankie moved behind him, shoved his head forward and swept the blade across the side of his neck, stepping neatly out of the way of the arterial spray that decorated the wall with scarlet.

Chapter Seventy-Five

Day 17

BILLY WALSH WAS RUNNING. Running for his life.

As soon as he heard Frankie's boys were looking for him, he fled, taking nothing from the squat in Darwin House apart from a handful of cash and a burner. He needed somewhere to go and realised he could be spotted by Frankie's men in the town centre. They would probably be watching the bus and railway stations, too. He decided to stay on the Eastside and use its warren of walkways and passages to hide. He had mates he could stay with, moving around every few days, although somebody might grass him up. He couldn't call the police and ask for protection. They wouldn't be interested, and Frankie would get to him anyway.

He was fucked. He knew it. He had to keep moving.

Billy was slinking along a walkway on the second floor of Rutherford House when he saw the black SUV pull up in front of the building. Four men got out and moved towards the flats. Frankie's men. He ran along the walkway, dodging rubbish dumped outside front doors. He tripped over a kid's broken scooter, knocking an array of empty lager bottles off the parapet. The fusillade of breaking glass caught the men's attention, and Billy saw them looking up and recognising him. Sick to his stomach he continued running, crashing into the stairwell and rushing up the vertical urinal that passed for the staircase.

He reached the tenth floor. If he could get to Flat 1066 before Frankie's men saw him, he might be able to hide. It was empty and the lock was broken. He reckoned he was well ahead of them, but when he got halfway along the walkway the door at the far end opened. Max the Plank stepped out and walked slowly towards him. Billy turned around. Jerome, holding a baseball bat, was approaching from the other staircase, his grin visible from many metres away.

Billy had never been a quick thinker, and the illicit pharmaceuticals he had assaulted his brain with over the years had slowed his mental processes down still further. But it took him only a few milliseconds to realise that the fate Frankie had in mind for him would be unimaginably horrific. So he pulled out his phone, switched it to video and recorded a couple of seconds of his would-be captors approaching. He shoved the phone into his pocket and, with a cry of 'Fuck you', threw himself over the parapet. The brief flapping of his hoodie in the wind was the last sound he heard.

———

'Frankie's not going to be happy about this,' said Jerome, looking scared. 'He said to bring him in alive and able to talk. He wanted a discussion with him.'

Max shrugged.

'The little shit must have known what was in store for him. He'd got more guts than I'd expected. Better get his phone.'

'We can't. People are filming and putting stuff on the internet.

We can't be seen here. It would have been fucked by the fall, anyway. And I don't reckon we should mention it to Frankie. Agreed?'

'Too fucking right,' said Max. 'We'd better give Frankie the bad news. And hope to fuck he's in a good mood when we get there.'

Jack Vaughan stepped away from the mess that had once been Billy Walsh and snapped into his phone.

'Get a tent up here. Fast. These vultures are filming everything.'

He turned to the crowd pressing up against the police tape.

'Who is he?'

Nobody answered.

'Come on. What's his name?'

No answer.

'For fuck's sake,' he raged. 'He was one of yours. Why won't you give me a fucking name? Do you think I'm gonna arrest him?'

'Billy. Billy Walsh. Darwin House,' a small voice said from inside the crowd, attracting glares from several residents.

The speaker hurried away before Jack could identify her. Despite the efforts of the four PCs accompanying Jack, the crowd refused to disperse until a forensic tent had been erected and inner and outer cordons had been established. It didn't take long for CSIs to photograph the scene and map the spatter of blood and other tissue around the remains. Dr Durbridge took a brief look at the body and suggested that Billy could have fallen from five floors or upwards, should the police wish to examine where he took flight. CSIs were duly dispatched, and two of the uniforms were sent to canvass Darwin House to obtain Billy's address.

By nightfall, all that remained was a few metres of police tape, tied to lampposts, that someone had tried to set on fire, and a half-cleaned stain where Billy had fallen that attracted the attentions of a couple of stray cats and a mangy fox.

Chapter Seventy-Six

HE LOVED THE PORSCHE. Not that it was his, of course, but in twelve years of twocking this was his favourite ride. He wished he'd seen the look on the bloke's face when he came back from paying for petrol and saw his motor scorching away. Stupid twat. Deserved to have it nicked for leaving it with the engine running, at the pump. Perhaps the white powder spilled on the passenger seat had something to do with it.

He knew he didn't have long. A car that distinctive would soon be picked up by police cameras and patrol cars. So he would make the most of his brief affair with a 911 and burn some rubber. Then he would dump it and nick something slower to get him back home.

The motorway would be ideal for a good burn, though he might not make it before the cops caught up with him. But there was the southern bypass that should be reasonably quiet at that time of night. So he headed south, keeping carefully to the speed limit until he reached the dual carriageway. Then he put his foot down.

Eighty... eighty-five... ninety...ninety-five... this was driving! This was living! He watched the needle creeping up to a hundred, exulting in the speed and power of the driving machine. Then he hit the small white van that pulled slowly onto the bypass in front of him.

'Christ, this is a messy one,' said Sergeant Pete Winwood. 'That Porsche must have been doing a ton at least.'

PC Chris Capaldi shrugged.

'The driver didn't have a chance and neither did the bloke in the van. They'll need DNA to confirm identities. There's nothing much recognisable of either of them.'

Winwood surveyed the two-hundred metres of closed-off dual carriageway, littered with bits of motor vehicles and body parts, blood glistening in the powerful lights set up by the roads policing unit.

'The investigators will be along in a minute,' he said, 'so we'd better leave things as they are. Worth taking a look at what's left of the van, though, in case it was carrying anything hazardous.'

The two officers approached the remains of the back of the van, carefully avoiding treading on any debris, human or mechanical.

'Hang on,' said Capaldi. 'What's that over there?'

A cardboard box, thrown out of the vehicle by the impact and smashed open when it hit the ground bore the label 'Konyo Bluetooth Headphones'. But visible through the ripped packaging were the gleaming butts of several small black pistols.

'Oh shit,' said Winwood. 'We'll need an AFO to sort this lot out. I'll call it in. So who the hell was driving the van?'

Chapter Seventy-Seven

Day 18

'GOOD MORNING, EVERYONE,' said Emma, at the start of the briefing. 'We've had a development in the armourer investigation. There was a serious RTC on the southern bypass last night. A van was hit by a speeding Porsche. The traffic guys found a box of starting pistols that the van was carrying. They were Retays, Turkish-made, and their importation and possession is illegal as they can be easily converted to fire live ammunition. My guess is that they were destined for our armourer. We've sent the serial numbers to NABIS and the NCA to see if there are any links with weapons already found.'

'So who was driving?' asked Kamal.

'We don't know who either of the drivers were,' replied Emma. 'They were too badly smashed up. Even dental records will be difficult. Fingerprints and DNA samples were taken, and we may get some IDs that way. Anyway, I've asked for any papers or documentation to be sent to the lab. They might find an address. The techies will also interrogate the van's computer to see where it's been, assuming that one was fitted and not smashed to smithereens. The Porsche was stolen, by the way. It looks like some bloody stupid twocker has given us a lead. I'd much rather we'd got it without two fatalities, though.'

The assembled detectives nodded or murmured their agreement.

'I've completed my examination of Billy Walsh's remains,' said Dr Durbridge, when Emma answered her phone. 'Unsurprisingly, he died from multiple injuries, incompatible with life, following a fall from height. A quick drug screen showed evidence of alcohol, cannabis and cocaine use. Do you want me to send off hair samples for a full screen?'

'I don't think so,' Emma replied. 'Not at this stage. The budget's too tight. But we'll retain the samples in case it becomes necessary in the future. I suppose you can't tell whether he jumped or was pushed?'

'Not a chance, I'm afraid. Too much damage. About the only thing I can tell you is that he wasn't shot or beheaded.'

Emma wasn't sure whether the pathologist was completely serious. Although friendly and affable, he wasn't known for cracking jokes about his work.

'Is there anything else?' she asked.

'He had a phone in his pocket. It was smashed up, but I manged to extract the bits. I gave it to the exhibits officer.'

'Thank you. There may be some contacts on it that could interest the drug squad. I'll ask Amira to take a look at it. Thanks again, doctor. I'll look forward to your report.'

She turned to the rest of the team and relayed the information from Dr Durbridge.

'Did the CSIs find anything where he fell from?'

'Nothing to suggest a struggle,' reported Jack. 'There was a possible scuff mark on the parapet from a trainer, halfway along the tenth-floor walkway, but that's not definite.'

'So do we think he jumped?'

'Either that or two people picked him up bodily and threw him clear. But if that was the case, he would have landed further from the building.'

'What about his home?'

'He was living in a squat in Darwin House. We found some weed and blow, enough to argue intent to supply, but no cash.'

'Perhaps he left in a hurry,' suggested Kamal. 'Maybe someone was after him.'

'Could be, I suppose,' said Emma. 'There's plenty of tension in that place. It didn't take me long to learn that when I first moved down here. But why would he kill himself?'

'Might that depend on who he was running from?' suggested Mel. 'If it was Garrett, for instance. Given his reputation, Billy might have preferred a relatively painless death to hours of torture. Just a thought.'

'Not a bad one,' said Jack. 'But he's not going to tell us. And neither is anyone else on that damn estate. No one saw or heard anything. And if they had, they sure as hell wouldn't tell us. Sometimes I wonder why we bother with that place.'

There were one or two murmurs of agreement.

'Anyway,' said Emma, 'we do need to keep asking. Promise people their names won't be mentioned if they help us. Tap our informants. Somebody must have seen something. That's it for now. Thank you, everyone.'

Mel and Kamal sifted through the flowers decorating the place where Billy had died, in case there was a clue to the reason for his demise. Some were bought, some had been uprooted from gardens elsewhere in Mexton and one bunch, clearly stolen from the cemetery, bore the message: 'Aunty Shirley, mother, grandma and soulmate to Fred. Passed five years ago today.'

'Charming,' said Kamal. 'They couldn't even be arsed to take the label off.'

Mel shrugged.

'I don't think Aunty Shirley will mind but her niece or nephew would be well pissed off if they found out what happened to their flowers.'

'Oi!' A small voice came from a space under an external stairway. 'Don't turn around. Pretend you're talking to each other. I know something.'

'Who are you?' asked Mel, pretending to address Kamal.

'Don't be stupid. No name, just a friend of Billy's.'

'What do you know?' Kamal asked, miming a deep conversation with Mel.

'Billy worked for Frankie. He used to do a bit around here, him and his sister. Frankie took over but his sister wouldn't play ball. Frankie's men fucked her up and she's in the nuthouse. He said he would get Frankie. I don't know what he did, but Frankie's men were on the estate, looking for him, just before he died. That's all I know.'

'Thank you. That's helpful. Can I just ask...?'

'No, you can't. That's all. And watch out. Frankie goes after coppers who meddle, too.'

Mel looked meaningfully at Kamal and shivered.

Chapter Seventy-Eight

'I've GOT something interesting from Billy's phone,' said Amira. 'I've printed off a list of his contacts and his recent call history, but it's this short video that caught my eye.'

She turned her laptop towards Emma and pressed play.

'It's only a few seconds long but look at these two blokes. They don't look very friendly.'

Emma studied the footage and asked Amira to replay it twice.

'I agree. They're not there to wish him happy birthday. I'll ask the team if anyone recognises them. Thanks for this, Amira. Can you send it to me?'

'Sure thing.'

'That's two of Frankie Garrett's heavies,' said Jack, when Emma projected the video onto the screen. 'Jerome Feynman and Max Pauli. Max is the thin one. I was looking at some stuff Portsmouth Serious Crime sent over. They're both pretty nasty, suspected of a shedload of assaults and at least three murders.'

'Lovely. We'd better pull them in and have a chat. They may have killed him. At the very least, they're witnesses. Any idea where we can find them?'

'Frankie recently bought a so-called gentleman's club, The Golden Thong. I reckon they hang out there.'

'OK. Take a couple of DCs and ask them politely to come in. Have a patrol car nearby in case anything kicks off, not that it should. Garrett's obviously trying to put up a front as an honest, albeit sleazy, businessman and he won't want any trouble at the club. There's a treat for you!' Emma smiled.

Jack grimaced.

'Not my thing. I'll take Kamal and Mel and let you know how we get on.'

No one was dancing at The Golden Thong at that time of day, and the detectives had to bang hard on a closed door to gain admittance. The unkempt individual who let them in curled his lip when he saw their warrant cards and asked them what they wanted.

'We'd like a chat with Max Pauli and Jerome Feynman, please.'

'Would you, now? What if they don't want to talk to you?'

'I couldn't care less whether they want to or not,' said Jack. 'Call them please.'

The man shrugged and pulled out a phone.

'I'll ask the boss,' he muttered, and retreated behind the bar to dial.

While they waited, the three officers looked around the club. A couple of shiny poles were fixed, somewhat wonkily, to a raised stage at the back of the club. Spotlights and a glitterball were visible but not in operation. Cheap tables and worn chairs were ranged around the room and the whole place smelled of stale beer, musty carpets and furtive ejaculations.

'Not exactly high end, is it?' commented Mel.

'Nope. I'll cross it off my list for a date night venue,' chuckled Kamal.

Before Jack could comment, a well-groomed, middle-aged man, in a three-piece suit, entered through a doorway beside the stage.

'Good afternoon, officers,' he said. 'I'm Francis Garrett and this is my establishment. May I see your warrant cards?'

Garrett made a show of examining their credentials, then produced a thin smile.

'And how may I help the police?'

'We need to talk to two of your employees, sir,' said Jack. 'Jerome Feynman and Maxwell Pauli.'

'And may I ask with what it is in connection?'

'I'm not prepared to give you the details, but we believe they may have witnessed a suspicious death.'

'Not that young man who fell from the flats? So tragic. But I believe both of them were here with me at the time. I'm not sure that they will be able to help you.'

'I think that's for us to decide, Mr Garrett. We have some video evidence to suggest that they were nearby. So, rather than waste any more time, perhaps you would send them out?'

'As you wish,' replied Garrett, clearly annoyed.

Ten minutes later, the two suspects appeared and stared impassively at the detectives.

'We'd like you to come to the police station for voluntary interviews, under caution,' said Jack. 'Are you prepared to co-operate?'

'If we must,' said Pauli. 'Mr Garrett said we should help you to clear up any misunderstandings.'

That's very obliging of him,' said Mel, dripping sarcasm. 'I'm sure we won't keep you from your duties for long.'

'If you think you need legal representation,' said Jack, 'now would be the time to arrange it.'

Neither answered, and both said nothing as they were conveyed to the police station in separate cars.

Chapter Seventy-Nine

THE FORMALITIES COMPLETED, Jack and Mel began questioning Pauli while Sally and Kamal interviewed Feynman in an adjacent room. Both suspects had declined the services of a solicitor.

'Mr Pauli,' began Jack. 'What can you tell us about the death of Billy Walsh?'

'It was tragic really. The poor kid just upped and jumped over the wall. We tried to save him, but we couldn't get to him in time. He was obviously disturbed.'

'Take a look at this video.' Jack showed Pauli the footage in a laptop. 'This was taken on his phone just before he died. It shows you and Jerome Feynman approaching him in what could be construed as a threatening manner. What can you say about that?'

'We weren't threatening him. Why would we be?'

'Can you say why Mr Feynman is holding a baseball bat?'

'He found it on the stairs and didn't want anyone to fall over it. It was a hazard,' Max replied, impassively.

'Did you and Jerome Feynman throw him over the parapet?'

'No.'

'Why were you there?' asked Mel.

'Mr Garrett wanted to offer him a job. He needed someone to help at the club, and we went there to give him the good news.'

'Then why would he film you before jumping? Or being murdered? Could it be to show us who killed him or made him jump?'

'I don't know. As I said, he was disturbed.'

'Mr Garrett has a reputation for brutality,' said Jack. 'Were you there to take Billy to Mr Garrett for some kind of punishment? In which case he might have preferred a quick death.'

'No. And, for your information, Mr Garrett has never been convicted of any violence. He is an honest businessman who wanted to help, in a small way, with the dreadful unemployment on the Eastside Estate.'

'Then why didn't you come forward and tell us what happened?'

'Mr Garrett said that we shouldn't get involved, as we couldn't help. He said people might jump to the wrong conclusions.'

'Didn't you think that, as the last people to see him alive, you had important information for us?'

'As I said, people might get the wrong idea. Like you have.'

'So it's only the fact that we found the video that made you talk to us.'

'Mr Garrett said we should set the record straight. Oh, and he's offered to pay for the kid's funeral.'

'Very generous, I'm sure,' said Mel.

'Is there anything else you'd like to say to us?' asked Jack.

'I have no further comment to make, and I'd like to leave.'

'Just wait a little longer while I confer with my colleague if you will. Interview suspended at sixteen thirty-two.'

Jack and Mel stepped out of the room.

'What do you think of that load of old bollocks?' said Mel.

'Triple-distilled, cask-conditioned bullshit,' replied Jack, just as Kamal and Sally joined them to compare notes.

It rapidly became obvious that the two suspects had provided almost identical answers to the questions, and that they had, presumably under Garrett's direction, prepared their responses.

'We've nothing to hold them on,' said Jack. 'We'd better let the bastards go. I'm convinced they had something to do with Billy's death, but we've no bloody proof. Get rid of them and we'll report back to Emma.'

Jack walked disgustedly back to the incident room.

'They're lying shits, and we had to release them,' said Jack to a furious Emma. 'They claimed to be there to offer Billy a job, but that's bollocks. We know he already worked for Frankie as a dealer. And they claimed that Feynman picked up the baseball bat to prevent someone from tripping over it on the stairs.'

Emma snorted and Jack continued.

'We've no idea what they wanted, but Billy was clearly scared.'

'D'you think it's something to do with the missing laptop?' she asked.

Jack shrugged.

'I can't see Billy stealing it. He's too low down the food chain. But I suppose he could have helped Crompton.'

'Maybe. See if Amira can find any phone calls between them. I suppose it's academic now, with both of them dead, but it could help to complete the picture. By the way, I've heard from Avon and Somerset drug squad. They know of the address where Crompton was supposed to have delivered the laptop. It's one of several Jasper Burnham uses. They don't think he keeps his supplies there, but they watch it from time to time. His home is a much flashier place on the outskirts of Bristol.'

'You know, we could be looking at a serious conflict between the gangs,' said Jack. 'Nicking Garrett's laptop could be the start.

With the information on that, Burnham would know where to strike, who to target. I really don't fancy Mexton becoming a battlefield.'

'Neither does the DCI. I think we definitely need a face-to-face with Avon and Somerset, perhaps with the NCA as well. Frankly, Jack, I'm bloody scared.'

Chapter Eighty

When Maurice Fermey left GCHQ under a cloud of unproven allegations, he needed an income. He knew a lot about electronic security, and a few things about national espionage operations, but he had no intention of betraying his country and selling his information to the Russians. He was only a small fish, anyway. Hardly a Philby or a Blunt. But his skills were valuable and, to use the business jargon, he needed to monetise them.

He could hardly put a card in a newsagent's window saying: 'Hacker for hire. Reasonable rates.' And he knew his former colleagues kept an eye on the dark web for rogue operators. But, he reasoned, there must be people out there who would pay him to fiddle, illicitly, with computers on their behalf. Finding them was the problem, though. He didn't move in criminal circles, and neither did his family. Any untoward associations would have raised a red flag when he was vetted, and he would never have been allowed anywhere near the Cheltenham Doughnut.

Aged twenty-six, he moved back to Bristol, where he had taken his degree, and spent most of his time smoking weed and listening to heavy metal. Four months later, when his money ran out, he managed to get a job in a computer repair shop and that was when opportunity knocked for him. Two men came into the shop one afternoon, one of whom complained that he'd forgotten the password for his laptop, an expensive model, which he placed on the counter. Could Maurice unlock it for him? It was clear, from the men's demeanour, that they weren't simply frustrated gamers, denied access to a session of electronic annihilation. What's more, Maurice recognised one of them as an occasional source of supply for his weed. Criminals, no doubt. And just the sort of people he wanted to meet.

'I'm sorry, sir,' he said. 'It's company policy not to unlock computers without proof of ownership. If you can bring in the necessary documentation, I'll be happy to help.'

Unseen by the shop's CCTV system, he wrote his mobile number on a piece of paper, added the words 'I can do it' and slipped it into the laptop before returning it to the disappointed customers. Then he waited.

At seven o'clock that evening he received a phone call inviting him to meet someone called Dave, in a Bedminster pub, The Flagon, to discuss a business transaction. He was to come alone and mention the meeting to no one. Excitedly, he stubbed out a half-smoked spliff, to ensure his head was clear, and prepared to, in his words, step into the shadows.

***

The pub was crowded when Maurice arrived, but he spotted the men from the shop in a secluded alcove. He bought himself a pint and approached. They motioned him to sit down and, without speaking, dropped a copy of the *Bristol Post* on the table in front of him. The front page featured the recovery of a body from Bristol's floating harbour and an account of the subsequent murder investigation. He began to feel uneasy and wondered whether he had been terminally stupid in contacting these men.

'He talked too much to the wrong people,' said one of the men, who Maurice presumed was Dave. 'Understand?'

'Y... yes,' gulped Maurice. 'Understood.'

'Right, then,' the man smiled. 'Can you get into this laptop?'

'No problem at all. It could take me an hour or so, and I'll need my gear, but I can do it. How much will you pay me?'

'A grand, if you can do it quickly. And we may have a few other jobs for you later on. Alright?'

'Yes, sure. How do you want to do this?'

'We'll bring the machine to you, and we'll watch you while you do it. What it contains doesn't concern you, so don't go snooping. Where do you live?'

Maurice gave him his address.

'Ten o'clock tonight. Enjoy your pint.'

The two men stood up and left the pub without looking back. Maurice drank his beer quickly wondering, once again, if he was being an idiot. But it was too late to back out. *Who knows, this could be the start of a successful illicit career* he thought, with a frisson of excitement, enhanced somewhat by the beer.

Chapter Eighty-One

'DAVE' and his companion rang Maurice's doorbell on the dot of ten. He showed them into his lounge, which was full of computer gear stacked on two long tables, and gingerly took hold of the proffered laptop. His first move was to copy the hard drive onto a machine of his own, giving him the opportunity to run password-cracking software without the risk of being permanently locked out of the laptop. While it was working, he attempted to engage them in small talk, failing miserably. They declined coffee, tea and beer and stood, stony-faced, while he watched the computer monitor. He tried to explain what he was doing, but quickly realised they had little understanding.

After about an hour, his computer pinged, and he reached for a notepad. He wrote down a series of letters and symbols and passed it to Dave.

'Here's the password. It should work. Do you know the username?'

They looked blankly at him.

'Never mind.'

Maurice returned to his keyboard and, a few seconds later, wrote down a name on another sheet.

'Do you want to try it?'

Dave nodded and typed the details Maurice had supplied into Frankie's laptop. There was a pause. Maurice started sweating. Then the screen flared into life displaying dozens of folders, meticulously arranged in rows and columns. Before Maurice could read any of the names, Dave turned the machine away from him and closed the lid.

'Nice job, mate,' he said, reaching slowly into his jacket.

Maurice froze. *Shit! He's gonna shoot me,* he thought. Instead of the expected pistol, Dave's hand held a scruffy envelope full of banknotes.

'Here you are. A grand, as agreed. And we may need you again.'

He picked up the laptop and the pieces of paper. As he left the flat, he turned back to Maurice and spoke.

'Remember. Tell no one. You don't want a swim in the floating harbour. It aint healthy.'

When the men had gone, Maurice let out a long sigh and helped himself to a can of beer. Had they realised he'd copied the contents of the laptop? He didn't think so. He hadn't told them that, and he could have been doing his tax return for all they seemed to understand. Should he take a look at the files they didn't want him to see? Dare he? He would think about it tomorrow. Now, he would roll himself a spliff, pour another beer and destroy a few hundred alien spaceships.

'So the kid did it,' said Jasper Burnham, gleefully. 'Frankie's empire is mine for the taking. That's gert lush.'

He paused and looked more serious.

'Can he be trusted? Did he know what was on the laptop?'

'We didn't let him see. And, yeah, he won't talk. I showed him that thing in the paper about the bloke found shot in the floating harbour. Let him know it could be him if he wasn't careful.'

'But that weren't to do with us.'

'Yeah, but he didn't know that.'

Jasper laughed.

'Nice one. Perhaps we'll use him again. Now, oi've got some plannin' to do.'

Chapter Eighty-Two

Day 19

'THE MAIN FOCUS OF THIS BRIEFING,' began DCI Farlowe, 'is Prison Officer Roy Markham. 'I'm sorry to have to tell you that he hanged himself in his cell last night. By the time he was found, it was too late to resuscitate him.'

'Was he Epsteined, guv? Helped on his way?' asked Mel.

'The post-mortem should determine whether he was physically restrained and hanged, but the prison doctor didn't notice any bruising, although that may not come out until later. The governor did say he was looking extremely scared while on remand and he kept being bumped into by some serious villains who whispered things to him.'

'So here's a theory,' said Sally. 'Garrett got word to him that if he didn't kill himself, Frankie would arrange for it to be done much more painfully. Or maybe he threatened to murder his wife. Or both.'

Several detectives nodded their heads in agreement.

'It's certainly possible,' admitted Farlowe, 'but impossible to prove. Though we do know that Garrett is good at getting others to kill people for him. Now, to other things…'

Before the DCI could move on, his mobile rang. He glanced at the screen and answered it.

'Good morning, Dr Durbridge. We were just discussing your latest customer, Roy Markham. Surely you haven't finished him yet?'

'No, I haven't started, but I've found something extremely interesting, and I think you'll want to hear about it immediately.'

'Hold on. I'll put you on speaker. Go ahead, please.'

'I took a quick look when I came in this morning,' continued the pathologist, and I noticed something odd about his throat. I fished around with some forceps and found a ball of paper, halfway down his oesophagus. It's possible he swallowed it immediately before he died. The interesting thing is the writing on it. It's in pencil and still legible. Shall I read it out?'

'Please do.'

'Frankie made me top myself or he would torture Tina to death. I killed Crompton for him for five grand. I couldn't refuse. I worked for him for years. I'm so sorry.'

'Shit,' muttered Mel. 'You were right, Sally.'

'Thank you very much, doctor,' said the DCI, ignoring Mel. 'That does bear out a theory one of my DCs has. We'll get an exhibits officer and observer to you for the PM. Much obliged to you. Goodbye.'

He ended the call and addressed the team.

'So, we've got some more work to do. We need to look at any incidents in prisons where Markham worked, and I think there are several, where Garrett could have been an instigator. Talk to the governors. The shanking of Crompton is an obvious example. That note will need to go to forensics to match the writing to Markham's. We need to confirm its evidential value. It would be useful to know who Markham was bumping into and where. He was supposed to be on Rule 43, with minimal contact, so he shouldn't have been at risk. Can you sort the jobs out, please, Jack?'

'Of course.'

'Now get yourselves some drinks. DI Thorpe wants you back here for a briefing in fifteen minutes. Thank you.'

———

'So where are we with the crashed van?' asked Emma, as the team sipped their coffees.

'We've had some success with electronics,' said Jack. 'The satnav wasn't fixed and was thrown clear in the collision. SOCOs found it on the grass verge, miraculously undamaged. Anyway, the last destination on the satnav was a deserted area beside the canal. My guess is it was heading there for a handover and never made it.'

'Hmm. I guess the armourer was too canny to have the consignment arrive at his factory,' mused Emma. 'Anything else?'

'The previous entry was for a transport café just outside Dover. I presume that's where the driver picked up the weapons. I've passed the location to Kent police in case they want to keep an eye on the place. The van's registered to an address in Reading. Thames Valley are sending someone to try and identify the driver and inform next of kin.'

'Thanks, Jack. The driver's DNA wasn't on the database but the twocker's was. He's been nicking cars since he was fourteen. Given his record, something like this was bound to happen sooner or later. Stupid bugger. His parents were devastated when Sally and Mel delivered the death message.' She paused, briefly. 'Now, ANPR.'

'We've picked him up on his way from Dover and through Mexton to the bypass,' replied Kamal, 'but it doesn't tell us anything we didn't already know. Amira did get something from the phone the SOCOs found. There were several calls to and from a burner we didn't already know about. Hopefully, that was the armourer, and we may be able to track it to somewhere significant. She's working on it at the moment.'

'Good. Let's hope she finds something. I'm getting increasingly frustrated with this bugger. We've found weapons, evidence that converted starting pistols have been used, and we know how Nathan got a pistol. But we've still no bloody idea where this menace lives or has his workshop. And all the NCA has been able to tell us is that there's a lot of these guns about. It's not bloody good enough.'

She sighed.

'OK. Keep working on CCTV and ANPR for the van, in case it's been here before, and dark Range Rovers with possibly cloned plates. Unless we get an informant, which is about as likely as Yorkshire changing its name to Lancashire, technical stuff is all we've got. So let's get to it. Thanks, everyone.'

Chapter Eighty-Three

AT TWO O'CLOCK, Amira stood at the front of the incident room and projected a map onto the screen.

'I've traced the movements of the burner phone the van driver called,' she began. 'It's not used much but, when it is, it's always on the south side of town. There's a couple of points of interest. A call was received from the van driver's phone at the time the van was recorded on ANPR at the transport café outside Dover. That could be the driver confirming that he'd picked up the weapons or, perhaps, seeking directions. Another, brief, connection was made as the van approached Mexton, possibly a confirmation of the arrival time at the meeting.'

'So there's little doubt that the call was to the armourer,' said Mel.

Amira nodded.

'The other interesting point is that several calls on the armourer's burner phone were made and received from this area.'

She circled a number of buildings on the screen.

'This could be either the target's home or workshop. Given that these buildings are mainly light industrial, I'd go for the latter.'

'He could have been phoning from a car,' objected Sally.

'Yes, but, if so, it was often parked in the same place. Probably outside his premises.'

'That's great work, Amira,' said DCI Farlowe. 'I think we need to take a look at those buildings, but discreetly. I don't want to provoke him to flee – or cause a firearms incident. Let's start by finding out who owns and rents the buildings. Get on to Open-Reach and see if they provide broadband. Contact other utilities as well.'

'How about surveillance, guv?' asked Kamal.

'We'll think about getting authorisation when we've identified a likely building. But it's worth checking any CCTV in the area for dark Range Rovers, as long as we can do so without arousing suspicion. There must be some on industrial premises. Right. You've got plenty to do. We'll meet up again at five o'clock. Thank you everyone.'

'What do you reckon,' said Mel to Sally as they got themselves coffee. 'A quick drive around? Take a look at the possible targets?'

'Not sure Mr Farlowe would approve. Anyway, we've got a load of trawling to do. Could do a drive-by after work, though.'

'You're on. Right, Martin's doing the utilities and I've got the Land Registry to look at. What's your job?'

'Local authority records. Oh the joy of being a detective!'

They both laughed and returned to their desks.

'A stroke of luck, guv,' said Kamal when the team reconvened. 'A motor parts supplier in the area was broken into a couple of days ago. Uniforms attended but there were no detectives or CSIs available at the time. We've got an excuse to ask for CCTV.'

'That's good, Kamal, thank you. We'll send teams out tomorrow. Most businesses will be closing up by now, I expect. So, what have the rest of you found?'

'There are four businesses in the area where the phone pinged, boss,' said Sally. 'A plastic windows company, a carpentry and joinery business, a light engineering firm and a small van hire outfit. They've all been there for some time, although the chippie and the engineers are the most recent. The firm that was broken into, Mexton Car Electronics, is just outside the zone, but CCTV from these four could be useful for investigating the offence.'

'How about ownership, Mel?'

'The whole site is owned by Mexton Commercial Estates, who lease out the individual units. I spoke to someone in their office, and they promised to get back to me with tenant details tomorrow morning, once they've cleared it with their lawyers.'

'The utilities were much the same,' said Martin. 'They didn't refuse but stalled pending legal advice.'

'We can get production orders, if necessary,' said the DCI. 'It'll just take longer. OK. Obviously, we need to talk to all four firms, and the electronics company, but a light engineering company would be best placed to convert firearms. They would have the tools and basic skills. But I'm jumping the gun.'

No one noticed the unintentional pun.

'That's all for now. Do the CCTV trawl tomorrow morning, and we'll reconvene around midday. I think, just to be on the safe side, I'll ask for an ARU to be put on standby in the area. Thank you.'

At six o'clock the commercial estate was all but deserted. The four premises of interest were closed, and only a light above a drop-box for returned van keys gave an indication that anything actually happened there. But eyes were watching Mel and Sally as they drove slowly past the buildings, and camera images were being recorded.

'Bit of a waste of time, this,' grumbled Sally. 'Helen's cooking tonight and I don't want to be late for dinner.'

'OK, OK,' replied Mel. 'It was just a long shot. Let's get you home. Tom's waiting for me, too.'

The unmarked car picked up speed and quickly joined the main road into town. But back on the estate one of the tenants was worried. *They looked like cops. Did they see anything? Have they spotted the Range Rover under the tarp? Do I need to take measures?* He thought for half an hour, then decided to make preparations for a quick exit. Just in case. And if he had to shoot a nosey copper or two to get clear, then so be it.

Chapter Eighty-Four

Day 20

ARRIVING at the industrial estate at eight am, the detectives split into two teams. Mel and Sally were to ask for CCTV footage at the carpenter's and the window firm, while Jack and Kamal took the engineering outfit and the van hire company.

The manager of Mexton Polywindows was co-operative, saying that they were welcome to view CCTV recordings when 'the lad who looks after that stuff' came in, later that morning.

Approaching the carpenter's unit, they were greeted by a tall, affable man, in overalls, who scrutinised their warrant cards, shook their hands and invited them in.

'Happy to help, officers,' he said, when they explained the purpose of their visit. 'Come through to the office. The gear's in there.'

He pulled open a door and they stepped into a windowless room, Mel in the lead. The door shut and Sally felt a tremendous shove in her back that sent her staggering into Mel, knocking both women off balance. They turned to find the man aiming a large, black pistol at them.

Oh fuck, thought Sally, *not again*, her knees and bladder threatening to give way.

'I knew who you were before you arrived this morning,' said the man. 'I saw you snooping last night. You had coppers written all over you, the way you were driving and casing the place. My question is, "How much do you know?" and you'd better give me an answer before I start shooting bits off you.'

'I wouldn't do that, if I were you,' replied Mel. 'There are other officers outside and armed police a few hundred yards away. We know who you are and what you do. That's all we're telling you,' she said, defiantly.

The gunman thought for a moment.

'OK. I suppose it doesn't make much difference. I made preparations and I'm leaving for a country with no extradition arrangements. I can't take you with me, so I'll have to keep you here. Now put your phones on that table and step back against the wall.'

Covering them with the pistol, he reached for the mobiles, dropped them on the concrete floor and stamped them to smithereens.

'Right. Come out here.'

He guided the two detectives into an open workshop area, keeping his distance so they were unable to reach either him or the weapon with foot or fist.

'You,' he indicated Mel. 'Tie her to that chair.'

He tossed a handful of cable ties at her.

Mel complied, leaving the ties as loose as she could get away with.

'Now tie your ankles and right wrist to the other one.'

Mel said nothing but did as she was told. As the armourer leaned in to secure her left wrist, she tried to head butt him, but he jerked away, smacked her on the side of the head with the pistol and finished the job. He then removed the lid from a plastic vessel of a greyish powder, poured the contents into an empty metal paint tin and tipped in a couple of handfuls of small, metallic objects. He replaced the lid on the tin and taped it down.

'I load my own cartridges,' he said, conversationally. 'And this tin is full of powder and primers. I'm giving it to you to look after.'

He placed it on Mel's lap then tied a nylon thread to a brick, which he balanced carefully on the back of Mel's chair, unspooling the line as he walked backwards to a bench. He clamped a cocked pistol in a vice on the bench, lined it up with the tin and looped the tightened thread around the butt, tying it to the trigger. He tied another thread to the trigger and walked towards the door.

'In case you're wondering what I'm doing,' he said, 'I'm arranging things so that if you move your chair the brick will drop, and the pistol will fire. And if your colleagues open the door after I've left, it will also fire. The bullet might kill one of you but the explosion when it hits that improvised bomb certainly will. Both of you. And there's no point shouting for help. No one will hear you outside, above all the traffic at this time of the day. Good morning, ladies. And goodbye.'

With that, he pulled the door shut, tied the thread to the door handle and sauntered out of the building's side entrance.

Chapter Eighty-Five

'How the fuck are we gonna get out of this alive?' Sally whispered to Mel, terrified, as they heard the car drive off. 'Any moment now, Jack or Kamal's gonna come through that door and blow us up.'

'I don't know. Can you get free at all? I tried to leave the ties as loose as possible.'

'Not loose enough. The chairs are tied together so, if I struggle, the brick will drop and sodding kill us.'

The two detectives looked around the workshop in the dim light from a pair of dirt-encrusted skylights immediately above them. The pistol on the workbench was far out of reach, on the dark side of the room, so any prospect of kicking it and shifting its aim was out of the question. Even if they could reach the bench with their feet, it was much too heavy to move. The nylon line gleamed, like the strand of a web that would unleash a deadly spider once disturbed. Neither of them could think of a way out, and cramp was setting in. And the arrival of one of their colleagues became ever more imminent.

'If we could just stop the brick from falling,' said Sally, 'I could maybe get my hand free. Then we could perhaps rock the chairs out of the way.'

'Yeah, right. I'll just fucking hypnotise, it, shall I? Can you think of a better way? Hang on, though. I've got an idea.'

Mel twisted as far as she could to her right, bringing her mouth tantalisingly close to the line where it passed over her shoulder, just out of reach. She stretched, an agonising pain developing in her neck. Still not far enough. With a redoubled effort, she managed to get her tongue under the line. As the line slipped away from her, they could just hear Kamal calling their names. He would come in at any moment. She tried again and managed to hook the line, drawing it into her mouth and manipulating it between her molars. She clamped her jaws tight.

'Et duh om irst' she said.

Sally looked puzzled and then nodded her understanding. She pulled and strained at the cable tie on her right wrist, trying to make her hand as small as possible. Slowly it scraped against the plastic until, with a heave and a shout from Sally, it came through, leaving a strip of bloody skin behind.

Sally knocked the bomb from Mel's lap. It clattered onto the floor and the women tensed, half expecting a detonation. The brick shifted slightly, and Mel froze. Sally tried to reach behind Mel to grab it, but it was too far away. Kamal's calls grew louder.

'OK,' Sally said, 'on my count of three. Rock the chairs and don't drop the fucking brick.' She smiled encouragingly.

When Sally got to three, Mel clamped down on the line as if her life depended on it. Which it did. They rocked the chairs forward, attempting to twist them out of the path of a bullet. The line slackened slightly. They'd almost managed it when the brick dropped down behind the chair.

The force nearly pulled two of Mel's teeth out and she screamed silently. Pain shot up the side of her neck. But she hung on. *I can't keep this up much longer,* she thought, as blood and saliva made the line slippery. *I've got to get the brick stable. Kamal will open the door any moment.*

She leant forward as far as she could, her head still facing sideways, terrified that she would slip and drop the brick. She felt it sliding up the back of the chair as she pulled, trying desperately not to take up the slack on the line attached to the pistol. Then the brick stuck.

She wept, silently. Tried again. And again. Finally, she felt the brick clear the back of the chair and drop behind her shoulders. She leaned back, pinning it in place and checked the tension in the line. Their movements had shifted the chairs enough to slacken off the line sufficiently for Mel to unclench her teeth and let it go. She spat blood, swore and called to Sally, her voice distorted by the pain in her jaw.

'Come on. Shift these things we're still in the line of fire.'

They rocked again and, just when they thought they were clear, the main door to the building started to open and the line tightened on the trigger.

Five minutes earlier

'What's happened to Mel and Sally?' asked Kamal, as they left the van hire depot. 'They're taking their time.'

'Must have found something useful' replied Jack. 'We'll join them when we've had a look at the engineers. I think they went to the carpenter's.'

Their speculations were interrupted by the roar of a car engine. A black Range Rover shot out of a side alley and drove straight at them. They threw themselves clear, avoiding the hurtling vehicle by millimetres. Jack managed to catch the last digits of the number plate before he thumped onto the ground. He ran to his car, grabbed an Airwave set and called it in.

'Suspect heading out of Mexton Industrial Estate in black Range Rover, index ending in kilo x-ray foxtrot. In pursuit. Suspect probably armed. Request backup.'

He shouted to Kamal to stay put, jumped into his car and accelerated after the suspect, reporting his location and direction continually.

The Range Rover flew past the parked armed response vehicle that took up the chase.

'He's moving south,' shouted Jack. 'Possibly heading for the bypass. Alert traffic patrols.'

Chapter Eighty-Six

THE CRASH of the gunshot half deafened them. A bullet whistled past Mel's head, hit the wall behind and ricocheted into Sally's back, lodging in a shoulder blade. Sally groaned and slumped in the chair. Mel called out, fearful that the weapon, a semi-automatic, could fire a second time if the line was released and pulled again.

'Wait. Don't move the bloody door,' she yelled. 'There's a thread tied to it attached to a gun. Use the side entrance. Sally's been shot. Hurry.'

Four seconds later the side door crashed open, and Kamal rushed in, looking stunned at the tableau in front of him. He ran to Sally first, checked that she was conscious, and cut the remaining cable ties with a knife picked up from the bench.

'My back. It fucking hurts. I think I'm bleeding.'

Kamal lowered her to the ground on her side, eased off her jacket and made a makeshift pad, from the sleeve of her shirt, which he pressed against the wound.

'Ambulance, please,' he shouted into his phone. 'Police officer shot. Urgent.'

While he was giving the address, he stepped away from Sally

for a few seconds to cut Mel's ties. Rubbing her wrists, she lifted the brick and placed it carefully on the bench, then crouched down beside her friend.

'You'll be alright, Sal,' she said, tenderly. 'We're bloody invincible, us two.'

Sally, still in shock, tried to answer but all she could manage was a groan and a tear trickling from her eye.

As they heard an ambulance and a police car draw up outside, Mel suddenly remembered.

'Quick, Kamal. Cut the line between the door handle and the pistol. Try not to fire it again. My ears won't stand it. Oh, and call for an AFO to make it safe. And the bomb squad for that thing over there.' She indicated the armourer's bomb. 'We'll also need forensics, a PolSA, weapons specialists – in fact, invite everyone. Let's have a fucking party.'

She started to laugh, maniacally, until a paramedic appeared and she regained her composure.

Sally was stretchered into the ambulance and blue-lighted to hospital, while a paramedic from a rapid response car dressed the lesions on Mel's wrists.

'Are you hurt anywhere else?' she asked.

'I might need a dentist,' Mel replied, 'assuming I can find one. Apart from that, I'm fine. Nothing that a hot bath and a large glass of wine won't fix. But I suppose I'd better get back to the station and write up a statement. Thanks a lot. Where's Jack, by the way?' she asked Kamal, as the paramedic left.

'He followed the black Range Rover that shot out of the side alley. No idea where he's got to.'

'Well, I hope he's got armed support. That bastard is not averse to killing coppers. Do you realise what he did here?'

Kamal shook his head and his jaw dropped progressively lower as Mel explained about the booby trap.

'What a total shit. It's not likely to go off, is it?' he asked, indicating the bomb, nervously.

'Not unless you stick it on the fire, crush it or fire a shot into it,' Mel reassured him. 'I read up quite a lot about bombs after that do in the shopping centre.'

'Yes. I heard you'd defused one. Respect! I'm not sure I'd have the nerve.'

'I didn't have much choice. But I can't pretend I wasn't shitting myself. Metaphorically,' she added when she saw his expression. 'Come on. Let's string up some police tape, ask the uniforms to guard it, get back to the nick, and grab a load of coffee. We're both going to need new phones and the bean counters are definitely not going to like that, especially on top of the wrecked car.'

Chapter Eighty-Seven

With the police obviously in pursuit, the armourer made no attempt to keep to speed limits or avoid attention. By the time he reached the bypass the Range Rover had shot through seven red lights, scraped the side of a supermarket delivery van, knocked two cyclists off their bikes and terrified a learner driver who decided, as result, that driving wasn't for him. It was only the blue lights and sirens on the chasing ARV, alerting drivers ahead, that prevented more serious collisions.

Patrols had managed to close off most of the slip roads feeding the bypass, so traffic was light. The Range Rover sped onto a three-mile section with no exits, reaching a hundred miles per hour. Untrained in high-speed pursuit, Jack dropped behind, leaving the ARV and a traffic car, which had joined them, to continue the chase.

As the convoy came round a bend, blue lights were visible up ahead. A row of police cars was blocking the carriageway. The armourer made no attempt to stop. The car ran over a stinger, laid across the road a hundred metres from the obstruction, which lacerated its tyres. Out of control, the vehicle swerved and rocked, the wheels screaming and grinding on the tarmac, until it came to rest on a grass verge. The traffic car pulled back, leaving the firearms officers to deal with the situation, as the armourer leapt out of the car, took cover behind an open door and aimed a pistol at the police.

For a moment, all was silent apart from the thrumming engine of the ARV. Then came the driver's command from a megaphone.

'Armed police. Throw down your weapon and walk towards the car with your hands on your head. Repeat, throw down your weapon and walk towards the car.'

PC Adeyomo just made out a muttered 'fuck off' when the first round from the armourer's pistol punched a hole in the ARV's door, narrowly missing his leg and burying itself in the seat. A second round skated across the windscreen, cracking the laminated glass, before hitting a tree on the opposite side of the road. Addy and the driver scrambled out of the vehicle and crouched behind it.

Shit! I've no option, thought Addy, preparing his carbine to fire.

'Last warning,' shouted the driver, to be greeted by another shot.

Addy took aim and fired twice, two rounds penetrating the Range Rover door and striking the armourer in the chest. The pistol clattered onto the edge of the tarmac, and the armourer slumped to the ground. By the time Addy reached him, his weapon still trained on the suspect and his finger close to the trigger, he was dead.

Chapter Eighty-Eight

Mel and Kamal were met with smiles when they entered the incident room, although the underlying mood was sombre.

'How's Sally?' was Mel's first question.

'She's had surgery,' replied Emma. 'Helen says she's comfortably numb at the moment and not really talking. The bullet lost a lot of energy when it ricocheted, but it still chipped the back of her shoulder blade and did a lot of muscle damage. She won't be doing much with that shoulder for quite a while. Apparently,' and Emma smiled grimly, 'just as the pre-med was beginning to take effect she told the doctor to tell us to drop her from the darts team.'

Several officers chuckled and Mel smiled.

'Where's the bastard behind this?' asked Kamal.

'Ah,' replied Emma. 'There's been a firearms incident on the southern bypass.'

'Is Jack alright?' interrupted Mel. 'Kamal said he was following the suspect.'

'Jack's fine. But the suspect was shot dead close to a roadblock. The stupid bugger fired at police. No one else was hurt.

Now tell us what happened to you. All we know is that there was some sort of trap involving a firearm and Sally was hit by a ricochet.'

Mel provided a concise, and relatively drama-free, account of her and Sally's ordeal, to be greeted with a round of applause as she finished.

'How are the guys getting on at the workshop?' she asked.

'Forensics will be ages yet,' replied Emma. 'The bomb squad took away the device for a controlled explosion somewhere. They said it was safe to fingerprint first, so we've got photos of some latents. There's a lot of firearms paraphernalia and metalworking tools that the lab will be examining, when they can remove them. AFOs made any actual weapons safe, and they've been seized. A good result – which would have been perfect if Sally hadn't been injured and the suspect hadn't been killed.'

'Do we know the suspect's name?' asked Kamal.

'Yes,' replied Emma. 'Thomas Garton. He's from Essex originally. I had a brief word with the local CID. He was discharged from the Army ten years ago, following allegations about smuggled weapons on returning from a tour abroad. Nothing was proven and no action was taken, although the Army decided it could do without him. He was a member of a shooting club in Chelmsford and held a firearms certificate for a couple of .22 rifles, and a shotgun certificate, until the local force declined to renew them. He's never been arrested but he was a known associate of some seriously dodgy people. That's all we know at the moment, but I'll be talking to Essex again, and also the NCA, tomorrow. So, that's one headache dealt with, apart from weeks of paperwork, of course. All we need to do now is deal with Frankie Garrett and his Bristol rivals.'

'Piece of cake!' called someone.

Emma smiled.

'That's all for now. There's a session in The Cat and Cushion with DI Chidgey tonight. All invited. Thanks, everyone.'

The team dispersed in search of coffee, several of them pressing Mel for more details of the morning's events – which she politely declined to provide.

Chapter Eighty-Nine

VICTORIA ADEYOMO RETURNED from the shops to find her husband slumped on the sofa, his head in his hands.

'What's the matter, love?' she said, putting her arm around his shoulder.

'It's finally happened. I've taken a life. And I didn't realise it would be like this.'

'Can you tell me about it?'

'Only in general terms. A suspect was shooting at us, and I had to return fire. Preservation of life. He died at once. I can't stop reliving those moments and I don't think I ever will. I mean, they try to prepare us for this, psychologically, in the training. But real life isn't like an exercise.'

'You poor love. I suppose I should feel sympathetic for the gunman, but if he was shooting at you, he deserved everything he got.'

She lifted up his face and kissed him.

'No one's going to blame you. You had to do it. I always wondered whether firearms was for you. You're such a decent man. So what happens now?'

'I'm suspended from duty while there's an inquiry. It's normal procedure. Nothing to worry about. It could take a few weeks, maybe months, before I'm back at work.'

'Oh that's awful, Sam. What are you going to do with yourself?'

He shrugged.

'I don't know. Paint the living room. Spend time at the gym. Visit my parents. There's counselling on offer and I think I'll take advantage of it. You know, I don't think I can do this again. I'm thinking of handing in my ticket and going back to CID. If they'll have me.'

She looked at him, a serious expression on her face.

'That might not be a bad idea, Sam.'

'Why?'

He looked concerned.

'I worry about you every time you go on shift. Will it be the last time I see you alive? I didn't want to interfere with your career, but I really don't want you shot in the line of duty. And if tomorrow's scan is OK, it matters all the more.'

'OK. That settles it. No more firearms. I'll call the Chief Inspector tomorrow.'

Victoria hugged him, tears in her eyes.

'Thank you, love. Thank you. Come on. I'll make us a cup of tea.'

Chapter Ninety

'Oh, yes. I remember Jasper Burnham,' said ex-DI Chidgey, supping his pint of Thatchers appreciatively, in The Cat and Cushion. 'Nasty little sod. Grew up in Hartcliffe and started thieving when he was about ten. Got himself banned from the local shops by the time he was twelve and began a career of underage drinking and ABH. Round about seventeen, he seemed to sort himself out. He wasn't coming to our attention so much, apart from the odd driving offence.'

'Nice chap,' said Emma, cradling a pint of Theakstons. 'Go on.'

'Some of my more naïve colleagues thought he'd gone more or less straight. Found the love of a good woman or some such bollocks. I didn't believe that, and I was proved right. He did some sort of college course – computers, I think – but all the time he was making plans. His education wasn't great, but he wasn't stupid. He had a lot of cunning, too. So by the time he was twenty-five he was controlling much of the drug trade on two estates in South Bristol. He'd done his research, recruited a posse of low-level dealers and persuaded the middlemen to give him a bulk discount. Before long, he was dealing direct with the major suppliers.'

'What was he dealing?' asked Mel.

'Cannabis and party drugs, mostly. He figured that, if he laid off the harder stuff, we'd leave him alone.'

'And did you?'

'Of course not. But he was bloody difficult to investigate. Most of his runners were underage and no one would talk about him to us. A few well-publicised woundings, attributed to him, ensured that people held their tongues. In truth, the drug squad was stretched dealing with heroin on the estates and cocaine in the clubs. They were the priorities. We would have gone after Jasper more forcefully if we'd had the resources, but we didn't. There was also a rumour that he had a couple of coppers on his payroll, but no one was caught. That's about all I can tell you, but I can give you the name of someone in Bristol Drug Squad who might be able to tell you more.'

'That's really helpful, Geoff,' said Emma. 'So what've you been up to in your retirement?'

'Keeping busy. The garden and so on. I'm thinking of writing my memoirs. There seems to be a thing for true crime these days. Perhaps I'll get a series on Netflix,' he joked. 'What's been going on in Mexton since I left, anyway?'

'Oh, not much,' replied Jack. 'A murdering MP kept us busy. You may have heard that Jenny Pike was killed.'

Chidgey nodded.

'We had that to deal with, and now we've got various scrotes killing each other, potential gang warfare, and, a now-deceased, underworld armourer flooding the place with converted starting pistols. Pretty much par for the course. Another pint?'

Chidgey smiled.

'I'm staying over, so I don't mind if I do.'

Chapter Ninety-One

'RIGHT, LADS,' said Jasper Burnham, addressing a motley crew of minor thugs in a disused farm building just outside Bristol. 'Tonight, we're gonna pay a visit to the Eastside and tweak Frankie Garrett's tail. Thanks to his laptop, we know who to look for and where they'll be. Here's your targets and where they operate.'

He handed round pieces of paper.

'Grab their stuff and cash. Take their phones so they can't call Frankie. Hurt them if you need to, but don't kill them. We don't want the cops looking for us. OK?'

Murmurs of assent greeted his instructions.

'We'll take two vans, cloned plates and road legal. We don't want to get pulled for defective lights. And keep to the speed limit. Oi'll follow in my car. One other thing. There's two blokes in Frankie's crew oi want to meet. One's tall and thin and they call him Max the Plank. The other's built like a brick shithouse and he's known as Speedy. If you find out where either of they's to, there's a bonus in it for you. OK? Good. We leave at nine o'clock.'

The small convoy reached Mexton at eleven and Jasper's crew dispersed, in pairs, to the given locations. They struck simultaneously, leaving seven of Frankie's street-level dealers injured, robbed of drugs and money, and terrified at Frankie's likely reaction. Just before midnight Jasper's phone buzzed.

'Boss? It's Ryan. That big bloke you wanted. I've seen him. Looks like he's trying to find someone.'

'Where is he?'

'There's a playground near the entrance to the estate. He's searching it. He's not been there long. I'm standing under a stairway, watching him.'

'Right. I'll pick you up. Then we'll get the bastard. Flash your phone torch when you see me.'

Five minutes later, Jasper picked up Ryan and told him to drive. He sat in the back, cradling a sawn-off shotgun in his gloved hands. It took two minutes to locate Speedy, who was walking away from the playground towards the main road. Ryan stopped the car alongside him and Jasper got out, the weapon hidden behind him.

'Speedy?' he called.

The man turned, his toothless glare just visible in the feeble streetlight.

'Who the fuck d'you think you are? Only my mates call me that and you aint my fucking mate.'

Jasper swung the shotgun towards him.

'Get in the car but, first, put these on.'

There was a jingle of metal and a gleam as Jasper threw a pair of handcuffs at Speedy. He fumbled for them and then hit the ground. As he bent to pick them up, Jasper stepped back out of range of any attack.

'Don't even fucking think of it,' he snarled, pulling the hammers back. 'Now get in the front. My shooter will be two inches from your head, so don't try jumping out or grabbing the wheel. Just do as you're fucking told.'

Speedy eased his bulk into the passenger seat, his head almost touching the roof of the car.

'You're that arsehole from Bristol,' he said. 'When Frankie gets you, you'll wish he'd killed you at the meet.'

Jasper laughed.

'Drive, Ryan. Find a nice quiet spot where oi can explain why we've taken this shit mountain. And you,' he tapped Speedy's head lightly with the shotgun, 'shut the fuck up.'

Fifteen minutes later, Ryan pulled the car into a picnic area on the edge of Mexton woods.

'Out,' commanded Jasper, 'and stand in the light from the headlights where we can see you.'

Speedy complied, radiating loathing and spitting out expletives, as well as making dire predictions about their fates when Frankie caught up with them.

'Why do you think oi've got you?' began Jasper.

'Fuck off.'

'Oi'll tell you. Does the name Shania Walsh mean anything to you?'

'What's this, a fucking police interview?'

'She was a street dealer. Frankie wanted her to work for him, but she wouldn't. So you and your mate raped her.'

'So what? She wasn't your mum. Street trash. Anyway, it was Frankie's business.'

'Now oi'm a tolerant man,' said Jasper, his contempt obvious. 'Oi don't mind murderers. In fact, a couple of my mates are murderers. But oi can't stand fucking raping scum like you.'

With that, he fired the first barrel of the shotgun into Speedy's groin at point blank range. Speedy howled and fell to his knees, clutching his crotch from which blood erupted in crimson spurts. He had a few seconds to lament the loss of his genitals before Jasper fired the second barrel into his head, killing him instantly.

'That'll teach the fuckerr,' said Jasper, his Bristol accent becoming more pronounced. He wiped the blood spatter from his hands and face, then dropped the weapon into a plastic bag before placing it in the boot of the car. His outer clothes went into a bin bag, he put on a beanie and climbed into a set of overalls before getting into the driver's seat.

'What about the body, boss?' asked Ryan.

'Leave it. Let the other rats eat him. It's more than he deserves.'

Unable to sleep, despite a large dose of brandy, Mel paced the living room. She'd had another argument with Tom who'd tried to persuade her to move to a different branch of the force where she was less likely to get shot or blown up. She had explained that she loved her job, despite the risks, and nothing satisfied her more than helping to bring a serious villain to justice. She pointed out, perhaps a little spitefully, that Tom's desk job hadn't prevented him from losing a hand. She had apologised but he was obviously hurt.

After checking on the parrots for the third time, and dismissing the idea of another drink, she lay on the sofa under a blanket, downloaded a *Guardian* cryptic crossword and wrestled with the clues until she finally fell asleep.

Chapter Ninety-Two

Day 21

FRANKIE RAGED. Normally mild in language, though vicious in action, he let fly a torrent of expletives that resounded around his office and made Max reel.

'You know what this is? It's fucking war. That fucking Bristol cider-monkey's invaded my fucking turf and fucked off back west with several grand's worth of fucking product. Seven of my dealers attacked, five of them in fucking hospital. And where the fuck's Speedy?'

'Don't know. I've not seen him since last night. D'you think he had anything to do with it, boss?' asked Max.

'No. He's loyal. We go way back. Anyway, he knows what I'd fucking do to him if he crossed me. Burnham has got the fucking laptop, though. That's how he knew who to target and where to find them.'

'Should I bring the dealers to you? Teach them a lesson?'

'No,' said Frankie, pragmatically. 'It was two against one. They had no chance. Anyway, I need them back out there, working. They need to make up the loss. And fucking quickly.'

'So what are we gonna do? Go down to Bristol and sort Jasper out?'

Calmer, now, Frankie shook his head.

'No. I don't know the city or how Burnham operates. There are other firms there I don't want to upset by mistake. Right now, I need you to find out as much as you can about Jasper fucking Burnham. Where he lives, where his premises are, where he drinks, who his relatives are and the name of his fucking dog. Everything. Then I'll get the bastard. Do it quick. I'm not having people think the arsehole can put one over me.'

'On it, boss.'

As Max turned to leave, the barman called up the stairs.

'There's two coppers here, boss. They say they need to talk to you.'

'What the fuck do they want?'

'Didn't say. Only that it's important.'

'OK. I'll be down.'

He straightened his tie, smoothed his suit jacket and joined his visitors in the empty club.

———

'Good morning, Mr Garrett,' said Mel. 'I'm afraid I have some bad news for you. One of your employees, Robert Newton, was found shot dead this morning, on the outskirts of Mexton.'

'Speedy? No.' Garrett's complexion darkened, and his knuckles whitened as he gripped the back of a chair.

'Do you have any leads?' he choked out.

'I'm afraid not, sir,' replied Kamal. 'We were hoping you might be able to help us. Do you know of anyone who might have wanted to kill him?'

'Certainly not. He was a big chap but a gentle soul. Never hurt anyone.'

'With respect, sir, that's not what his criminal record shows.

Numerous convictions for violent offences and several prison terms.'

'All misunderstandings, I assure you. He could be a little exuberant but, because he was so large, people always assumed he was the violent one. Completely unfair. Do you know when he was killed?'

'Sometime last night,' replied Mel. 'We can't say exactly when. Did you see him at all yesterday evening?'

'Yes. He was working here. He left the club about eleven, saying he had a headache and was going home. I didn't hear from him after that.'

'So you've no idea of his movements?'

'Sorry, no. I will ask my employees if they know anything, of course. I'll let you know.'

'Do you know anything about his next of kin? We'd like to contact them.'

'He had a brother, I believe. I'll text you his number if I can find it. Is there anything else, officers?'

'One more thing,' said Kamal. 'Several low-level drug dealers on the Eastside ended up in hospital last night. I wonder whether you can tell us anything about that?'

'Nothing whatsoever. As you can see,' he gestured around the sleazy club, 'I'm in the entertainment business. I don't allow drugs on my premises, and I prohibit my employees from using them.'

'Thank you, Mr Garrett,' said Mel, hiding her disbelief. 'I'm sure we'll be in touch again. Good morning.'

As soon as the detectives had left Frankie Garrett picked up a chair. He threw it across the bar, smashing several bottles of knocked-off spirits, two dozen glasses and a large mirror. Without a word he stalked back upstairs, slammed his office door and was heard to sob.

Half an hour later, a composed but pale Frankie called Max and Jerome into his office.

'Somebody killed Speedy last night. The police don't know who, but it must have been Burnham, or his boys. This has gone way beyond treading on my turf. He's got to go. But before that, he has to suffer. Jerome, tap that bent copper. Tell him to find out what the Bristol lot know about Burnham's operations, without tipping them off. Burnham may have his own people in the force. Get him to search the police computer. Find a few addresses. Then pick someone up. I'll interview them personally and then I'll decide what to do. Get on with it.'

The others simply nodded and left the office.

Chapter Ninety-Three

'Is this the start of gang warfare?' asked Mel, as DCI Farlowe began the briefing.

'I'm afraid it looks like it,' he replied. 'No one's saying much, but it seems a group of men with Bristol accents attacked some of Frankie Garrett's dealers last night, beating and robbing them. It was a co-ordinated exercise, all attacks taking place at the same time. Furthermore, one of Garrett's lieutenants, Robert Newton, known as Speedy, was killed. Shot twice at close range with a shotgun, once in the groin and once in the head.'

'That doesn't sound like a simple execution, does it, guv?' said Kamal. 'That wound in the groin means something. The woman who spoke to us at the flats said a couple of Frankie's men, quote, fucked up, Billy's sister. Perhaps the victim raped the girl and this was revenge.'

'Good point,' said Farlowe. 'But, assuming this was all part of the attacks by the Bristol crew, why would Jasper Burnham care about what happened to a woman on the Eastside?'

No one answered.

'Right. Do ANPR checks on the vehicles Bristol Drug Squad told us Burnham and his gang use. Find out if they were in

Mexton at the time of the offences. Look for CCTV as well. See if you can pick up any images of Newton.'

'Garrett said he left the club at eleven, heading for home, but that's not necessarily true,' said Mel. 'I suppose it's a start.'

'OK. We'll need to interview Garrett formally at some point, though I doubt he'll tell us anything. Make it clear to him that we won't tolerate warfare on the streets of Mexton. I'll liaise with Bristol Major Crimes to let them know what's happened and to expect reprisals. I'd like to have Frankie watched. We've got grounds for surveillance but getting the resources will be difficult. I'll have a word with the Super. That will do for now. Plenty to do. Thank you, everybody.'

Jerome's phone pinged as a WhatsApp message arrived. Two names, two mugshots and the words: 'The Flagon. Bedminster. Most Fridays.' He reported the information to Frankie, phoned Max, and at eight o'clock in the evening, Max and Jerome headed west in a dark van with cloned plates. Both carried pistols, and a holdall in the back of the van contained a length of rope, cable ties and a baseball bat. Frankie's warning to 'not screw things up' resonated in their heads as they headed off in search of their prey. Whatever happened, someone would be hurt tonight.

Jasper Burnham was crowing.

'Wish oi'd seen that bugger's face when he found out what we done,' he chortled, downing his second pint of cider. 'Seven in one night and his fat friend done, too. Frankie must be fucking screaming.'

'So what d'you reckon he'll do, Jas?' asked Darren Ridgeway, Jasper's second in command.

'Don't give a stuff. If he comes down here, we'll do 'im. None of that safe conduct bollocks.'

'He must realise you've got the laptop.'

Jasper shrugged.

'There's not much he can do about it, is there? And we're gonna use it again. Next time we'll go after his suppliers as well as his dealers. Convince them we'll be running Mexton and will pay a bit more for product. Cut Frankie fucking Garrett out completely. It's all on the laptop, the idiot. Oi mean, what kind of twat puts all his business on a computer? Does he think he's selling fucking sweeties?'

Darren laughed.

'He is pissed off though. He's got a rep and there's no knowing what he'll do.'

'Yeah. We'd better alert the lads. Tell them to be careful. But we've got the advantage. We knows everything about his operations. He knows fuck all about us. So oi reckons we're pretty safe. Go and get me a bit of blow, Darren, oi'm celebrating.'

Ricky Mason walked unsteadily out of The Flagon, unaware of the dark van parked a few dozen metres from the pub. Jasper had given everyone a few extra quid to celebrate, and he'd chosen to spend it in his local rather than with the rest of the gang. He'd had his eye on the barmaid for a while, and he thought flashing the cash might impress her. It didn't.

The van followed him, at a distance, as he approached the bridge carrying the railway line by Bedminster station. It stopped and two men got out, following him under the bridge. A train rumbled overhead so he didn't hear them approach until they were right behind him.

'Ricky? Ricky Mason?' one of the men called out.

'Er. Yeah,' he replied, suddenly feeling apprehensive.

The viciously swung baseball bat caught him on the side of his face, knocking him to the ground and crushing bone. Above the excruciating pain, he felt himself being dragged along the ground, lifted into the van, and tied up with his hands bound behind him. The next two hours were sheer hell for Ricky Mason, made worse by the fact that he had absolutely no idea who had taken him or where he was going. Which was probably just as well.

Chapter Ninety-Four

'WE'VE GOT one of them, boss,' said Max when Frankie answered his phone. 'Ricky Mason.'

'Good. What state is he in?'

'Reasonable. Jerome broke his jaw but he's conscious. And shitting himself.'

'I can work with that jaw. A hammer and a pair of pliers should do it. Then there's the blowtorch. OK. Take him to the warehouse for a discussion. How long will you be?'

'Two hours, max.'

'Keep to the limit. Don't get pulled.'

'Sure, boss,' said Max, wondering for the nth time exactly what sort of psychopath he was working for.

It took less than ten minutes of Frankie's attentions for Ricky to tell him everything he knew. Frankie would have liked more, but Ricky was pretty low down the food chain and only knew about some of Burnham's operations. Satisfied that he'd got everything he could, Frankie slid a thin-bladed knife through the spinal cord in Ricky's neck and instructed Max and Jerome to get rid of the body.'

'Take it back to Bristol and leave it somewhere public. Send a message. Then torch the van. I've arrangements to make, and we'll strike tomorrow.'

<hr>

Day 22

At four in the morning the centre of Bristol was quiet, although a few clubbers, too intoxicated to take much notice of the van, were making their way home. Jerome and Max had been driving around for half an hour, looking for somewhere suitable to dump Ricky's body. CCTV cameras proliferated, ruling out a number of promising locations. Recordings wouldn't be a problem – the van would be a burnt-out wreck before anybody viewed them – but a monitored live feed could lead to an arrest.

As they drove past the hospital complex down towards the city centre, Max spotted a flight of steps.

'That'll do,' he called.

Jerome stopped the van, and it took them nine seconds to get Ricky's body out and throw it down the steps. Ten minutes later they were on the M32, heading home.

Ricky's body was found at seven am by a nurse, climbing Christmas Steps on her way to work at Bristol Children's Hospital. Within a couple of hours her grim discovery was all over the online edition of the *Bristol Post*. Jasper didn't find out until lunchtime and, when he did, he was incandescent.

'It's Frankie fucking Garrett. Oi'li fucking 'ave 'im, oi will. Tell the lads to arm up, Darren. We're goin' to Mexton tonight.'

'Guv,' said Kamal, knocking on Emma's open office door, 'I think there's been another gang-related killing.'

Emma looked up from a pile of paperwork.

'So what's happened?'

'The body of a young male, showing signs of torture, was found in Bristol early this morning.'

'OK, but what's the link with Mexton?'

'Cameras picked up a van with false plates driving around in the early hours of the morning, looking a bit iffy. Avon and Somerset tracked it up the M32, onto the M4 and onwards towards Mexton. A similar van was found torched in Mexton Woods early today.'

'So we're thinking Frankie Garrett was responsible? The torture certainly looks like his MO. Can you find out who the victim was? Did he have any links to Burnham?'

'I already did, guv. His name was Ricky Mason, a known associate of Burnham. He had a number of drug-related convictions and spent a few months in prison for ABH last year. My contact didn't think he was high up in Burnham's organisation. As far as they could determine, he was drinking in a Bristol pub yesterday evening and hasn't been seen since he left.'

'Looks like Garrett snatched him, tortured and killed him, and had his body dumped to send a message to Burnham.'

'In retaliation for Newton's death, presumably,' added Kamal.

Emma nodded.

'Thanks, Kamal. Well done. The DCI's got a meeting with DSup Gorman later this afternoon. He needs to know this. Things are obviously getting worse, and it looks like a shitstorm's on the way. And how the hell are we going to cope, with so bloody few officers?'

Kamal didn't answer but quietly closed the door behind him.

<hr>

Late evening

Kevin Partridge was tired. Incredibly, mind-numbingly tired. He'd got no sleep on the ferry because the crossing was unusually rough, and he'd barely stopped since he'd left Fishguard, grabbing a burger and coffee to consume in his lorry *en route*. He knew he should take a break, but his load had to be in Swindon by late evening. A mate had disconnected the tacho for him, so he wasn't worried about getting into trouble with his boss, as long as he delivered on time.

He'd just passed Bath when his vision began to blur, and his eyelids drooped. The lights in front of him, glaring in the twilight, confused him. He started to swerve erratically. And he didn't see the Army low-loader, carrying a tank, until he smashed into its side.

Kevin's artic jack-knifed, then turned over, sliding along the carriageway on its side and ripping up tarmac. Diesel spilled from his fuel tank forming a lethal slick across two lanes. A small van carrying medical radioisotopes braked sharply and pirouetted into the underside of the lorry as the driver lost control on the slippery surface. The doors flew open, and its contents spilled out. A dozen other vehicles crashed into each other, adding to the chaos and spilling more fuel on the road. The battery of a crashed electric SUV started to smoke, dangerously close to a pool of petrol, and a boy racer in a Mazda swerved to avoid the pile-up and hit a bridge support, blocking the hard shoulder.

Within half an hour, eastbound traffic had tailed back for five miles, although the westbound side of the motorway, by some miracle, was still clear. In the middle of the tailback, two vans full of Bristol gangsters, hyped up on testosterone and amphetamines, sat motionless while their occupants fumed with frustration.

'What the fuck's goin' on, Darren?' cursed Jasper Burnham. 'Why're we stuck?'

'Dunno, boss. Some prick's crashed, I s'pose. I'll check the satnav.'

While Darren fiddled with his phone, a convoy of emergency vehicles shot past along the hard shoulder. Five police cars, three ambulances, four fire engines and a van bearing radiation warning symbols passed in quick succession. Two helicopters, their spotlights illuminating the stationary vehicles, swept overhead, the noise of their rotors splitting the silence.

Darren finally managed to locate a news feed. 'Major incident on M4,' he read. 'Multiple collisions and possible radiation hazard. Motorway closed between Bath and Chippenham eastbound, and westbound lanes to be closed imminently to facilitate rescue. Motorists are advised to avoid the M4 in the area until further notice.'

He showed his phone to Jasper.

'Fuck, fuck and fuck,' was the response. 'How're we gonna sort out Frankie now?'

'We'll just have to wait, boss. They didn't say when the motorway will be open again. Could be hours. I don't like the sound of that radiation.'

'Oi doesn't care about no fucking radiation. Oi wants to fuck up Frankie and oi wants to do it tonight.'

Darren simply shrugged. Neither of the two men noticed, just before the police closed the westbound carriageway, two vans carrying Frankie's men heading towards Bristol.

Chapter Ninety-Six

Josh Norton bitterly regretted that he'd volunteered to guard Jasper's barn. The seemingly disused farm building, set down a narrow lane outside Bristol, held most of his boss's product. Although it was fitted out with alarms and discreet CCTV, monitoring anyone approaching along the lane, Jasper insisted that a human presence was necessary. Josh had offered to do guard duty because he didn't fancy the planned battle in Mexton. But now, bleeding out from two pistol rounds in his chest, he realised his mistake.

They had come down the lane in the dark, in two vans. At first, he'd thought it was a delivery, but Jasper hadn't mentioned one. He'd picked up his shotgun and walked towards the vehicles, shouting that it was private property and they should leave. He heard someone laugh and saw a tall, thin man stepping out of the leading vehicle. He didn't speak but simply drew a pistol and fired twice, which was why Josh had collapsed at the side of the lane and had only moments to live.

Max took a set of keys from Josh's pocket and opened the padlock that secured the barn door. Dragging it open, he was pleased to see the doorway was wide enough to accommodate one of the vans. Frankie joined him and, by the light of a series of battery-powered, powerful LEDs set up inside the building, they surveyed the room. It was clearly a workshop as well as a store. Cardboard boxes of small plastic bags were piled up against one wall and trays held filled baggies of heroin. Plastic-wrapped blocks of cocaine were arranged on shelves and dustbins held bags of tablets of various colours. The heady smell of cannabis emanated from a corner where plants were heaped up into large piles.

'Jackpot!' said Max, turning to Frankie and grinning.

Frankie nodded.

'So Jasper is selling my product range. We'd better get a move on. The kid said there were alarms and cameras. Jasper could be on his way. Grab the charlie and the filled baggies. We don't have time to load the rest. You know what to do with the van.'

It took less than five minutes for Frankie's men to seize Jasper's product and load it into the larger of the vans, which they had turned round to enable a swift departure. The smaller van they drove into the barn. Max opened the valves on the four cylinders of butane in the back of the van and heaped a handful of purple crystals beside them. He poured a viscous liquid from a bottle, kept warm in his breast pocket, onto the pile and ran, pulling the barn door shut behind him and jumping into the waiting van that took off down the lane at speed.

Inside the barn the mixture of chemicals started to heat up, Wisps of smoke began to appear. A pale lilac flame burst from the pile, igniting the cloud of gas. The resulting explosion blew the door and roof off the building and started a conflagration that destroyed all Jasper's remaining stock and sent clouds of intoxicating fumes over the fields. Several cows, grazing downwind, felt extremely odd when a cloud of cannabis fumes engulfed them and an owl, caught in the smoke pouring through the roof, fell out of the sky, succumbing to the effects of vaporised heroin. Frankie smiled broadly at the sight of the blaze in the rear view mirror. *Just the beginning,* he thought. *Just the beginning.*

It was half past three in the morning before the police managed to get the stranded motorists off the M4, instructing them to turn round and drive back to the Bath junction. Dealing with the spilled radioisotopes that, fortunately, hadn't leaked, took priority. It would be midday before the road could open again, as part of it needed resurfacing. Jasper, abandoning his planned assault on Frankie's crew, arrived home at five o'clock and collapsed into bed after swallowing a tumbler of whisky. It wasn't until mid-morning that he noticed the alarms at his store had gone off during the night. Panicking, he checked the CCTV recordings and, on seeing the blaze, went into a total meltdown.

He raged around the lounge of his luxury home, smashing everything in reach and hurling the sixty-inch TV at the wall. He grabbed his shotgun and pumped round after round into the walls and even fired at his rottweiler, which had enough sense to get out of the way before he pulled the trigger. His wife, cowering under the bed, phoned Darren.

'Come quickly,' she whispered, 'he's gone mad. He's smashing everything and shooting. I'm terrified he'll kill me.'

By the time Darren arrived, Jasper's rage had subsided into cold fury.

'Darren,' he said. 'Frankie crossed another line last night. He torched the fuckin' barn. Check the news for what the cops found. We can't go down there, obviously. Last night we was gonna grab a few more of his dealers, nick some product and rough him up a bit. But it's changed. Oi'm gonna fucking kill him and as many of the fuckers who work for him as we can find. It's war, cousin. It's fuckin' war.'

Chapter Ninety-Seven

Day 23

'HAVE we got anything more on Jasper Burnham?' asked DCI Farlowe, at the start of the briefing.

'Something interesting, guv,' replied Mel. 'A couple of reg numbers for vehicles with cloned plates he's known to use were picked up on the M4 heading in our general direction. They got held up by a major RTC this side of Bath and returned to Bristol several hours later when traffic was sent back to the Bath junction.'

'Was he coming for Frankie, do you think?'

'Maybe. It's a bit stupid to use vans with identifiable plates, though. But Geoff Chidgey did say that Jasper isn't the brightest star in the criminal firmament. Presumably he didn't know the police had the cloned numbers. One other thing. A barn-load of drugs blew up outside Bristol last night and a male was found dead just outside, shot twice. The local drug squad reckon it was Jasper's storage depot, and the dead man was one of his crew. The fire wasn't an accident. There were gas canisters in the wreckage

315

of a van, inside the barn, which, their SOCOs believed, formed some kind of bomb.'

'Frankie Garrett, do you reckon?' asked the DCI.

'Very likely,' said Jack. 'If he blames Burnham for the attack on his dealers and the death of Newton, which he probably will, he will want revenge. I think he's upped the stakes.'

'Then we've got a vengeful and highly dangerous individual likely to come to Mexton to spread mayhem. Whatever reason he had for coming here last night, it's going to be multiplied by the attack on his supplies. We need to watch out for him and his gang, ladies and gentlemen, and we need to be very careful indeed. It looks like a bloodbath is on the way.'

No one spoke, reflecting on the horrific prospects of carnage on the streets of Mexton.

Detective Sergeant Peter Carter was bent. He'd been on Jasper Burnham's payroll ever since he was a PC. They'd been at the same school and knocked around together, getting up to the usual sorts of mischief young lads growing up on deprived housing estates tend to do. As Jasper's path veered towards more overt and serious criminality, they had drifted apart, and Peter had never come to the attention of the authorities. He wasn't snowy white – he had done some illegal things – but he just hadn't been caught. His family managed to move away from Hartcliffe, and he broke many of his old ties. So, when he decided to join the police, there was nothing recorded that could lead to his application being rejected.

Jasper's first thought, when he found out, was that Peter had betrayed him and the others he had grown up with. Joining the enemy was something you just didn't do. But it occurred to him that having a tame copper could be useful, if not now, then in the future. Getting Peter on board was easy. He asked Peter's mum to let him know when Peter was due to visit and intercepted him as he approached the parental home.

'Hi Pete. 'Ow's it going.'

'All right, Jasper,' Peter replied, guardedly.

'Long time no see. Oi hears you're doin' well for yourself, in the filth an' all.'

'I've changed, Jasper. I like my job. I don't reckon we've got much in common anymore. I've heard what you're up to.'

'What? You're turning your back on an old mate? Too good for me now?'

'No, Jasper, it's...'

'Now listen Pee See Farter,' sneered Jasper, his tone becoming more hostile. 'There may come a time when oi needs a friend in the force and, guess what? You've got the job.'

'Sorry, Jasper, I can't help you. And I've got a good career ahead of me.'

'Yeah? And what would happen to your fuckin' career if your bosses found out about those cars we torched and the weed we used to sell at school?'

Peter's face was ashen.

'I've put all that behind me. There's no proof, anyway. Your word against mine, and they wouldn't take any notice of anonymous tip-offs.'

'Funny you should say that. Next time I get pulled oi could always mention your past fun and games. Bargain for a reduced charge or something. Or, oi could send the photos to someone.'

'What photos?'

'Course, we didn't have phones to take films in those days. But oi had me little Instamatic. I've a family album, of sorts. It's good to have memories and look back at things we did. And you're there, clear as fucking day, doing that Mercedes. You're in a few others, too, but that's the clearest. You didn't know oi was a photographer, did you?'

Peter all but collapsed and leant against a wall to steady himself.

'What do you want?'

'For the moment, just the odd tip-off. What your lot are up to. If I'm gonna be raided. Just small stuff. Later on, who knows, But I'll pay you. Oi aint lookin' for anything for free.'

'I don't want your bloody money.'

'Oi insist. You're on my payroll. Get used to it. Oi'll be in touch.'

As Jasper drove away, Peter stood, trembling and hardly daring to join the parents who were so proud of him. His life had changed, irrevocably, and he had no choice but to comply with Jasper's demands.

Chapter Ninety-Eight

After a string of sleepless nights, Maurice decided to act. He'd spent hours looking at the files he'd downloaded from the laptop, wondering what he should do. They were obviously to do with criminal activity on a staggering scale. Drugs were clearly involved, and a town called Mexton. He had vaguely heard of it. Something to do with Albanians, he thought. He realised, with some relief, that Jasper Burnham didn't know he had copied the files. The thugs who watched him crack the password had no idea what he was doing, but it had been necessary in case there was a program on it that would wipe the machine if someone tried to hack it. But if he found out, Maurice would be in serious trouble. The files could be a ticking bomb.

Finally, he came to a decision. He copied the files from the laptop onto two separate external hard drives, one of which he posted to Mexton Drug Squad and the other he sent to the National Crime Agency. Then he saved all his own computer files onto external drives and reformatted his internal hard drive, removing all traces of the laptop, before reinstalling his files. If Dave asked for his help again, he would try to refuse. But he knew, deep inside, that he would probably have no choice in the matter.

***

For years Peter provided Jasper with titbits of information. A planned raid here, the impending arrest of a rival there and, occasionally, the reg numbers of unmarked police cars new to the area. He also managed to lose evidence on occasions, but the one request he always turned down was the identity of undercover officers – not that he knew them, as they always came from another force. He convinced himself that what he was doing wasn't so bad. No one really got hurt. But when he realised that Jasper, enraged by Frankie's attacks, was planning an all-out war, he knew he had to act. Enough was enough.

Over the years he had kept detailed notes of Jasper's activities. He had downplayed his own role, but he knew that anyone examining the file would realise that he had been involved somehow. His career would be over, and he would end up in jail, unless he could disappear. His parents were dead, he was divorced and had no children, so he had no ties to the UK. The money Jasper had given him, plus his savings, would keep him going until he could find another source of income. Flight seemed a logical step.

It took him a couple of days to make the arrangements. He printed off copies of the file, got them ready to post, and also arranged for electronic copies to be sent to three different departments in his own force, as well as the NCA and Mexton CID, at a predetermined time. He instructed his solicitor to sell his house and pay the proceeds into a Cayman Islands account.

On his last day, Pete posted the hard copies on his way to work and put his go-bag in the boot of his car. The electronic copies would be sent at midnight, by which time he would be in the air to somewhere safe, the car abandoned at Bristol Airport.

He sat down at his desk and logged on for the last time, aware that there was something odd about the atmosphere in the office. He noticed a couple of uniformed officers standing at the door, which was unusual, and the look on his DCI's face as he approached was one Pete had never seen before.

'Pete,' he said. 'Professional Standards have some questions for you. Come with me please.'

He realised that he must have been under suspicion. It had been going on so long that he must have got careless. He knew that he was headed for several types of hell and the only way to mitigate the consequences would be to co-operate fully.

'Yes, sir,' he replied. 'I have some things I need to tell them.'

Chapter Ninety-Nine

'So how do you want to play this, Jasper?' asked Darren, in an attempt to get his boss to think logically. 'We can't just storm into Mexton with all guns blazing. The cops have weapons, too. Perhaps we could start with something a bit more subtle. Then go for Frankie when his resources are running low. Is there anything on that laptop that might help?'

Jasper scratched his head and thought for a moment.

'Spose there might be. We've got the names of his suppliers. We could pay them a visit. Tell them we're takin' over and not to supply Frankie anymore. He'd be right pissed off at that. Right pissed off.'

Jasper brightened up a little.

'Darren, moi lad. We're goin' on a trip to sunny Swindon. Just you and me. See what the bloke who supplies his gear has to say to us.'

'And why the fook,' said the massive Liverpudlian with the razor scar across his forehead, 'should I end a profitable deal with

Frankie Garrett, just on your say-so? You look like a scruff, you speak as though you've just fallen off a bleedin' hay wagon and you've got the fooking cheek to come to my office and interfere with my business. Ave you got a fookin' death wish or something?'

'Frankie Garrett is on 'is way out. We've got details of 'is finances, 'is dealers and,' Jasper looked pointedly at the Scouser, ''is suppliers. The stupid arsehole kept it all on a laptop that oive got.'

The Liverpudlian raised his eyebrows as far as the scar permitted.

'Somewhere safe,' he added. 'Anyways, we've started turning his dealers, we've taken out one of his top guys and oil get Frankie 'imself before long. It's got personal.'

'What makes you think you can handle my product.'

'I already distributes most of the weed and Es in Mexton, and half of Bristol. I'm diversifyin' me product range.'

'What's to stop me tellin' Frankie what's goin' on?'

Jasper shrugged.

'I reckons 'e already knows. We've 'ad our clashes. But with 'im gone, you'll lose an outlet. Oi can fill the gap. And, as a sign of goodwill, oi'll pay you ten percent more than Frankie does until he's out of the picture. What do you reckon?'

The Liverpudlian conferred with an equally scarred companion, then turned back to Jasper.

'I'll think about it. It could make business sense. I'll check you out and get back to you. Give me a number. And don't fookin' come here uninvited again.'

Two hours later, Frankie Garrett paced the floor of The Golden Thong, completely ignoring the naked women wrapping themselves around the wonky poles. He muttered angrily into his phone and, when the call ended, he dialled Max's number.

'Those bloody Scousers,' he hissed. 'They're putting the price of gear up by twenty percent. They say they've got a better offer and if I want them to continue supplying me, I've got to pay up. They also said to watch my back.'

'It's obviously Burnham,' said Max. 'He's got the name from your laptop and is trying to put us out of business. What're you going to do?'

'I'll get back to them and tell them Burnham will be dead within the week, and that I'm not prepared to pay over the odds. We could go direct to the Turks, if necessary, but it's convenient dealing with this lot. I want you and Jerome in the club at eight tonight, and I'll decide how we're going to deal with Burnham. He's crossed so many lines he's playing hopscotch with us, and I won't have it.'

Chapter One Hundred

'Did you hear about Addy?' asked Mel, as she sat beside Sally in the visitors' room at the hospital. 'He's applying to come back to CID. He gave me a call last night.'

'How come? I thought he was doing OK as an AFO.'

'So did I but killing Garton traumatised him and he decided it wasn't for him. He's got to wait until after the inquiry until he can return to duty, but I've invited him down the pub next time we go. It would be good to see him without a carbine in his hands for a change.'

'True enough. I never fancied firearms myself. I don't like loud noises.'

'I did wonder about it,' said Mel, 'but the sword attack that damaged my shoulder kind of put paid to that. I still get the odd twinge in my shoulder. I'm happy as a detective, though. Jack keeps urging me to go for DS but I'm not sure I'm ready. I'll study for the exams when we get a quiet patch and see where it goes.'

'Oh dear. Does that mean I'll have to call you "Sarge"?' Sally said, pretending to look worried.

'Not at all. I'll expect you to stand up and salute when I come into the room, though.'

'In your dreams, Mel. In your dreams.'

The two women laughed as Mel stood up.

'Anyway, I've got to go. Plenty to do at the station. I'm glad to see you're on the mend, and everyone sends their love. See you again soon.'

Sally waved goodbye as Mel left, wincing at the twinge in her injured arm and wondering whether she really wanted to return to duty.

***

'Oi've heard from them fuckin' Scousers,' said Jasper. 'The bastards said that if oi'm still alive by the middle of next week they'd consider my offer. For now, they'll continue supplying Frankie. The fuckin' cheek of it. They must have talked to 'im.'

'So what now? Try and do the same with the mob that supplies his blow?' asked Darren. 'Or take out Frankie once and for all?'

'We gotta make a statement. Prove to those Scouse gits we're serious. And competent. But oi wants to make Frankie suffer before we does him. Right. Here's what we'll do. We killed one of his top guys. There's two others. And oi particularly wants this one.'

He threw a blurred photo onto the pub table.

'So, we're goin' to Mexton, just you, me and one other. And we'll take this arsehole and do something public with him. Just like those fuckers did with our Ricky.'

***

Max the Plank stepped out of The Golden Thong just after midnight and felt uneasy. Something wasn't right. That bloke leaning against the lamppost? No, just a drunk throwing up a kebab and the night's alcohol. That Skoda, parked along the street? No, that was an unmarked police car carrying out the intermittent, unproductive, surveillance the gang was used to. But that SUV just over the road. It didn't fit. Sliding his hand into his pocket and grasping the butt of his pistol, he crossed over to investigate.

The vehicle appeared to be empty but, as he drew close, the passenger door was flung open, smashing him in the face. Stunned, he didn't have time to draw his weapon before someone stepped out of the car and hit him hard in the solar plexus. He collapsed to the floor, unable to resist as he was shoved into the back of the SUV. He felt the muzzle of a gun pressed against his ribs as someone searched him. He heard his own pistol clatter on the tarmac as it was thrown out of the car. And he heard Jasper's triumphant voice coming from the driver's seat.

'Do up your seatbelt, Max. 'Oi wouldn't want you to get hurt if oi has an accident.'

Jasper's malevolent chuckle rang in Max's ears as the vehicle pulled smoothly away. Max tried not to think about what was likely to happen to him. But, knowing what had happened to Speedy, he had a pretty good idea. And the thought terrified him.

'Did you see that?' asked DC Plummer, turning round in the police Skoda and watching Jasper's car disappearing into the distance.

'What?' said DC Carpenter.

'I noticed that SUV in my mirror. It looked like someone was being snatched and shoved in the back.'

'Probably just a drunk being helped in by his mates. Did you get the plate?'

'No. Too dark. I think I'll take a look. Stretch my legs a bit.'

Plummer stepped out of the car and walked back to where the SUV had been parked, shining his torch along the ground. He didn't really expect to find any signs of a struggle, but it alleviated the boredom. He stopped, suddenly. Gleaming dully in the light of his torch, close to the opposite side of the road, was a semi-automatic pistol.

'Oh shit,' he muttered, reaching for his phone. 'It's DC Plummer,' he said, when Control answered. 'I need an AFO to retrieve a weapon. I'm outside The Golden Thong, Loseley Street. Also, I may have seen a possible kidnapping.'

He ran back to the car and extracted a traffic cone and a hi-vis jacket from the boot. He placed the cone carefully over the weapon, put the jacket on and stood guard, shivering in the chilly night air until a specialist officer arrived.

So much for covert surveillance, he thought. *I bet they know who we are anyway. Bloody waste of time, watching the club. Still, finding that weapon could be useful, I suppose.*

Chapter One Hundred One

Day 24

'Oh, shit. That's nasty,' said Emma as she contemplated Max's naked body. 'Can someone get a tent over it, please? As soon as.'

The corpse, tied to a plank of wood and with a large nail sticking out of his groin, had been dumped in a skip some fifty yards from The Golden Thong. A large hole in the chest, from a close-range shotgun blast, testified to the probable cause of death, but whether the other injury occurred before or after the shot would not be determined until later.

Uniformed officers cordoned off a large section of the street, politely deflecting questions from curious onlookers and dissuading them from filming the scene on their phones. SOCOs busied themselves within the inner cordon, erecting a tent, taking photographs and establishing a common approach path to the skip, while PC Halligan, feeling queasy at the sight of the body, clutched the scene log. Business as usual for the initial stages of a homicide investigation.

Emma called the team together after lunch, by which time Max's body had been removed to the mortuary.

'OK, everybody. We've got another murder. Maxwell Pauli, or Max the Plank, found naked and dead in a skip near his place of work, The Golden Thong, early this morning by a security guard after his shift. The deceased had been shot in the chest, and a nail had been hammered through his scrotum.'

Most of the male members of the team winced at that.

'He's under the care of Dr Durbridge now, and he expects to provide us with the PM report tomorrow morning. DC Plummer, a drug squad officer watching the club in an unmarked car, thought he saw someone being abducted, so talk to him and find out what he witnessed. So, we need door-to-doors in the area, not that there's much residential property around there, and CCTV trawling. We may have more luck with that. Can we get incident boards with a contact number, please? I'll ask for a couple of uniforms on the night shift to ask people passing by between, say, two o'clock and dawn if they use that street regularly and whether they saw anything odd. I want a couple of you to interview Frankie Garrett again, please. Pauli and Robert Newton were his right-hand men and it's clear this was directed at him. I doubt that the bugger'll say anything, but we have to try. My money's on Jasper Burnham and his crew. OK. Plenty to do. Any questions?'

'One thing, guv,' said Kamal. 'Why Max the Plank? Is he particularly thick?'

Emma smiled.

'No, Kamal. He is – rather, was – tall and very thin with few apparent muscles. That didn't stop him being a vicious bastard. He was much stronger than he looked and mean with it. OK? Thanks, everyone.'

Chapter One Hundred Two

Frankie Garrett slipped the freshly cleaned and oiled Browning Hi-Power semi-automatic into his desk drawer when the barman announced that the police wanted to speak to him. He adjusted his waistcoat, smoothed down his immaculately tailored trousers and descended the stairs into the club.

'What do you want, officers?' he asked, somewhat testily. 'As you know, I've lost another of my trusted employees, and I have a lot to deal with.'

'That's what we wanted to talk to you about,' replied Mel. 'Can you think why anyone would want to torture and kill Mr Pauli?'

'No. Certainly not. He was a respected member of my team. He may have made enemies in his private life but none in his employment with me.'

'Well, again, there's a discrepancy,' said Jack. 'As was the case with Robert Newton. Mr Pauli had a history of violence and other criminal activities, from quite an early age.'

'That's true, sergeant, but he's never been convicted of anything since he's worked for me. I believe in giving people a second chance, and, with Maxwell, it was fully justified. We will all miss him badly.'

'There is another similarity with Mr Newton,' said Mel. 'Both suffered genital mutilations before they were killed. We were wondering if that had anything to do with the rape of a young drug dealer on the Eastside Estate a few months ago.'

'Inconceivable, Miss Cotton. I will not tolerate abuse of women by my employees. All the girls who work here,' he gestured to a dyed blonde lurching listlessly around a pole, 'are treated with respect.'

The detectives looked sceptical.

'I see you have a CCTV camera outside the club, Mr Garrett,' said Mel. 'May we see the footage from last night?'

'I'm afraid it doesn't work. It's there for show. I'm sure you understand that some of our clientele might not wish to be recorded.'

'Can you tell us about your relationship with Jasper Burnham?' asked Jack.

'I have no relationship with Jasper Burnham. As I understand it, he's a common criminal from somewhere in the West Country. Why do you ask?'

'Our intelligence suggests that he is challenging you for the drugs market in Mexton, and gang warfare is imminent, which we will not tolerate.'

'Poppycock. Is this some kind of warning, sergeant? And if you are accusing me of some kind of illegal activity, I will need my solicitor present. I should warn you that I play golf occasionally with your Assistant Chief Constable. Now if there is nothing else, I have matters to attend to.'

'That's all for the moment, sir,' said Jack. 'We'll probably need to speak to you again. If you know of Mr Pauli's next of kin, we'd be obliged if you would send us the details.'

Frankie Garrett walked away without further comment.

'God, he really pissed me off, making out that Newton and Pauli were fucking angels,' said Mel. 'Two Grade-A thugs who would sell their grannies, and he tells us they were fine upstanding citizens. Makes me sick.'

'Yes, he's a slick bastard, isn't he?' replied Jack. 'But he did look edgy when I mentioned Burnham. There's something brewing, definitely. And it scares the shit out of me.'

Frankie sat in his office planning. The loss of Speedy had affected him and he was also furious at the loss of Max. Jerome could step up and do some of the jobs the others did, but he was still short of at least one reliable lieutenant. He would have to recruit from the ranks. Ethan, who was keeping an eye on things in Portsmouth, might do, but that was something for the future. The priority was to deal with Jasper Burnham, in a way that would repair his reputation and reassert his authority.

For once in his career, Frankie was at a loss. He ruled out open warfare on the streets. Too much attention from the police and he could lose even more soldiers. He briefly considered getting Jasper arrested but rejected the idea. He was not a grass and would never do that, not even to a sworn enemy. Jasper had to die, and publicly. Finally, he hit on a solution. He called a former weapons officer he knew from the navy. There was nothing that man didn't know about bombs, and Frankie knew exactly how to recruit him.

'Hello, Clive,' he said. 'I've got a little job needs doing. There's cash and gear in it for you. Interested?'

Chapter One Hundred Three

THE DETECTIVES HAD JUST FINISHED the first round of drinks in The Cat and Cushion when Addy joined them, almost bouncing with excitement.

'I have news! Big news! Let me get the drinks and I'll tell you all about it!'

With glasses duly replenished they waited for Addy to speak.

'It's Vic. She's pregnant. I'm going to be a dad!'

Congratulations flowed and Addy beamed.

'When's it due?' asked Emma.

'A few months yet. We've just had the twelve-week scan and everything looks fine. We're so excited!'

'Is that why you're leaving firearms?' asked Kamal.

'Partly,' replied Addy, turning serious. 'But I'd already decided to leave before we got the results. I just can't get over killing Garton. So,' he said, brightening up. 'I'll be back with you guys before long.'

'Good news, Addy, on both accounts,' said Mel. 'Have you started thinking about names yet?'

'We have lists, but it's difficult because relatives would like to see their names used. We don't want to offend people, but we can't use them all. We haven't told them yet. Also, we want to embody some of our own culture in the names. We'll probably wait till the baby arrives and see which names fit.'

'One thing I can tell you,' said Emma, 'is that your life will never be the same again. You'll be constantly knackered, frequently covered in sick, and worrying on overdrive. But believe me, it's all worth it. I wouldn't be without Genevieve for the world. By the way, I've found out the name of my job share. A DI Jessop. He's starting next month.'

'Christ, no! Not Paul Jessop, surely?' asked Mel.

'Why?' asked Emma, looking puzzled.

'Because he worked with us a few years back, on secondment from the Met. He was a drunken, incompetent twat who nearly screwed a case by mishandling evidence.'

'Ah. Mr Farlowe said he'd been here before and had had a few problems. Apparently, he sobered up, performed well thereafter, and passed the promotion board for Inspector. The boss also hinted that Jessop had – quote – found Jesus, which should be... interesting.'

'Didn't know he went missing,' muttered Mel, which attracted a few chuckles and one disapproving look.

'Anyway,' continued Emma, 'I should be finding things a little easier in future.'

'Careful!' warned Jack. 'That's almost like using the Q word.'

Emma laughed.

'Right. I'd better be off. See you all bright and early tomorrow.'

The others finished their drinks and slowly drifted off. Sally and Mel left the pub together and waited in the car park for Tom to pick them up.

'Do you and Tom want children, Mel?' Kamal asked.

Mel looked grave.

'We've discussed it, and almost rowed about it. I don't think it's a good idea. Just look at the way society's going and the type of people in charge,' she said, bitterly. 'And the way the planet is being dragged down the toilet by billionaires and fossil fuel companies. It wouldn't be fair to bring a child into this shitstorm. By the time things improve, if they ever do, my eggs will have dried up.'

'But Tom feels differently?'

'Yes. He would like children. It's odd, because we usually agree about everything and I don't understand it. I get the feeling there's something he's not telling me, which makes me uneasy.'

Kamal grimaced.

'I hope we can compromise on adoption, a few years down the road,' Mel continued. 'It would be lovely to have a family, but I don't think it's fair to bring a new child into the world when there are so many without loving parents. Anyway,' she smiled briefly, 'enough of Tom's and my differences. Here's my lift.'

Day 25

'Bloody hell! Father Christmas has come early!'

Emma nearly danced around her office when she ended the call, much to Jack's puzzlement.

'That was Derek Palmer. Someone's sent the Drug Squad Frankie Garrett's files, presumably the ones on his laptop. We now have access to everything he's up to in Mexton: who his suppliers are, the buildings he operates from and who he uses on the streets. We've really got the bugger now!'

'Whoa! Steady on. That's a massive job, taking down a big enterprise like Frankie's. We're not gonna do it with a few dozen DCs, a depleted uniformed strength and a couple of ARUs. It'll take ages to plan an operation.'

'I quite agree, Jack. But Derek told me that the NCA received the files as well. So there'll be a joint op. Hampshire Police may be involved as well, if there's anything in the files about his Portsmouth activities. You're right about the length of time required, though, but with the prospect of gang warfare in the offing, we need to act fast. OK. We'll brief the troops this afternoon. I've got a meeting now with Colin and a DI from Avon and Somerset who's got something to tell us about Jasper Burnham.'

Emma left her office with a spring in her step. Jack looked worried.

'This is DI Rosie Frankley,' said DCI Farlowe, introducing the smartly suited woman standing beside his desk to Emma. The women smiled at each other and shook hands, then Farlowe invited them to sit.

'We've had a development in Bristol,' Frankley began, 'which affects you in Mexton. One of our long-serving officers has just confessed to being a mole for Jasper Burnham.'

A look of contempt flickered across Emma's face.

'Over the years, he's tipped off Burnham to raids, provided other information on police activities and, occasionally, mislaid evidence. He was coerced, initially, but has been taking bribes as well. We don't believe he's been involved directly in Burnham's operations, such as selling drugs, but he is in serious trouble, nonetheless. Anyway, he has provided us with full details of Jasper's activities over the years. He was planning to leave the country and posted paper files to be delivered once he was free and clear. He also sent electronic copies to arrive once he was in the air. Professional Standards got to him first, though. They'd been watching him for a while, with no firm evidence of wrongdoing, but he started acting suspiciously a couple of days ago, so they wanted a chat. He confessed to everything.'

'So why did he give it all up?' asked Emma.

'He realised that Burnham was headed for a violent clash with Frankie Garrett. He saw that lives had already been lost and wanted no further part in it. He thought he could get away and make a new start, somewhere he couldn't be extradited from.'

'What's happening to him now?'

'Officially, he's on leave. Contrary to all normal procedures, we decided not to arrest him or start formal disciplinary action in case it tipped off Burnham. That'll all come later. For the moment, we think he could help to prevent a bloodbath.'

'How so?' asked Farlowe.

'Burnham is intent on a confrontation with Garrett. Quite frankly, he's an out-of-control maniac, especially since his drug storage depot was blown up, presumably by Garrett. So, I wondered if we could lure him and his crew into a trap, here in Mexton, and arrest the lot. He would believe a tipoff from his mole, who would say he'd heard about a meeting of Frankie's men from a mate in Mexton CID. If we can get him and some of his thugs into custody on weapons charges, and they're bound to be armed, we can use the information provided by our bent DS to dismantle the rest of his operation at leisure – working with you, of course, as we know he sells drugs in Mexton.'

Emma looked taken aback and Farlowe looked doubtful. It was the DCI who spoke.

'That could put our officers at risk, and I'm not sure the high-ups would wear it. I'll raise it with the DSup this afternoon. We have a particularly acute resource issue, as well. Someone has provided us with details of Frankie Garrett's operations in Mexton. Apparently, they were on a laptop that Burnham had stolen from him. Although the NCA has offered to help us take him down, we're too stretched to tackle both gangs at once.'

'I understand,' said DI Frankley. 'My boss has authorised me to offer help in the form of manpower, including some AFOs. But if the idea is acceptable, we need to move fast before Burnham charges into Mexton, tooled up and murderous.'

'I think we could do it, Colin,' interjected Emma. 'As long as we can find a contained location to minimise the risks of harm to our people and stray rounds hitting the public. I've got a couple of possible locations in mind already. And we need to find another reason for out-of-town officers descending on Mexton, in case of leaks.'

'All right,' said Farlowe. 'I believe it could work, subject to the appropriate risk assessments. I'll see if the DSup's available this afternoon and push the idea. If it'll prevent Mexton from turning into 1920s Chicago, I think he'll support it. And if we can deal with Garrett simultaneously, that would be a bonus.'

He turned to his visitor.

'Thanks very much for coming, Rosie. You're welcome to stay for lunch in the canteen. I'll get back to you as soon as I have a decision.'

'I'll pass on the canteen, I think. If it's anything like ours, a motorway services would be a better bet.'

Emma smiled and showed her out to reception.

Chapter One Hundred Five

Despite his, managed, use of heroin, Clive Crawley hadn't lost all the skills he'd acquired serving his country. He had scoped out Jasper Burnham's luxury home outside Bristol, using satellite images on the internet, and noted a concealed approach route via an adjacent patch of woodland. He sneered when he arrived and saw a substantial branch overhanging the perimeter fence. *What kind of idiot didn't spot that and prune it!* he wondered and promptly used it to gain access to the garden.

He commando-crawled across the lawn, slowly in case of motion sensors, and inched around a couple of flowerbeds. He slithered across a concrete patio and drew himself upright, at the side of a pair of French doors, confident that he couldn't be seen from within. Jasper was in the room, throwing darts at a dartboard and drinking from a silver tankard. A woman, presumably his wife, sat watching television. Domestic bliss, which Jack was about to disrupt, terminally. He was just about to slip his rucksack off his shoulder and prime the device when he heard a growl.

Helpful as the satellite images were, they couldn't provide Jack with every detail about the premises. A crucial detail missing was the presence of Jasper's rottweiler, a creature with a serious anxiety problem following his owner's recent frenzied firing of a shotgun. The dog would normally have launched itself at the intruder, as Jasper had intended, but now the unfortunate animal contented itself with a growl and bared teeth.

Clive saw the flash of fangs in the light from the patio doors. He had seen what big dogs could do and decided that retreat was the only option. Moving slowly and steadily at first, he increased his speed as he approached the perimeter, fearful that the dog was following. He didn't look back to find out and, when he reached the fence, he threw his rucksack onto the barbed wire that ran along the top. The minor shock would not have been sufficient to set off his bomb. But the rucksack formed a bridge between the barbed wire and the electrically live wire beneath it. The burst of current instantly triggered the firing mechanism and a kilo of Semtex destroyed the fence, blew the tree over and turned Clive Crawley to mush. In the cold distance, a dog began to howl.

Chapter One Hundred Six

Day 26

'Jasper. It's Pete. I've got something for you. And it's big.'

'Wassatt? You've woken me up. It's six in the fuckin' morning. Some arsehole tried to blow me up last night and oi've had no bleedin' sleep. This'd better be good.'

'It is. I've got a mate in Mexton CID. They've been monitoring Frankie Garrett's phone. He's right pissed off at what you did to his guys and he's coming for you.'

Jasper chuckled.

'Good. I expected that. But what's so important you're ringing me now?'

'My mate says he's getting some muscle up from Portsmouth. They're all meeting up in a car park in Mexton, tonight at eleven. Then they're coming down our way. But here's the thing. Frankie and his main guys will be there from half-ten. Frankie in his Merc and the others in SUVs. Now, I've looked at the site on a map and if you wanted to take Frankie out it's a good place for an ambush. And there's nothing much around. No witnesses.'

'Why the fuck are you tellin' me this?'

'I may be your mate, Jasper, but I'm also a cop and we don't want shoot-outs in Bristol. Innocent people could get hurt. And Frankie's a piece of shit we'd all be better off without. So there it is. Take it or leave it.'

'OK. Where's this car park to? Oi'll take a look. Are the Mexton cops planning anything? Did your mate say?'

'He thinks they're planning a joint operation with my force. They'll intercept them on the motorway as soon as they enter the Avon and Somerset area. They reckon there'll be less chance of a firefight that way.'

'What about the car park? Won't they be there?'

'They're keeping away in case it spooks Frankie. They'll pick up his vehicles on the way out of town. There's a camera on a lamppost on the way in, but if you take it out with a shotgun you could do the job and be on your way before anyone knows what's happening. Change your plates as soon as you get clear, though.'

Jasper thought for a while.

'OK, Pete. If this works, oil owe you. There'll be a grand in it.'

'Thanks. Could come in handy. Anyway, here's the address. Let me know how it goes.'

Pete recited a postcode and switched off his burner.

'Do you think he'll fall for that bollocks?' he asked DI Frankley, who was sitting next to him in the police headquarters at Portishead. 'I mean, if he knew how we would really handle a situation like that, he would know it was crap.'

'True,' the DI replied, 'but it's worth a try. You said he's not that bright and he's desperate to get Frankie Garrett. I hope desperation overrules caution. Now go home and wait to hear from us. And let me know if Jasper contacts you.'

She watched Carter leave with a mixture of hope and disgust. A corrupt officer was anathema to his colleagues, but his actions just might save lives.

Chapter One Hundred Seven

THE SMALL CONVOY of two white vans and Jasper's car approached the rugby ground car park at precisely ten-thirty, driving slowly so as to minimise noise. The fifteen occupants of the vehicles sweated, some with fear and some, fuelled by coke or speed, with gleeful anticipation. The CCTV camera, with its blinking red light, was an easy target for Jasper's shotgun. The blast was the cue for action. Engines roared. The car and vans hurtled forward, throwing a fusillade of gravel into the air. Jasper's car headed straight for the Mercedes saloon while his vans went left and right in a pincer movement, flanking the two black people-carriers that bracketed the Merc. Jasper's car slewed sideways and stopped. He leapt out, took cover behind it, and yelled.

'Frankie fucking Garrett, where are you?'

The response sent him into a volcanic rage.

Spotlights flared and the whole scene lit up. He heard the clang of a barrier pole being dropped into position across the entrance. Police officers poured out of the people carriers, carbines at the ready. And the voice of the Tactical Firearms Commander blared out through a megaphone.

'Armed police. You are surrounded. Throw down your weapons. Get out of your vehicles with your hands on your heads and lie on the ground. Do exactly as I say and you will not be harmed. I repeat, armed police. You are surrounded.'

'What do we do, boss?' asked Darren, crouching beside him

'Do as 'e fucking sez. That fucking Pete Carter's betrayed me. Oi'll fuckin' 'ave 'e, you see if oi don't.'

Darren and the other occupants of the car stood up slowly with their hands on their heads. The men in the van followed suit and, while attention was focussed on the row of villains lowering themselves to the ground, Jasper remained crouching behind the vehicle then threw his shotgun high into the air and bolted for the gate. When the cocked weapon hit the ground the impact made it fire, pellets peppering Jasper's car. He had almost reached the entrance when a bulky uniformed sergeant from the Avon and Somerset force rugby tackled him to the ground, breaking a couple of his ribs in the process. Handcuffed and turned over, he gazed with dismay at the familiar face above him.

'You bastard! I thought you were one of mine.'

'Not tonight, Jasper. Not tonight. You are fucking nicked.'

The officer chuckled.

'I've always wanted to say that. But, Jasper Burnham, I am arresting you on suspicion of conspiracy to murder. You do not have to say anything but...'

Jasper couldn't believe what was happening. He hardly noticed the caution. He hardly noticed anything. And all he had the energy to respond with was 'Fuck you.'

Chapter One Hundred Eight

FRANKIE GARRETT KNEW something was wrong. Whether it was the sudden lack of traffic in the road outside the club, the unfamiliar vehicles cruising by, or just the instinct honed through many years of avoiding arrest, he couldn't say. But he thought it would be a good idea to be somewhere else for a while. He swapped his bespoke suit for a pair of scruffy joggers, a T-shirt and a hoodie. Five hundred pounds worth of the cobbler's craft went into a bin, to be replaced by a pair of old trainers. He tucked the Browning into the back of his waistband, splashed some whisky on his clothes and slunk out of the club, heading for his escape vehicle, parked a couple of streets away.

He had just reached the end of the road when a police officer stepped in front of him.

'Just a minute, sir. May I ask where you're going?'

'Home, ossifer,' Frankie replied, feigning drunkenness.

'Have you just come from The Golden Thong?'

'Yes. Bin watching the girlies.' He frowned. 'You won't tell the missus, will you?'

'Do you have any identification on you?' asked the PC, ignoring the question.

Frankie proffered a food-smeared, fake driving licence, which the PC examined disdainfully.

'That's OK, sir. You'd better be on your way. You're not driving, are you?'

'No, Shanks's pony for me. Don't drink and drive. Might hit something.'

The constable made a note of the name on the licence and watched Frankie shamble off into the night, unaware that he might just have signed a fellow officer's death warrant.

'Have you seen *The Usual Suspects*, Kamal?' asked Mel, as they waited in an unmarked police car, two hundred metres from The Golden Thong.

'Yes, why? Is this a movie quiz?' he smiled.

'Remember that bit at the end. The bloke's stumbling along and then starts walking normally.'

'Ye-es. So what?'

'Well, that drunk who just staggered past has suddenly sobered up. I'm going to have a chat with him. Keep an eye on the club and call me when the guys go in.'

'OK. But don't take any chances.'

'I'm prudence personified,' replied Mel, prompting a derisive raspberry from Kamal.

She climbed out of the car and walked briskly after the sober drunk who disappeared round a corner before she could reach him. Five minutes later, when she hadn't returned, Kamal followed. He turned the corner and his heart nearly stopped. Mel had disappeared completely. Frantically, he rushed along the empty street, looking in cars, doorways and alleys for any sign of her. And when he saw the debris of Mel's phone, in a distinctive case with a picture of a parrot on the back, the dreadful realisation hit him. Mel had been taken.

Five minutes earlier

'Excuse me, sir,' called Mel, turning the corner after her quarry. 'Police. Can I talk to you?'

The man took no notice and quickened his pace, drawing level with a row of parked cars.

'Sir! Please stop. I need to speak to you.'

The man slowed down, keeping his face turned away from Mel. Just as she reached him, he whipped round and jabbed her hard in the solar plexus with the barrel of the Browning Hi-Power. Winded, she stumbled back against a Toyota Prius and fumbled for her phone. Garrett knocked it out of her hand, and it tumbled into the road where a passing van crushed it. He put the keys to the Prius on the car's roof and stepped back so Mel couldn't reach the pistol.

'Get in the driver's seat Miss Cotton,' he snarled, 'and don't piss about.'

As Mel complied, he slid into the back of the car, keeping the weapon trained on Mel's head.

'Drive. And don't do anything to draw attention to us or I'll shoot you dead.'

Chapter One Hundred Nine

THE RAID on The Golden Thong, synchronised with the arrest of Jasper Burnham's crew, began quietly. Uniformed officers, under the watchful eyes of two AFOs, shepherded the punters and staff into the street, two or three at a time, guiding them beyond the cordon of police tape. Their identities were checked, no one was allowed to leave the scene, and they were told not to use their phones, an instruction with which few people complied. Two dancers, freezing in lingerie, were allowed to sit in a police car for warmth.

'Armed police. Come down the stairs slowly, with your hands on your heads, shouted the TFO.'

There was no reply. He repeated the call, again receiving no response.

'OK. Send up the dogs,' he instructed. The dogs bounded up the stairs to the office and halted outside the door, barking furiously.

'You have nowhere to go. There are armed officers in the club and at the bottom of the fire escape. Come out, leave your weapons behind, and no one needs to get hurt. I repeat, you have nowhere to go.'

There was a silence apart from the growling of the firearms dogs. Eventually a voice was heard.

'Call off the fucking dogs and we'll come out.'

The handlers complied and the office door slowly opened. The AFOs at the bottom of the stairs tensed, ready to fire. Two individuals shuffled out with their hands on their heads, radiating hatred. They were arrested, handcuffed and cautioned while AFOs searched the office for weapons.

'Where's Frankie Garrett?' demanded Jack, when the suspects had been removed from the premises.

'Wouldn't you like to fucking know,' hissed Jerome.

His companion said nothing.

Jack called Farlowe.

'Frankie's in the wind. He wasn't in the club when we raided it. He must have slipped out before we struck. And another thing. Mel's disappeared. She went to talk to a drunk who seemed to have suddenly sobered up. Her broken phone was lying in the road. Kamal thinks she's been taken.

'Then you'd better bloody find her. Divert some uniforms from the club. She's the priority, now.'

A distraught Kamal handed Jack Mel's phone in a plastic evidence bag.

'This was in the road over there,' he pointed, 'and there is a space in this row of parked cars where a vehicle could have been parked. But there's no CCTV or doorbell cameras, no passing buses, nothing. I've driven up and down this street, and the others nearby. I've checked alleys, bins and doorways. No trace of her. Fuck, I wish I'd gone with her.'

'Don't blame yourself, Kamal,' replied Jack. 'Mel's always been a bit impetuous, and she probably thought there was no serious risk. We all assumed that Frankie was in the club. And

I've no fucking doubt that it's Frankie who's got her, which is bloody awful news. Have you talked to the uniform on the cordon?'

'Yes. The tape wasn't up when this drunk wandered down the road from the club. He checked the man's identity, but the driving licence he showed has proved to be fake. The PC's kicking himself for not detaining the drunk, but he seemed pissed out of his head and harmless.'

'Well, the idiot will know better next time, which won't help Mel in the least. Right, phone the station and get people looking at traffic cameras around the area for vehicles moving at the time Mel went AWOL. A long shot, but we may get something,' as traffic is quiet. Go through the info we have on Frankie to see if he has other premises. Check the files from his laptop – look for rental or purchase details. Either he's taken her there or he's planning to leave the country, keeping her as a hostage in the meantime. Or,' he said grimly, 'he's already killed her and she's lying dead in a ditch somewhere. And nobody goes home until we've found her.'

Chapter One Hundred Ten

Mel said nothing as she drove Garrett's Prius, merely nodding in response to his directions. She concentrated on memorising the route as they headed into increasingly unfamiliar parts of Mexton's outskirts. She had no illusions about Garrett letting her go. The fact that she was driving, rather than blindfolded or locked in the boot, told her unequivocally that this would be a one-way journey. She also knew that no one would be coming to rescue her – with no phone to trace or witnesses to her abduction, her colleagues wouldn't have a clue where she had been taken. She would have to find a way of overpowering him. But he had a powerful semi-automatic and knew to keep his distance. If she did get a chance, it would be only one. So she bottled up her mounting terror, tried to present the image of someone totally defeated and watched every move Garrett made, for that single chance.

'Turn in here,' said Garrett, indicating the entrance to a disused building supplies warehouse, secured by padlocked steel gates. A dilapidated sign, bearing the legend Hawker and Lovelace, Building Supplies, hung unevenly from the façade. He passed a key to her.

'Get out, unlock the padlock, open the gates, then drive in. I should warn you that I'm an excellent shot. You will be less than twelve feet from me and, should you try to run, you won't get half a yard.'

Fuck! No chance there, thought Mel.

She complied with Garrett's instructions and stopped the car in front of a steel door beside the main roller shutter. He tossed her another key once they had got out.

'Open the door and enter. The light switch is in the wall to your left. Don't think of running.'

The first thing Mel noticed inside the warehouse was the smell. Stale blood, urine and faeces combined to produce an evil olfactory cocktail. Then she noticed an array of tools and kitchen implements on a bench, with a bloodstained chair next to it. She nearly threw up.

'So what the fuck's this all about, Frankie,' she said, dully. 'Someone sent us the contents of your laptop, so we know everything about your criminal activities. Whatever you're planning, you're done.'

'I'm afraid you're wrong. My contingency plans aren't on the computer. They're in my head and in the go-bag in the back of the car. No, what this is about is me enjoying myself and sending a message to interfering police officers. Such as DCI Farlowe, DI Thorpe and DS Vaughan.'

'How do you know their names? Have you got a bent copper on the Mexton force?'

'Not exactly. But Assistant Chief Constable Collins is a golfing friend of that upstanding businessman Mr Francis Garrett, with whom he passes many a convivial evening. He does like his brandy. Anyway, if you think you can keep me talking long enough for someone to come and rescue you, like in the films, you're wasting your time.'

He removed his hoodie to reveal a thin T-shirt.

'You're going to fasten yourself to that chair and I'm going to send bits of you to the three colleagues of yours I mentioned. Come to think of it, I'll send a bit to ACC Collins. Something for him to remember me by when I'm thousands of miles away. Now, sit!'

'Oh God! No! I'm going to be sick.'

Mel stumbled over to the bench, heaving, and managed to bring up some bitter liquid. In doing so, she knocked over some tools and sent instruments flying.

'Sit down, you stupid bitch. Fix your left hand to the arm of that chair with one of the cable ties on the seat. Tightly. And you can drop the knife you just grabbed from the bench.'

As the knife clattered to the floor, Mel looked into Garrett's eyes with an expression of total despair.

Chapter One Hundred Eleven

'Have you got anything? Anything at all?' asked DCI Farlowe, desperation in his voice, as he entered the incident room where a dozen officers were pounding laptops.

'Nothing of any use, guv,' replied Kamal. 'Forty-seven vehicles were moving away from the area at the time Mel was taken but, given the spacing of the cameras, they could have come from anywhere. We're working through the owners at the moment, but they all seem legit. Hang on, though.' He paused as information appeared on his screen. 'There's a Toyota Prius here with false plates. They belong to a Nissan Micra. It was heading east. Worth taking a closer look.'

'Definitely. Tag it and check ANPR along its direction of travel. I'll get an ARU on standby. But keep looking at the others in case this is something unrelated. Good spot. How about the laptop files?'

'Nothing so far,' replied Martin. 'There does seem to be references to various premises but they're cryptic – Pompey One, Pompey Two – that sort of thing. Portsmouth places, no doubt. Locally, we've got Mexton Gold – that's obviously the club – Mexton Paint, and Mexton Forest. No idea what they mean.'

'Keep at it. Maybe ask Jack. He likes puzzles and quizzes, doesn't he? Keep me informed of any developments as soon as they occur. I'll be in my office.'

'It's no good, guv,' said Jack, his eyes moist. 'We've lost the Prius, and I can't make any sense of the premises' names. Paint could refer to a gallery and forest to a caravan or cabin, but there's nothing to support either. I'm afraid Mel's on her own. And if he's harmed her, I'll hunt the bastard down and fucking kill him. And I don't care whether you heard that or not.'

He slammed Farlowe's office door and rushed out to the car park, setting off to drive around Mexton in an, almost certainly futile, attempt to find his friend and colleague before Frankie killed her.

Chapter One Hundred Twelve

'Yeeeaaargh!' screamed Mel as Frankie Garrett bent over her, a second cable tie in his hand.

Startled, he stepped back slightly. But not quickly enough to avoid the Stanley knife blade that Mel stuck into the back of his gun hand.

Garrett swore and switched the weapon to his left. He prepared to aim, but Mel was already moving. She leapt to her feet and spun around. The chair, attached to her hand by the cable tie, swung through the air like a medieval flail, connecting with the side of Garrett's head. His shot went wild, the crash of the report echoing around the steel walls of the warehouse. Dazed, he tried to aim again, but Mel stepped aside and lashed a foot into his kidney. He doubled over in agony, dropping the weapon, then lunged for Mel in blind fury. She jerked the chair up into his face, breaking several teeth. But still he came on, fuelled by adrenaline and hate.

Garrett smashed into Mel, knocking her to the ground and splintering the chair. She broke her wrist as she fell, and a vicious pain coursed along her arm. He crouched, groping for the pistol, but Mel rolled and kicked it out of reach. He grabbed a long-bladed hunting knife, knocked off the bench during Mel's feigned vomiting and staggered to his feet. He raised the knife and snarled. 'You fucking...' He never completed the sentence. Mel swept his feet from under him in a scything motion and rolled away. As Garrett fell, a sharp length of broken chair leg, sticking up from the floor, penetrated his T-shirt, slipped between his ribs, entered his left ventricle and stopped his heart.

Mel looked at the dead gangster, impaled on the remains of the chair. She turned him over, checked for a pulse and started to laugh hysterically.

'Oh Buffy, where art thou?' she muttered, then composed herself. Her wrist sending bolts of agony up her arm, she used the knife to cut the cable tie and retrieved Garrett's phone from his hoody. Using his thumb to unlock it, she checked her location and dialled.

Jack Vaughan, driving aimlessly around Mexton, frowned at the unknown number that appeared on his screen. He didn't have time for junk calls, but he answered it anyway. A quavering voice came over the car's speaker.

'Can I get an Uber to the police station, please?'

'Mel? What the fuck's going on? We thought we'd lost you.'

He pulled into the side of the road.

'I'm at an old building supplies warehouse,' she replied, 'Hawker and Lovelace, on the outskirts of town. She gave him the co-ordinates. 'Garrett took me, but I seem to have done a Van Helsing on him.'

'I've no idea what you're talking about. Are you OK?'

'Sorry. I guess I'm in shock. Probably sound a bit silly. I've got a broken wrist and a bleeding hand, that's all. Right, so, can you send a team to that location? We need SOCOs, an AFO to deal with a pistol, and a paramedic for me, preferably one carrying a bottle of brandy. Dr Durbridge may want to attend. Garrett fell onto a piece of wood sticking up from a broken chair on the ground. His body weight pushed it into his chest and he's dead. Something for his unusual deaths collection.

'This place looks as though it's been used for torturing people, so it will need a thorough going over. Please hurry. I feel like shit, and I really need to sit down somewhere warm, quiet and blood-stain free.'

'We're on our way, Mel. I'm so fucking glad you're OK. You had us all worried.'

'Not half as worried as me, mate. See you soon.'

Mel looked around the derelict warehouse, at the evidence of Frankie's cruelty and at his dead body, slowly oozing blood from the chest wound. The pieces of broken chair stuck out of his chest like some old-fashioned TV aerial, and she almost laughed. *What is it about me? Why do I keep getting into situations like this? Am I some kind of shit magnet?* Unable to answer herself, she stumbled out of the warehouse, breathed the fresh air and sat on a concrete bollard to await her colleagues with tears streaming down her face.

Chapter One Hundred Thireteen

Three days later

'GOOD MORNING, EVERYONE,' began DCI Farlowe. 'This briefing is to bring you up to date with recent developments. Firstly, you'll be pleased to know that Sally is recovering well. We don't have a date for her return. Mel, as you can see, is already back at work.'

Mel waved her cast-enveloped wrist at the rest of the team.

'Trevor is also recovering, although we don't know if and when he will be able to return. He will welcome visitors at home, but please telephone beforehand. Susie is extremely grateful for all the support you have shown.

'Jasper Burnham has been charged with murder and a number of other offences. We are working with Avon and Somerset to establish the extent of his activities and arrest other persons as appropriate. Those arrested at the rugby club car park have already been charged with firearms, and other, offences and remanded. We found a blood-stained baseball bat, in one of their vehicles, which could have been the weapon used to injure

Trevor. It's with forensics now and we hope to be able to prosecute whoever used it.

'We are collaborating with Hampshire Police to dismantle Frankie Garrett's empire, both here and in Portsmouth. The NCA will be going after his suppliers, and we will be offering what help we can. They were sent copies of the files on his laptop at the same time as we were. There is, of course, a huge amount of paperwork to complete, and it will be months before cases go to trial, but the hardest jobs are done.

'All in all, I think we have achieved a terrific result, with, fortunately, minimal loss of life. I congratulate you all on a tremendous team effort. The traditional celebrations were postponed until Mel could join in, but DSup Gorman has given me a significant sum to put behind the bar at The Cat and Cushion tonight. I hope as many of you as possible will come along. Thank you everyone.'

Epilogue

After a prolonged series of investigations, and lengthy trials, members of the two gangs were convicted of numerous offences and given lengthy prison terms. Jasper Burnham was found guilty of the murders of Speedy and Max, and of conspiracy to murder Frankie Garrett at the rugby club car park. He received a whole life tariff.

Marcus Forrest was convicted of the attempted murder of Sally, several firearms offences and possession of controlled drugs with intent to supply. He received a long prison sentence.

The killers of Shane Hopton and Tyson Harper were never formally identified but it was assumed that they were Frankie's men.

Forensic evidence on the baseball bat led to Wayne Fletcher's conviction for the attempted murder of Trevor. He received a twelve-year sentence.

Clare Miller was found guilty of murdering Jenny Pike and sentenced to life with a minimum term of fifteen years. Several law firms launched appeals against the convictions of their clients, where her work had been presented at trial, on the grounds that she was incompetent. One appeal was successful, but all the other convictions were upheld.

Pete Carter received a four-year sentence for corruption and misconduct in public office. It would have been longer had he not co-operated.

An IOPC investigation found that no blame for Frankie Garrett's death should be attributed to Mel.

Sally eventually returned to work with no permanent damage, apart from an occasional ache in her shoulder that worsened in cold weather. She continued to receive counselling.

Trevor returned after a long convalescence. He was physically and mentally fit, apart from a slight speech impediment consequent upon his injury.

Addy was welcomed back to CID once the inquiry into the shooting had concluded and attributed no blame to him.

Assistant Chief Constable Roger Collins took early retirement, and his wife left him shortly afterwards.

Burnham's traumatised dog was rehomed with a firearms-free family.

Glossary of Police Terms

AFO: Authorised Firearms Officer
ANPR: Automatic Number Plate Recognition (camera)
APT: Anatomical Pathology Technologist
ARU: Armed Response Unit
ARV: Armed Response Vehicle
Carbine: Short-barrelled rifle used by AFOs
CHIS: Covert Human Intelligence Source
CI: Civilian Investigator
CPS: Crown Prosecution Service
Cut and shut: The process of welding two halves of damaged cars together to make a functioning vehicle
DBS: Disclosure and Barring Service
Directed surveillance: Planned, covert observation of somebody (*see* RIPA)
DVLA: Driver and Vehicle Licensing Agency
DWP: Department for Work and Pensions
GDPR: General Data Protection Regulations
GCHQ: Government Communications Headquarters – electronic intelligence gathering establishment in Cheltenham
HMRC: His Majesty's Revenue and Customs

HOLMES2: Home Office Large Major Enquiry System –
national police IT system for investigating major crimes
IED: Improvised Explosive Device
IOPC: Independent Office for Police Conduct
Locard's Principle: Basis of forensic science: every contact leaves
a trace
Met (the): Metropolitan Police Service
NABIS: National Ballistics Intelligence Service
NCA: National Crime Agency
OCG: Organised Crime Group
PolSA: Police Search Advisor
PSNI: Police Service of Northern Ireland
Q word: Police officers are never supposed to say 'It's quiet
tonight' because then all hell breaks loose
QGM: Queen's Gallantry Medal
RIPA: Regulation of Investigatory Powers Act
RTC: road traffic collision
SOCO: Scene Of Crime Officer (aka CSI)
TIE: Trace, Interview, Eliminate (possible suspects)
VIN: Vehicle Identification Number, stamped on the chassis of
every motor vehicle

Acknowledgments

Thanks are due to Zoe Sharp for checking fight scenes, Kate Bendelow for answering a CSI query and, as ever, my wife, Jen, who turned my draft into something worth submitting for publication by spotting errors, improving my English and pointing out when things just wouldn't work. I'm also constantly grateful to Rebecca and Adrian at Hobeck Books for continuing to publish my work. Thanks also to Jayne Mapp for another great cover.

BRIAN PRICE

About the Author

Brian Price is a writer living in the South West of England. A scientist by training, he worked for the Environment Agency for twelve years and has also worked as an environmental consultant, a pharmacy technician and, for twenty-six years, as an Open University tutor.

Fatal Trade was his first full-length novel and has quickly been followed by more novels featuring DC Mel Cotton. He has also contributed to a number of short stories to a local writing group's anthology, called *Cuckoo*. He is the author of *Crime Writing: How To Write the Science*, a guide for authors on the scientific aspects of crime. He has a website on the topic **www.crimewriterscience.co.uk** and advises crime writers on how to avoid scientific mistakes in their books. He was once credited with keeping author M.W. Craven out of jail, as a result of advice given.

Brian reads a wide range of crime fiction and also enjoys Terry Pratchett, Genevieve Cogman and Philip Pullman. He may sometimes be found listening to rock, folk and 1960s psychedelic music. He is married and has four grown-up children.

To find out more about Brian and his crime fiction writing please visit his website: **www.brianpriceauthor.co.uk**.

The Mel Cotton Crime Series

Fatal Trade

Fatal Hate

Fatal Dose

Fatal Blow

Fatal Image

Fatal Shot

Available from book retailers.

Fatal Beginnings – a free prequel novella available if you subscribe to Hobeck Books www.hobeck.net.

Also by Brian Price

A Pocketful of Poisons: A. Collection of Deadly Short Stories

Available from book retailers.

Hobeck Books - the home of great stories

We hope you've enjoyed reading this novel by Brian Price. To keep up to date on Brian's fiction writing please subscribe to his website: **www.brianpriceauthor.co.uk**.

Hobeck Books offers a number of short stories and novellas, including *Fatal Beginnings* by Brian Price, free for subscribers in the compilation *Crime Bites*.

Also please visit the Hobeck Books website for details of our other superb authors and their books, and if you would like to get in touch, we would love to hear from you.

Hobeck Books also presents a weekly podcast, the Hobcast, where founders Adrian Hobart and Rebecca Collins discuss all things book related, key issues from each week, including the ups and downs of running a creative business. Each episode includes an interview with one of the people who make Hobeck possible: the editors, the authors, the cover designers. These are the people who help Hobeck bring great stories to life. Without them, Hobeck wouldn't exist. The Hobcast can be listened to from all the usual platforms but it can also be found on the Hobeck website: **www.hobeck.net/hobcast**.